ACCLAIM FOR Thomas McGuane's

The Cadence of Grass

"A fine, quirky, funny, startling novel . . . with witty dialogue and hilarious moments and sudden violence and awful betrayals."   —*The Miami Herald*

"McGuane is a terrific writer, a great chronicler of the vanishing West."   —*The Orlando Sentinel*

"There is a raw exuberance to this hard-edged novel. . . . McGuane proves that he is still an accomplished cowpuncher with words."
                    —*Seattle Post-Intelligencer*

"McGuane's unflagging invention is consistently engaging. . . . He is remarkably attuned to the psychological discomfort and indirect jousting underlying routine social interactions, and his language is rich, varied and effortless."
                    —*The San Diego Union-Tribune*

"When McGuane dissects his characters to their squirming core, *The Cadence of Grass* is downright hilarious."   —*St. Petersburg Times*

Thomas McGuane

The Cadence of Grass

Thomas McGuane lives in Sweet Grass County, Montana. He is the author of numerous novels and a collection of stories, as well as two collections of essays.

ALSO BY THOMAS McGUANE

The Longest Silence: A Life in Fishing

Some Horses

Nothing but Blue Skies

Keep the Change

To Skin a Cat

Something to Be Desired

Nobody's Angel

An Outside Chance

Panama

Ninety-two in the Shade

The Bushwhacked Piano

The Sporting Club

The Cadence of Grass

The Cadence of Grass

Thomas McGuane

VINTAGE CONTEMPORARIES

VINTAGE BOOKS

A DIVISION OF RANDOM HOUSE, INC.

NEW YORK

FIRST VINTAGE CONTEMPORARIES EDITION, MAY 2003

Copyright © 2002 by Thomas McGuane

Portions of this novel originally appeared in somewhat different form
as the following pieces: "A Black Dress" in *GQ*; "Boom and Bust"
in *The Harvard Review*; "Family" and "War and Peace" in
The New Yorker; "Bees" in *Open City*.

The Library of Congress has cataloged the Knopf edition as follows:
McGuane, Thomas.
The cadence of grass / by Thomas McGuane.—1st ed.
p. cm.
1. Family-owned business enterprises—Fiction. 2. Inheritance and succession—
Fiction. 3. Montana—Fiction. I. Title.
PS3563.A3114 C33 2002
813'.54—dc21
2001050623

Vintage ISBN: 0-679-76745-2

Book design by Robert C. Olsson

www.vintagebooks.com

Printed in the United States of America
10 9 8 7 6 5 4 3 2 1

In memory of my sister Marion

A savage place! as holy and enchanted
As e'er beneath a waning moon was haunted
By woman wailing for her demon lover.

—"Kubla Khan"

The Cadence of Grass

IN MOST WAYS, old man Whitelaw's funeral was just another scene in the family's life. Paul Crusoe, estranged from Whitelaw's daughter Evelyn, a strong young woman with black hair that hung straight to her collar, was led to his mother-in-law's sitting room by Evelyn herself. Mrs. Whitelaw, who could act as oblivious as someone nearly blind, sat with Evelyn's sister, Natalie, whom Paul viewed as a high-strung, nasty girl who once caused all his problems and who for her part despised him unstintingly. On the side table was a *Stockman's Journal* and a CPR handbook. Natalie smoked and looked at Paul over her raised cigarette. The red hair was certainly not genuine.

Bill Champion, an old rancher and longtime partner of the deceased, looked in briefly. He was dressed for the occasion but the clothes belonged to an earlier era. His forehead was much paler than the rest of his face and his blue eyes were startling. From the cuffs of his jacket, once part of a suit, projected hands that looked too big. He exchanged a concerned glance with Mrs. Whitelaw, then left the family alone.

"Mother, you haven't said a word to Paul," Evelyn said with an anxious smile once Bill was gone.

"Oh, Paul," said Mrs. Whitelaw, seeming to awaken, "you're so considerate to have come." Evelyn toyed with the porcelain birds and turtles on the mantel while keeping a watchful eye on her mother.

"It's unfathomable," said Natalie.

Mrs. Whitelaw turned slowly toward her.

"*I* don't think so," said Mrs. Whitelaw blindly toward Paul. "Jim and Paul had so much in common, an adventurous spirit! So suspicious of everything too," she said. "It made the rest of us *or*dinary people feel we were in a wonderf—"

"A wonderful play," said Natalie.

"—ful whodunnit. But Paul, Father was much saddened by your divorce—"

"Saddened, illuminated, chastened," said Natalie. "Where are we going with this?"

"I liked you better when you were on drugs," Paul whispered to Natalie.

Natalie had recently graduated from rehab in Arizona, a pleasant milieu with celebrities arriving by helicopter.

"It was not drugs," she hissed. "It was rage. *Justified rage*. In any case, I wouldn't have otherwise flown a thousand miles to eat from a steam table, to share a room and to wear a breezy outfit that tied in back."

"No worries," said Paul. "It's behind you now, mate."

With feverish preoccupation, Evelyn tended to her mother, refilling tea and holding a tray of cookies at eye level. In truth, she was no more prepared for her father's funeral than she'd been for his death. And both she and her sister would soon discover how incomplete his departure had been.

"What exactly *are* you doing these days, Paul?" Natalie asked. "Anything illuminating for Mother at this very rough time in her life?"

"I, I—"

"Ay-yi-yi-yi? Is this the Mexican hat dance?"

"I was doing a project with . . . a firm—underwriters, really—doing debentures pertinent to the lumber business, or the *wood products* business would be more like it. . . ." Paul knew perfectly well, if too late, that Natalie was well informed in these areas.

"*Wood products debentures?*"

"Something of a by-product of the days with those stock pickers, you remember, the small-capital and emerging-nations guys that—"

"Paul, you have no job, have you?"

"Not at the moment. Not much of anything. A bit of a day trader. I hope to return to the bottling plant."

Evelyn moved away in embarrassment, Paul's eyes following her.

"I'm sure you'll find something," said Natalie, holding her cigarette to her mouth and relighting it. "And Evelyn," she said, turning to her sister, "I was touched by your little grimace of sympathy, your pained embarrassment at *all this unease*. Paul, she still cares!"

Mrs. Whitelaw's eyes seemed to search around the room for the source of the discord. "Natalie," she said hopelessly, knowing there was never any cautioning Natalie, whose latest fear was that she had stopped emitting pheromones.

"Perhaps we both still care," said Paul. A touching remark, made to comfort Mrs. Whitelaw in her widowhood since neither of them cared anymore at all. It was surprising, really, that Natalie seemed to take him seriously enough to go on challenging the idea. Evelyn occasionally noted a visceral inclination toward her estranged husband, though it was not at all unmanageable.

"But all that water under the bridge! The otherwise admirable but nonmeshing complexities of character, the lack of the children, the—evidently!—dimming prospects of a nonstarter in the workplace!"

She was rolling now and Paul had her in his sights. Natalie found it difficult to listen while others were speaking, and her attention darted among trivia—silverware, matchbook covers, her napkin—practically anything in order to avoid listening. Whenever she herself spoke, she fastened on the listener's eyes, feeling that only absolute vigilance could prevent their attention from escaping.

"Natalie," Paul interrupted, "when you were on drugs, at least there was the initial euphoria. Perhaps we were insufficiently appreciative of that during the days of rage when you sought to recapture the original high. And certainly we remained unaware of the depth of your situation until you installed the *cat* door at your apartment so as to receive packages from your connection without burdensome conversations."

Natalie smiled at this recollection. "That was good, wasn't it?"

It was a sincere question, and reluctantly Paul's admiration of Natalie came back. They'd once had what she called quality sex, and perhaps its lingering tonalities were what now gave Evelyn such a lost look. She had been thrilled to be rid of Paul but would have preferred dumping him more felicitously than upon her own sister, who gave him an entirely too greedy welcome.

Mrs. Whitelaw, having fled the present scene into her own thoughts, capitalized on this first real pause to steer the conversation elsewhere, whether they liked it or not. The three of them knew ahead of time that what followed would be an analogue every bit as opaque as the most ancient aphorism.

"Explain this to me," Mrs. Whitelaw said with a certain eagerness. "I read in the *Chronicle* that a boat speeding down the Sewanee River—the Sewanee River!—hit a wave made by a water-skier and flew right through the window of a second-story condominium! Paul, you tell the girls and me: How can these things happen?"

"Mrs. Whitelaw, I—"

"Surely you know Stephen Foster's *Way Down Upon the Sewanee River*!"

Natalie left the cigarette dangling from her lips. "Mama, evidently times have changed way down upon the Sewanee—"

"How on earth does a speedboat fly into the *second story* of a condominium?"

"I don't know," Paul said as though genuinely puzzled. Actually, he was staring at the old Harry Winston choker bedecking Mrs. Whitelaw's bosom, wondering how it would fare in a death tax appraisal. All of them thought Mrs. Whitelaw had finished her venture in analogies, but in this they were not correct.

"According to the same issue of the *Chronicle,* a chicken, a pet, escapes its hutch in Greeley, Colorado, and walks forty miles to the other side of Denver through traffic, strip malls, gas stations, parking lots, followed everywhere by rumors and news reports. At one point they had a helicopter looking for this chicken, and the owner, an older gal, a waitress, trudged and rode and followed the rumor trail until *fate* brought this chicken to bay in the parking lot of Blockbuster Video! There—and this just makes me want to bawl—it was reunited with the old waitress. Who was no dope, because before she even fed that worn-out bird which I saw on TV and which looked like a piece of rag, before she'd even given this poor broken little thing a dish of water, she sold the film rights to Hollywood! No *wonder* my husband was ready to go!"

"Still, Mrs. Whitelaw," said Paul, who had rarely been this mentally bankrupt, "there's so much to be thankful for."

"*Oh, Paul,*" said Natalie with contempt and pity as Mrs. Whitelaw belly laughed and pulled a handkerchief from her reticule with which to undampen her eyes.

Evelyn, looking on, recalled feeling that Paul Crusoe had never really been ready for this family. This sort of customary byplay between Paul and the sisters was nothing new and not nearly as resonant as it would become after Jim Whitelaw's will was read. For now, they lived on in a fool's paradise, brought together as a family by the apparently complete lack of feeling for the deceased.

Earlier, at the funeral itself, Mrs. Whitelaw, seated next to Paul during the long and tiresome service, wanted to know a few things about him; sotto voce, like a conspirator, she seemed not to be thinking about her husband at all.

"Were you a Boy Scout, Paul?"

"No."

"It wouldn't have mattered when you were young, of course, but the Boy Scouts are in hot water with the queers. It was in the *Chronicle*. Can you tell me briefly, Paul, why your marriage to Evelyn failed so suddenly? And be sure to make it brief."

"It wasn't sud—"

"It was the lack of children, wasn't it?"

"Actually, we—"

"I have no right to make these sorts of guesses, Paul. Other people's lives, even your own children's, are a com-*plete* mystery."

"Actually, we bo—"

"What's that?"

"We bored each other!"

"Don't raise your voice to me, Paul. Do you need money?"

"Not yours."

"Whatever could you mean by that?" Mrs. Whitelaw turned her attention to the service. "Isn't there going to be some sort of music?"

"I have no idea."

Paul's mother, Dr. Edith Crusoe, a Westernist at the University of Colorado at Boulder, chose this moment for a quiet arrival. She was not to stay for long. Indeed, she remained in her mackintosh, whose wide lapels rose around her ears as she sat quizzically regarding the coffin, her face lively and discontented. She murmured something that caused Alice Whitelaw to smile in modest gratitude, nodded rather formally to her son and snubbed Evelyn entirely.

Evelyn understood that had Dr. Crusoe not found something thematic in the funeral, something emblematic about low rainfall, say, she wouldn't have come at all. Evelyn surmised that as her father had owned a bottling plant Dr. Crusoe may have viewed him as an oligarch of moisture hoarding, and she imagined the passage wherein the descendants of mammoth hunters are bludgeoned into an ecological black hole by waves of coercive white men on horseback wielding Coca-Cola bottles. Partisan hyperbole had made Dr. Crusoe not just a professor but a public intellectual in the Northern Rockies, but Evelyn's views of her were unreasonable. She had never married and Paul was her only child. When the priest began to speak of the deceased and the meaning of his life, Dr. Crusoe rose sharply to her feet and departed, the crown of her head barely visible above the lapels of her coat.

The priest addressed his remarks to the coffin. Having not listened to anything until now, Paul and Mrs. Whitelaw found this completely baffling. Evelyn was discomfited to recognize in the sermon whole passages from that year's *Farmers' Almanac*.

"I see where they've made another movie about the *Titanic*," said Mrs. Whitelaw.

"That's right," Paul said, his eyes widening.

"What can they possibly add?"

"This time it floats," he said wearily.

"Oh, Paul, I find your humor rather extreme."

"Pay attention to your husband's funeral," he snapped. Mrs. Whitelaw looked at him, then suddenly crumpled and began sniveling into her handkerchief.

"This is what it feels like to be doomed," she said miserably.

"Oh, Mrs. Whitelaw, I'm so sorry."

"You will look after me, won't you, Paul?" Later he would wonder if her remark contained some premonition.

"Yes, Mrs. Whitelaw."

"I was doing so well, so detached—"

"Yes."

"Remarkably well, in view of circumstances. Now it is all falling, falling, falling, falling." Knowing that it would be only a short time before Mrs. Whitelaw was on the muscle again, Paul attempted to hold and comfort her, a dismal exercise. "What a shame we're losing you to our family, Paul. I'm glad Jim wasn't quite aware of it, he was so enfeebled toward the end, always with a hat on his head. *Never* wore a hat during his life unless it was dangerously cold out, but at the end it was always these awful red watch caps. He looked homeless. Perhaps when people reach that point they *are* homeless, aren't they, Paul? Are they finished up there?"

It looked as though they were. The priest had just finished saying something and had clasped his hands. It must have been something very good about heaven for him to chance such a puckish demeanor. But no, good God; he was addressing Mrs. Whitelaw, who hadn't heard a word he'd said. "I hope my words weren't inadequate, Mrs. Whitelaw. I remember Jim's opinion on long speeches all too well."

She gazed at him as though he were a pesky employee.

"That's not just Jim," said Mrs. Whitelaw with sudden authority. "That's the way the whole world feels."

The family was obliged to meet over and over again just to understand how the estate was to be probated because the last will and testament of the deceased was a "minefield," according to the attorney who drafted it. The daughters were so fixated on the attorney's dramatic hairdo that they often couldn't remember his name, but they recognized the will as pure Sunny Jim Whitelaw, attempting to bind his family to his wishes from beyond the grave. Alice was bequeathed a living from the bottling plant, of which Paul was appointed president and chief operating officer, at a handsome salary. Not a guaranteed red cent for anyone else. A provision, however, existed for the alteration of the conditions thus imposed. Should Paul and Evelyn cancel their plans for divorce, the profits of the business could be shared among all family members, or it could be sold and the proceeds divided. In any event, while it wouldn't make any of them wealthy, a degree of comfort and security was probable if, as the obnoxious attorney suggested, they behaved themselves. Natalie's husband, Stuart, said that the will reminded him of the Iron Maiden. Natalie called it proof of her father's hatred and emitted penetrating howls in the chambers of the probate judge. Stuart gave her a calming shoulder rub. Evelyn exhaled and said, "Ooh, boy," as her intention to divorce Paul was the single greatest act of defiance she had ever directed at her father. Paul had, through the confidences of Sunny Jim, known all along that if he stayed in the marriage, stayed in the family business, he could be reasonably expected to keep his trap shut. He had a copy of the will and put the cash-flow schematics in his wallet as though they were real money. Alice Whitelaw said that she felt secure and offered loans to her children. Knowing what a cheapskate she was, this provided scarce comfort to anyone; and when Paul gave her a congratulatory pat on the back, Evelyn heaved a sigh of heartfelt disgust.

The probate judge, a decent old man with snow white hair, found himself agitated by all the ill will and complication in this family. While offering them formal best wishes and the ongoing availability of his advice, he quietly and desperately hoped he never saw these people again, then darted off like a fugitive, describing the situation to the first colleague he ran into as "a chandelle off a shithouse."

Paul had been out of prison only a little more than a year. He was still occasionally in touch with his two cell mates, who had named themselves Kahuna and Moondoggie after characters in *Gidget;* and while he had sometimes been afraid of the other prisoners, they themselves were chiefly afraid of freedom, though they experimented with it, between sentences, like a dangerous drug. He had served his time for a manslaughter conviction, years stolen from his life but economic opportunity of a kind he might not otherwise have enjoyed. Driving back from a Masons' banquet with his father-in-law passed out on the front seat, Paul had rear-ended a motorcycle at ninety-five miles an hour, liquidating its driver. On the way home from the dilapidated county jail out from which Sunny Jim had bailed him, Paul devised a remarkable conversation.

"Why were you going so fast?" Sunny Jim asked reasonably.

"I wasn't."

"What's that supposed to mean?"

"*You* were."

Sunny Jim slowed down to concentrate on the talk. "I'm not following you," he said.

"You were driving," said Paul. "You killed the motor-cyclist."

As Sunny Jim pulled over, the hiss of pavement changed to gravel popping under the tires. He was silent.

"I dragged you over to the passenger's side and sat at the wheel till the Highway Patrol arrived."

Sunny Jim studied every pore on Paul's face.

"Why would you do that?"

"Why? Because you have more to lose than me and you're too old to go to prison, which is where I'm undoubtedly headed."

Sunny Jim turned the engine off and let traffic flash past behind him. He seemed far away. Paul was thinking of an old country song, "Wreck on the Highway," and its chorus, "I didn't hear nobody pray." This was a special moment, and Paul hoped that over the long haul it would pay like a slot machine.

"I won't forget this, Paul," said Sunny Jim, a faint vibration stirring his accustomed baritone. "I'll never forget what you've done."

Paul was now due for his weekly appointment with Geraldine, his parole officer. He was fascinated by the atmosphere of the office itself, which, with a stern recep-tionist in front and offices on either side, was somewhat like the waiting room of a dentist's office. There were usu-ally several parolees in attendance, including a few "short leashes" as Geraldine called them, who went to the farthest office on the right, which handled electronic monitoring and chemical castration.

He did not want to suggest to her—at all!—that he was

taking advantage of the intimacy that had grown between them. Paul was well dressed, straight from work, transformed from ex-con to CEO in a matter of a few short blocks. He was on top of the situation in terms of heading off any clever remarks he might make on impulse. But she was glad to see him and greeted him with real warmth, right in front of her secretary, whom Paul had already checked out and scratched for the bench knees she so unwisely revealed below her skirt. Geraldine even held the door for him! When they sat down, she behind her desk, he in a small, disadvantageous chair so deep he felt he was gazing out over his own pelvis, she moved to the corner of her desk to make him more comfortable. Geraldine was a big-boned, good-looking girl whose slightly out-of-date teased hair put her at risk in Paul's eyes. When he'd pointed her out to Natalie late one night, she'd said, "Baby, let's kiss those seventies good-bye!"

"I think I can update these forms almost without talking to you."

"Well, I haven't been anywhere, just working."

"But things *have* changed, Paul."

"Yeah, and like I'm rolling in it."

"You got a bit of training, I guess, under your former father-in-law . . . ?"

"Uh-huh, he was sure grateful I did the time."

"Well, it looks to me that this is all a fairly happy outcome."

"You mean, I'm getting the time *back*?"

"You'll have to talk to God about that," said Geraldine with an alarming laugh.

Paul wasn't having it. "Is that who you work for?" he said with a hard, level gaze.

"Sorry, Paul, my powers are more limited. I just work for the State of Montana." At length, Geraldine continued, her eyes on an empty portion of her desk. "I enjoyed our evening together, Paul."

He was still smarting over the flippant reference to his lost years, and his previous resolutions were dust. Let her get away with this piece of nauseating sentiment and she'd be asking, "But what about *us*?"

He waited for her to look up, then said, "You know something, Geraldine? You look great on your back. It's your best side."

She began to write on forms from the file folder in front of her. "I have only myself to blame."

"Oh? Well, when they locked me away, I didn't know who to blame."

"I'm sure you didn't."

Geraldine looked contrite, even a little shaken. Paul saw that she actually cared for him and wondered where he could go with this, only he wasn't interested. Instead, he resolved never to see her again, or not to see her in that way, even though she was pretty good at it and put plenty into her work; but if she couldn't behave like a real professional, there was no point in acting lively and objective when you got within ten feet of a desk. He was going to be keeping these appointments for a while and had to make a binding resolution with the State of Montana Parole Board; he didn't need her half-goofy on the far side of his file folder.

"I don't think there's anything new for you," he said, indicating the forms. "My work situation, as discussed, is much improved. I'm still in my apartment, but I'm looking at houses. I'm looking at a new car. When the conditions of my parole so allow, I plan to travel the Pacific Rim which, as far as I'm concerned, is where it's at, but not until I am so allowed. I would like to go to New York for some threads—" he smiled "—but only with your permission."

"And your domestic situation?" She abruptly flipped several pages over.

Paul smiled at this little diversion. "Under the terms of my father-in-law's will, there is considerable motivation for me to reconcile with my wife." He declined to add that as sex-sherpa to the Whitelaw sisters he would no longer have time for her.

"You know, I've never actually—"

"But I don't see that as a real possibility."

"—seen her, though I know she lives right around here."

"Beautiful."

"What?"

"She's beautiful. Inside and out. Yeah, she lives around here. Her deal is cows, et cetera, her horse."

"Well, it's so nice that . . . she's beautiful," said Geraldine. "I like horses myself."

"You know, Geraldine, beauty is only skin deep, but *ugly* goes to the bone." Paul considered this and enjoyed watching her squirm. People are so hard nowadays that you can't buy a good squirm if you try. But he decided to let her off the hook.

"Evelyn always smells like the animals. That's sort of a turnoff. She really smells when they've been worming cattle, with this gross stuff they dump on their backs. Maybe there's some things I do miss but that doesn't include having a fridge full of cattle vaccine." Paul thought you could cut the air in here with a knife. Geraldine didn't seem to know what to do with her face, and her imitations of casual interest in this information were repellent. This would be a good time to get her off the hot seat by pouring his heart out.

"Look, unless Evelyn and I get back together, I can't sell that bottle plant, okay? Unless we get back together, the plant can't be houses in other countries, okay? Or the beach. I'm not so twisted I *don't* want to live on the beach. I was down in San Diego once with a friend. We drove along the houses and I mean upscale *all* the way and he like kept his thumb on the garage door opener until he found the one that was his home. How cool is that? I liked it down there because it was so blue and futuristic and you're walking around with thirty-five SPF sunblock all over you just checking everything out. It was way different than prison, I can tell you, with these creeps that look like they fell out of a bad dream." Paul remembered when those creeps had suddenly become his friends, once he'd turned on the snitches and they'd invented a board game they'd named Where the Fuck Is Carmen Santiago. He'd never achieved such popularity anywhere.

"You want to lock the door and get it on?" he inquired.

"No, Paul, there's a time and a place for that."

He couldn't imagine what he would've done had she said yes. But she sure knew how to turn a guy off. *There's a time and a place.* Obviously, once you're a bureaucrat you start losing all your vital juices and you turn into a *cactus.* "Would you say that you've behaved like a professional in handling my case?"

"Paul, I must have said something to offend you." She smiled a little and raised her eyebrows.

He chuckled. "I've got to go," he said, "but please don't

torment yourself that I haven't enjoyed myself here. I know I'm not the easiest case you've got. I've mired myself in the Seven Deadly Sins." He got up and Geraldine too thought she would rise and see him off. It was clear now that she had made a big mistake with Paul, and in admitting to herself that she'd been had, she remembered how something about him had captivated her against all her best judgment, not just his very good looks, his compact physique and fine features, the particular way his black hair was combed in a kind of 1930s look, and his quickness of mind. There was really something infernal about Paul, but it was only this very sulfurousness that made her act so out of character and believe that they were entitled to a harmless good time together. The last time they'd made love and she'd asked him if she was "good," he'd replied that it was the thought that counted, adding, as he finished dressing, "Feets, don't fail me now." It was clear to her that Paul's contempt for her was based on his belief that she had fallen from grace and was now somehow on his level. He was wrong about that.

Following their appointment, Paul drove no more than five blocks and stopped to buy an ice cream. Across the street, a Little League game spun along, two squads of uniformed children and a small group of towering grown-ups, strangely inconsequential looking against the small squads of activists. Paul licked his cone avidly and watched each successive batter, dense with sporting affectations, swing at the ball with surprising vehemence. One angel-faced boy hit a stand-up double, and Paul observed both the pitcher's nearly operatic despair and the disgusted whirl of his coach. The hitter stood on second base with the detachment of a broadly successful person, doing a few stretches, presumably for the final sprint to home plate, but generally taking in the benevolence of Indian summer in the mountains. This was so much like the baseball-stopped time of his own childhood, when he had been such an utterly different human being that he could, tongue against the ice cream, ponder this in curious stupefaction.

Paul did not want to eat the remainder of the dry cone now, but since two little athletes were watching him, he couldn't very well throw it on the ground and was forced to cram it into his mouth.

Crossing a country road, Paul saw numerous nearly identical new homes gnawed through old grain fields toward the Bridger Mountains, one after the other like a caterpillar. A combine made its way while holding up homebound suburban traffic, exasperation in every direction, the guilt of the farmer evident in his slouch and his avoidance of all eye contact, his deafness to horns and abrupt passings. The sign in front of a new subdivision invited the buyer to "select from over eighteen models."

Paul pulled into Stuart and Natalie's driveway, parking directly behind Stuart's well-kept Fairlane and Natalie's Mustang with its MSTNG SLLY vanity plates, a car Paul thought too young for her. Stuart came around the house operating a leaf blower and wearing ear protection. When Stuart saw him, he turned off his blower with an amiable smile, propped it against the house with his ear protectors slung over its handle, swept the grass clippings from his trousers and came toward Paul with a pigeon-toed lurch. Paul watched his approach with raised eyebrows. He actually liked Stuart's personality for its lack of surprises, for the rolled-up sleeves of his shirts and for the shoes that had been nursed through several changes of style by careful care. The ones he wore today resembled the ones you saw in portraits of the Pilgrims. He knew as well that Stuart was sometimes rather hard done by in his relations with Natalie. He'd once arrived unexpectedly and found Natalie, arms stiff at her sides, shouting at Stuart, "*Please* don't say 'davenport'! Just this once for me, say '*sofa*'!" Sometimes, Paul had got the disquieting feeling that Stuart was watching him. If Paul was to take over the life of the family, he wasn't going to be keen on having this feeling.

"Paul, hey, what's up?"

"Not much. Just grabbed an ice cream. Been watching Little League."

Stuart glanced at his watch. "They're nearly done. Ace Hardware wins today and they clinch a playoff slot."

"Where's Nat?"

"She's at her mother's. The cruise is only a couple of days away."

"Yeah, I bought Mother Whitelaw a little going-away present."

Stuart seemed to flinch. "I wonder if I should've gotten something. I didn't even think about it."

"Trade beads."

"Oh, Paul."

Paul caught a whiff of Stuart's appraisal in his self-discounting body language. In prison you look for every trace of these things so some babyface doesn't push a sharpened utensil through your liver. It was one thing to be observant and quite another to be absolutely awake. That's where Paul had gotten by dint of long effort, and that's where he intended to stay. Certain conflicts lay inevitably ahead. Just now it was time to lay some assurance and bon voyage on the old lady, the holdout being a certain warm feeling that might beguile the rest of them.

"I'm just glad Alice is getting away, Stu. She'll learn some real changes."

"I wish I were so sure," Stuart said.

"You can't believe how adaptable women are. They're like chameleons. Match the color of any background, including plaid."

"You can't say that about Natalie."

"Nat's the exception that proves the rule. The others just wear themselves out trying."

Stuart turned to resume his work, ending the conversation. Paul wasn't sure there wasn't a message here. He frowned slightly and called, "Catch you later," thinking that if Stuart were any measure, Paul's vow upon release from prison—of not settling for being less than larger than life—was coming true. He drove across town to his mother-in-law's house, which Sunny Jim, in an access of imperial ego, had named "Whitelaw." After consideration, he declined to knock upon the brass and varnish surface of the door, smelling the heat on the russet brick and thinking, Alaska, that's a good one, and simply strolled in, in order to see Mrs. Whitelaw off, the former Alice Nyoka Smoot, and give her something to trade with the Eskimos. But no, it turned out a little traveler's portfolio was more like it. Thinking about what she might appreciate and training his mind away from chilblain cures, folklore of the Gold Rush, et cetera, he felt an odd affection for the old bag who'd had a hard time of it in her brutish marriage. It was rumored that, at fifteen, she had been flung from her white-trash household to fend for herself. When she received her gift, he recited, "There are strange things done 'neath the midnight sun" while thinking, How thin her hair has become!

Discovering Natalie in eavesdropping range by the pantry offered little in the way of surprise; she faded from view and was next seen gathered around Mother White-law's rather good Georgian tea service, which when Paul was in jail had represented, in his mind, if not the good life, then the unconfined life; and once he'd heard it appraised in the spinning portrait of value called "the estate," he immediately concluded it would be even handsomer in cash form than it had been during its two hundred years on an Edinburgh sideboard before Sunny Jim swept it to the Rockies on the wings of his credit card. When in unla-mented down-and-out days Paul had suggested to Evelyn that she possibly gather it unto him, she cried "Never!" and thus differentiated herself from her own sister, who at the behest of a discomposed main man would've jogged off with the whole kit and kaboodle.

"Good afternoon, Natalie."

"Paul." She seemed unable to fathom his warm and admiring gaze. Alice Whitelaw got up to fill the teapot, trailing a cloud of Joy perfume behind her. When the spring-loaded door to the kitchen quit flashing, Paul said to Natalie, "Stop by later and I'll throw a good one into you."

"Give it a rest, Paul."

Paul parted the drapes absentmindedly. "Around eightish would be good." Then, to Alice, who'd just returned with the exaggerated difficulty meant to highlight her hospital-ity, "I hope you've packed plenty of warm things, Mrs. Whitelaw!"

"Nice black English breakfast," said Alice Whitelaw. "Yes, I have, Paul, all I'll need."

"You're going to Alaska, you know."

"Yes, I do."

"Icebergs, igloos, killer whales with the big fin." He sailed on, completely twisted in Natalie's view but merely baffling in her mother's. "In a ship with a casino, four ball-rooms, six restaurants and *a putting green,* you will be insulated from the very worst of the people who wish to take such a trip." And hopefully all memories of Papa in his final days, the dribbling fuckwit who'd once ruled them with such might and incomprehension.

"I don't know about *that*. *I* wish to be on this trip. Paul, I hope to be dis*or*iented by comfort and services. I don't want to suffer, but I don't want to be around here before I can make sense of things."

"What do you mean 'sense of things'?"

"Just what I said. We're not having the easiest time of this, Paul. And we hear quite frequently from the employees. Maybe you can see our point of view."

Paul was aware of the discontent but thought, I'm going to kick ass and take names. "Of course I can," said Paul with surprising mildness. "I find it very awkward, and I hope that by running things profitably and intelligently that I will win your confidence."

"As a businessman," Alice Whitelaw said, "you already have it."

Paul was not about to go digging around about what other areas might lie in Ma Whitelaw's omissions when it was far better to pour tincture on her remark and treat it like blanket approval. At all events the bottom line was the bucks.

While Natalie watched in amazement, he beamed like Howdy Doody and stated his gratitude. He said nothing whatsoever about what it was to be chained to the bottling plant for as far into the future as he could see, or to go through life as an ex-convict in a Paul Stuart Canadian twill suit and a hundred-dollar shantung tie. What chance was there of persuading her that he had a stain which no money could reach, and which was perhaps not entirely visible to someone heading for an Alaskan cruise in a haze of thousand-dollar-an-ounce perfume?

Aware of their gazes crossing somewhere in front of him, Paul felt rather hemmed in and took a geographer's note of the form and movement of altocumulus clouds through the garden window, some starting to stream in from the north. He knew perfectly well that he would forever feel the gust of his predatory urges. To stay the course, he wasn't anxious to dance with the devil; he wanted to find smaller, more efficient bottling plants, to hog the franchises, the relationships, the new containers, to get both the kids and the tavern rats, to score with the celebrities who visited each summer, big Hollywood guys who were willing to put their name on some pork-and-bean microbrewery just to be part of things in the West. And all for what? So Mother Whitelaw can see a hundred and give him a watch? He didn't think so. Even this house, which he now wanted out of fast, was deader than a federal correctional facility, where life, after a fashion, ran riot. At least there you could sleep and not fear waking up crazy in the way that marked his first days of freedom, a fear that ended only when fortune gave him a going concern and the family that depended upon it. There was some poetry here.

He rattled off a few hopes for plant expansion, alluding to a simple and remunerative harvest of opportunity, and had managed to create an atmosphere of fiscal security by the time he bade Mrs. Whitelaw good-bye. Natalie silently raised a hand in sardonic farewell, and Paul drove to the bottling plant, noting with satisfaction that his name had been applied to his parking space. When he got out of the car, he could smell the fresh paint; he looked up at his factory and smiled.

On Monday, freed from the mood of resentment surrounding Mrs. Whitelaw and Natalie—a true horn dog!—he felt entirely relieved and happier still as he walked around the plant among his workers. He found his erstwhile brother-in-law, the "vice president of sales," as per Paul's spontaneous invention, talking with the maintenance supervisor, Herman Schmitz, who wiped his hands on his shop apron in the unlikely event that the boss wanted to shake hands. "Herman," said Paul, stepping back a bit, "I am very aware that the one thing we don't bottle around here is water." He said "water" with an aspect of astonishing sourness. He had been raised by a mother for whom water was almost the only subject. Amidst the violent tinklings and forklift rumbles of the thriving bottle plant, Herman seemed unable to reply, and so Stuart butted right in.

"Well, Paul, we have such good water in our area. Even at that, we treat it with ferrous sulfate, hydrated lime and chlorine, then run it back through the filters. It's crystal pure."

"Our area" is what particularly stuck in Paul's craw, the very idea of drinking water without the messages, interactions and fairly binding deals that ensued once you got the stuff into a bottle. "It may be that we have good water, but thinking like that drives no business. We are encircled by a very remunerative world of designer water, Stuart. So, anyway: floor space."

"How's this?"

"*Floor space*. Do we have the *space* for a small plant?"

"We cou—"

"One simple complex for washing, filling, capping and conveying at, let's say, four thousand bottles an hour. But it takes *floor space*."

"Maybe we could find a few hundred square f—"

"Get me some quotes."

"The onl—"

"And make sure it's a stand-alone in case the thing goes tits up. We should be looking at some bigger containers too, with, you know, tamper-evident snap closures, leak-proof low-density polyethylene. And I mean, make it thick! Like thirty-eight millimeters, which is the industry standard. Stuart, you and Herman both look like you fell out of your high chairs."

Herman tried to contribute. "Maybe the tamper thing with plain water—"

"Tampering? Tampering is on the way. That's all we have in America: *tampering*."

At four, Paul went for a smoke behind the buildings. Guys from other plants were in the alleyway smoking too. Smoke in back, talk in your car, relieve yourself in the john; it was always something. Someday, all you'd do in these buildings would be work. But it was nice to get some air and see the sky at the top of the alley and enjoy the quiet glee he'd always felt, yes, even in prison where the patterned movements of the men were broken by hot spells of peril that had been, with some awful exceptions, an adventure.

He kept walking, soaking in the pleasures of what peered at him in the form of nature: mushrooms at the base of steel bins, an effulgent cloudscape way down toward the RV lot, children playing in front of a very run-down day care center, children soon to grow old, wave after wave of them in a town as ordinary as the flat earth, waxing, waning, pushing each other off the edge into the abyss and no God to care. But in the meanwhile, a rather rich and detailed picture! All of this, thought Paul, is why we must hunt down the wherewithal that held irritation at bay, not that it saved so much as an ant from oblivion, but for its anesthetic properties in a phenomenally bleak deal handed down to the human race by the Joker. However, money was another thing: Money brings us closer to nature.

In his special views of beauty and nature, Paul sought the semi-eternity that helped make up for the security that sort of *atomized* in sixth grade, when his mother told him the disturbing story of his conception involving a father she described as little more than a worthless stranger, an all-consuming vacancy that suddenly gave his young life a cartoonish quality complete with flying faces, dither, interruptions and babble. He also missed the God that had been described in his small-town grade school, a terrible old tyrant who seemed to demand all the wheedlings and importunings mankind could send his way.

When Paul noticed movement behind the green bin that secured trash for the Marvel Foundry, not far along the alley from the back of his own factory, he suspected it was the striped russet mutt he'd observed lurking around most mornings. He hung over the bin to peer into the space between the Dumpster and the wall, and immediately found himself looking into a bright pair of eyes belonging to the suspected dog. Scouring the garbage, Paul retrieved a burger fragment with matching bun halves and tooth marks. This was all it took to lure out a narrow-faced and expressive mutt, more brindle than anything and possessing an elevated indecisive curlicue tail over its back. Paul gave it the wasted meat and managed to get a hand on its back with only a suggestion of lips raised over teeth before the contact of Paul's hand and murmuring voice reassured it, "You eat like a cannibal." Further rummaging produced a length of wrapping twine with which Paul devised a noose and leash and to which he attached the still dining dog. But towing it was not easy as the dog reared back and fishtailed at the end of the twine, revealing an endearingly freckled belly. Paul, obliged to hold the twine with both hands, towed the dog the short distance into the back door of his plant where, in front of all employees, another battle of wills ensued. Once things quieted down, he called out an order to Herman while peeling a twenty-dollar bill from his wallet: "*T-Bone!*" then added, "You may call him Whitelaw!"

"I don't see how you figured this out on your own," said Evelyn. She was grilling poor Bill Champion about horses all over again. The first of every month, she helped him update his cattle records. Getting out to this unprofitable little ranch had been the most important part of Evelyn's life since the days of childhood when her father sent her here to learn to ride. It was an unsurprising piece of shortgrass prairie yet had a strange hold upon her imagination.

"I never said I did. There's always a lot of folks gone before. And, you know, I had Robert Wood. I don't know who *he* had, but I'm sure neither one of them made it up either."

Evelyn had seen a picture of Robert Wood hanging in a cowboy bar on the south side of Billings. He had long uncut white hair and looked like George Washington. "I guess he was your hero."

"He was *a* horseman. Said he got it all in Nevada, had 'em up in a bridle rolling a copper cricket."

Evelyn understood the peculiarities of Bill's language, like calling the accelerator the "foot feed." When Paul had been in the picture, Bill would scarcely talk to her and certainly not about anything important. Maybe a cow, or farming, but no chance of horses nor their pride and beauty. While Paul may have earned his enmity, it must be said that Bill disliked him the first time he saw him. It was quite unreasonable. But right now it was different; she wasn't going back to Paul and Bill was at peace.

"It was the last Mother's Day before I went to the navy . . ." Here was another of his tantalizations: never a word about the war except vague references to his Cheyenne friend, a chief petty officer named Red Wolf. The only decoration in Bill's house was an old black-and-white photograph of the light cruiser he'd served on in the Pacific, and references to Red Wolf ran throughout all the years Evelyn had come here. If Bill said he had an appointment with Red Wolf, it meant he was busy and didn't have time to explain why. If the truck broke down, it was Red Wolf, and sometimes it was Red Wolf who came around disguised as the tax assessor. But evidently there really had been a man named Red Wolf, a strangely unforgotten part of Bill's life. "You and Nat was just little bitty." Here was another one. Evelyn couldn't quite understand why she and her sister kept appearing in these early stories, other than that her father had thought farms and ranches were repositories of basic virtue and had sent his girls out to Bill every chance he got. But still, that was early. "I want to tell you a little story about what a hand Robert Wood was." Evelyn had a feeling that Bill needed to tell these stories. He'd had a brief marriage and had two kids from that whom he might just as well not have had. All he said about his wife was "Somebody throwed a switch, turned her out on a blind siding and she never got back on the main line." They almost never visited him, and when they did, it was mostly hoping to stumble on something they could take. About ten years ago, the girl, Karen, came up with some friends and tried to make methamphetamine in the old line shack, but they claimed she'd changed her ways and had a family of her own, living near Powderville with a good cowboy she'd met at the Calgary Stampede. The boy, Clay, sold cars in Glendive and was a gloomy type who hated winters and stayed close to his mother, who had inherited the local Penney's store; together they were paying on a lot in Mesa, Arizona. All Bill ever said was that no thanks to him, they'd turned out good.

"We had just got our horses up for the year. They was out all winter and the saddles didn't fit and them horses would buck all hell west and crooked till we could get 'em rode. I was down in the ranch yard and Leo, the illegal worked for me then, said some old-timer had arrived on a wild horse and rolled out his bedroll under the loading chute, put his head on his saddle and gone to sleep. I had an idea it was Robert Wood, and it was. Course I didn't find him asleep, just caught his eye and told him I would see him in the morning. I pretty much knew what he was after. He had a band of mares up on the bench behind our ranch, you know, Ev, where that tank went dry, mares that was running out with wild horses there, not real mustangs but just cayuses folks had turned out when they went to war and they'd reverted and was all outright broncs. I'd promised to gather 'em for Robert when we had a full complement of help, because it wasn't going to be easy in any way, shape or form. Well, Robert lost patience with me . . ."

By this time, Evelyn had sunk full length into the couch, and the only thing that moved were her extremely attentive eyes. She was afraid that if she moved she would make some sound and lose a word or two and that was just out of the question. She had long wished to know about all the disappeared horses of the surrounding hills.

"Robert's horses were quick, and the only safe place around them was on their backs. They was quiet in a herd of cattle and had the lightest noses in the West. It always looked like he'd put high-volt lights in their eyes. Robert showed them all the little connections between what he asked them to do and their jobs, and it was so pretty the way they'd look for a cow. O. C. Drury hauled cattle as a sideline, and he hated to haul Robert's calves. Invariably, he'd arrive in the ranch yard mid-October and Robert would start whining, 'O. C., anyone can see I'm so short-handed just now. You want to catch up old bay and help me bring these cattle in? We'll sort 'em off right here and now and call this year done.' O. C. didn't want to do it, in fact his blood ran cold. But he *had* to. So, he'd climb up on old bay or old sorrelly who'd know right then and there this wasn't Robert Wood: one false move and the wreck was on.

"Back to Mother's Day, I let Robert sleep through the night and by the time I woke, just before sunup, I could smell his fire and coffee. Then in a bit I heard Leo's voice and knew the two of them throwed in and was layin' a plan. I made something decent for the three of us, mostly just to buy some time in the hopes Robert would quit this idea to bring his broncs off the bench with just me, him and Leo, a small fellow out of Sonora who listened to this kinda like polka music when he was homesick. Hair fell in his face in bangs, hard, square hands, and no sense of humor. Couldn't read nor write but he had a perfect memory. If you lost something, could be a week ago, he'd walk straight to where you put it down.

"Robert Wood was just an old puncher who'd outlived his day. Thought the Old West could be brought back if they'd just quit dammin' up water to make alfalfa. He hated alfalfa and would go a long way out of his way to keep from seein' it. I suppose he was seventy-five years old 'cause I seen in the papers when he died about ten years ago he'd made ninety or better. Wore a Stetson right out of the box, no crease, no nothin'. He wouldn't wear a straw hat in the summer, said it was a farmer's hat.

"Robert said, 'Here is the deal. We'll go up the switch-back together to the bench and when we get there I'll ride around and see if I can't stop them.' The right place to get their attention was that big earthquake fault, you know, where we seen that lynx last summer, which no man could cross with a horse. That slope beyond it could've been a good escape route for those mares. 'And *hide* in the brush and don't show even the end of your nose else they'll see it.

Then you two get around them mares and start 'em home. I'll make sure they come back down the trail. When they get down to the flat *somebody* will have to get outside these horses and thataway turn 'em into your corrals. I hope you don't mind me borrowin' your corrals.'

"Ev, you've seen that crack in the ground. It's a long way to the bottom. I really doubted Robert would turn those horses there. Wild horses and canners like these just as soon jump it and break their necks, whereas a horse and rider would never do such a thing. I guessed it would end there and we'd turn 'em down off the bench and lock 'em up at the neighbors. *Then* we'd have time to get a proper crew together."

Evelyn started to speak, but thought better of it.

"When the horses got out on the flat, somebody'd have to ride out around that wild band, outrun them on broken ground, turn them into the corrals. And I wondered how all of this might look to Robert, who kind of despised our horsemanship. I mean Robert Wood worked for the Hash Knife, the N Bar, the Pitchfork, the Matador. And sure always rode a *finished* horse, but it had to be tough as whang leather or he just wouldn't have it around. Horse needed to stand up in that bridle and *look* for work.

"First off, we had to get crooked old Robert on his horse. He led his sorrel mare out of the pen behind the scales and tied her to a plank of the chute. She was a little sickle-hocked, which I'm sure he preferred, and she had good withers, short pasterns, kind of coon-footed, low-croup cow-horse look to her, ears pricked forward, even whickered at him quick as she seen him.

"It was just painful to watch him saddle this horse. He threw the Navajo up all right, but when he lifted that old slick-fork saddle, we felt how it hurt him and yet knew we ought not to help. He bridled her up in a little grazer bit and led her around to the front of the chute. He threw one rein around the horn and wrapped the other around the corner post of the loading chute. She stood all right—I mean, he'd dare her not to stand—but that wasn't no kid's horse, bad as anything he'd force O. C. onto, nose blowed out and white around her eyes. Cross a horse like that and she drives you into the ground like a picketpin.

"Then Robert walks around to the holding pen, squeaks the old gate open, goes inside and next time we see him, he's crawling up the chute, out the end and onto his horse. She snorted and backed away and he hung down around her neck to catch his other rein. When he sat up in the saddle, he had both reins plaited through the fingers of his left hand and just lifted his hand about three-sixteenths of an inch and she sat down on her hocks and backed clear across the ranch yard in a cloud of dust. Then he straightened up, threw her some slack and she stood square to the world, ready for work. Had of been O. C. his ass'd be over the granary. I rode a dun gelding I'd broke and was hopin' Robert'd tell me what a great job I'd did, but he didn't say *nothin'*.

"Up we go single file and I stay to watch Robert. His shoulders were back and he sat ramrod straight in the middle of his saddle, boots plumb home in iron oxbows, reins hangin' soft over the side of his left hand. In the other hand he's got a string with a knot for every mare. He turned real slow in his saddle and give my Mexican a good hard look. It wasn't long before we were on top. When Leo loped out to the west and made a little dust, I could see Robert was gonna quit worryin' about him. Leo made a big ride around the horses, which had wheeled up to watch him, and only began to disperse and feed as the circle he made came to seem too grand to concern them. By the time I rode back to the far side of the bench, Leo was closin' in my direction and two miles off, them horses began to drift away. There was sixteen horses, and about ten of them was pretty uniform-looking sorrel horses that looked kin to Robert's mount. The remainder was nothin' but dog feed with Roman noses and big hairy feet. They'd hurt your eyes. My old man sent thousands just like them on the train to Owens Brothers in Kansas City. The good ones went to the Boer War and the Frenchmen ate the rest.

"The first part of our plan to come apart was where we's gonna ease 'em on out of there because they plumb took off. In two jumps they was smokin' across the flattop and our horses caught that gust off of them and liked to get out from under us. Leo had to pull his mount in some hard circles to keep him from buckin' with him, and mine had his head in my lap to where I'd liked to broke something over it, but pretty quick I had the best of him and he's look-ing straight through his bridle like a gentleman. Leo was foggin' it about a mile off, a big cloud of dust driftin' away like a grass fire.

"It was pretty clear there was no smart way to turn 'em down the road even if Robert had been prepared to do so, but he was nowhere in sight. So the best we could do was throw them off the slope ahead and scatter them out among those little ranches along the river, where they would just play hell with the alfalfa. Them farmers would just shoot 'em down.

"That's where everything changed. Robert broke out of the brush on his horse way past that crack in the ground, his sorrel mare comin' out in a flurry of sage and grease-wood cracking off in the air around her. Them broncs froze at the *sight* of her. They could either leap that crack and fly past him, or Robert could jump the crack himself and turn 'em toward my house. It was my corrals or the alfalfa; it was that simple.

"Presently they came boilin' back and we whooped and hollered. Leo took down his slicker and got them bunched up once more toward the trail where they *did not* want to go and Robert's yellin', 'Drive 'em, boys!' till they advanced his way like a bright-colored little cyclone tryin' to break right around him. We almost lost 'em right there. Robert stretched up over his mare's neck and she closed on that crack just burnin' a hole in the wind, and when she reached it she soared up into the air, Robert easing back into the saddle with his stirrups pushed out in front toward the landing he hoped they would both make."

At this, Bill stopped and went across the room to the fire-place, where he rapped the grate with a poker to make the cold ashes fall through.

"I can still see that black hole in the ground, which was really s'posed to be Robert's grave, but that old man float-ing beyond its grasp, that smart old mare reaching her long beautiful legs for the far shore. Leo told me he thought she'd been in the air for an hour.

"Well, they make it. And she sits down into her stop in a cloud of dust and confounds them wild horses who was turned into lambs with their ears hangin' ever which way. Robert leans up with both hands on the pommel, deep slack of reins hanging under the sorrel's neck, and he takes time to count off them mares on his string. Then we re-sume a very orderly jog down the ranch road gazin' over the packed, hurryin' backs of them mares who recognized they was back in Mr. Robert Wood's remuda and was very well behaved. You could see they liked it. They wanted to be there. It was okay.

"When they was corralled, Robert says in his singsong voice, 'That sure is a relief. I have to be honest, I was worried they'd give us trouble.' He rode over to where he left his bedroll. 'Bill,' he said, 'I was gonna ask your Mexican to cheek this mare while I slide off, but I'm confusing her with her mother. She was bad to paw at you when you got down. And one other thing, Billy, when you ask a green horse like yours to stop and turn, you need to start his nose first and just let him pour through. You got him handlin' like *a plank*.'"

Bill threw his head back and laughed. Evelyn would have joined him, but she was still thinking.

There were things about her treatment of her husband that Natalie regretted, but they did not include the endless pains she'd taken to protect him from her father and his conviction that Stuart would never go anywhere at all. It was remarkable that Sunny Jim would have settled all his hopes on Paul, who at the funeral owned the driest eye in the house, and completely pass over Stuart, who was loved by the workers at the bottling plant while Paul was loathed as a treacherous and authoritarian opportunist.

Natalie was less proud of the fact that she was so unwilling to join Stuart at the things he loved. It was just that she found him so very, very tiresome. She felt she needed to leave sticky notes for him everywhere just to keep him on course. And she regretted her fury at his remark that her father was "gone but not forgotten," which, it's true, was delivered in a singsong that suggested Stuart had a streak of independence. After the funeral, she tried to bend a little and agreed to sail with him for a day at Canyon Ferry, where he kept his sloop on a narrow wooden dock over green water. *Miss Annie* had been named for a pretty girl at the plant on whom Stuart had a harmless crush. Natalie had never been sufficiently interested to ask about the name, and Stuart liked having the secret that he thought might be expanded, perhaps to an exchange of small kind-nesses, if ever he took the real Annie for a sail.

Winter was almost upon them and snatching this warm day from such a short autumn was exciting. Natalie dangled her legs over the water with her omnipresent fat paperback while Stuart prepared the boat. He sponged the rainwater out of the bilges, pulled the sail cover off the main and let the condensation evaporate; he scrubbed bird droppings from the painted canvas deck, then rinsed it down with buckets of cold, fresh lake water that ran around the coam-ing and out over the transom. He was eager to "take the old girl out for a gallop," as his easygoing father used to say.

No one of his in-laws would have understood such a thought, except maybe Evelyn with her horses. He found these people rather twisted, but he was far too mild to make much of it. He presumed it to be part of the Western Way. Most of the Whitelaws failed to appreciate Stuart's quiet self-knowledge and would have been surprised at how often his idlest daydreams featured detailed accounts of their complete humiliation. He still resented the fact that Natalie had long ago forbidden him to sing any of the sea chanties he'd so painstakingly memorized. Once the decks dried and everything was in order, Stuart said, "Shall we sail?" And without a word, Natalie turned down a corner of her potboiler, got to her feet and stretched. "This will be very pleasant," she said fretfully.

Stuart helped her aboard, then ran his eye around the inside of the boat, making certain everything was in order, fingers reaching out to touch white oak ribs, curves of cedar. Natalie picked a quiet spot in the cockpit so as not to be in Stuart's way, made herself comfortable with her hands up the sleeves of an old sailing sweater. Stuart untied all the lines, coiled and stowed them in the forepeak, then walked the sloop the length of the dock, gave her a shove toward open water and jumped aboard. He let the main sheet run free while he raised the sail, putting the halyard on the winch and hoisting it tight. The boat began slowly to forge toward Confederate Gulch, a steady chugging sound against the hull as they worked their way across the vanished riverbed, whiffs of pine and barbecue, farm trucks in the distance and a dust cloud following a tractor. Stuart raised the jib, sat back in the cockpit with his hand on the tiller, looked over at his wife and said, "There."

Natalie seemed contemplative, certainly not desperate. Clearly the death of her father was always on her mind. But Whitelaw had never been close to his girls and at the end was quite senile, interested mostly in filling the birdfeeders around the house and keeping his wife constantly in sight. Yes, said the court to suggestions of senility, but of insufficient duration: the will was binding, its various booby traps ascribable to eccentricity not mental incompetence. Seeing him pottering around in his red watch cap, his family occasionally forgot what he had done to their lives. Natalie had even exclaimed that he was "adorable," an epithet Evelyn could not quite go along with.

From Confederate Gulch they tacked to the old brick grain silos on the west side of the lake, then east again toward the great bend north of the village of Winston, the lee rail just compressing against the swell and the rise and fall of the stem slicing forward into the water, quiet and thrilling. From time to time Natalie turned to watch the water race past. The sun was over the whole lake now, and the breeze carried the spray across the deck. Several other boats had set out, their sails vivid and white against the grain fields of the far shore. Stuart felt a lovely hum come up the rudder and through the tiller as the sloop began to sail itself. Later, he would keep going back to that picture: the sloop at its perfect angle, the flow of water along the rudder, the silver spray in the air, and Natalie taking it all in, curled up in her sweater, trying to picture how she might leave him.

A school of fish broke the surface off the bow, and they saw, beneath the hull, their small shapes hurrying away. They drew abreast of abandoned grassy hills where deer grazed in bright sun. Stuart sailed from cat's paw to cat's paw, working his way to an anchorage, a nice piece of work lost on Natalie, whose mind lingered on the handsome stranger in her book who had just turned up in the lives of the three young heiresses. At last the anchor was down, and the sloop swung close to the steep beach and its mantle of wild berries.

Natalie stretched and looked around as though awakening and discovering her surroundings. "Is it too early for a drink?" she asked.

"Yes, my dear, it is."

"Stuart, you're always looking out for me, aren't you?" Her musing tone successfully concealed her loathing. " 'Put on your sweater. Get out of the wind. No drink till five. Try to see Dad's good side. Be patient with your mother. . . .'" He glanced at her warily, but she really meant this.

"Those sound like club rules. I hope I'm not oppressing you."

"Oh, not at all, it's like being tucked in. Apart from the indication that I need help in performing these obvious things." As a kind of internal joke, she was pretending to address all of her remarks to a cigar-store Indian.

"Nat—"

"But my worst trait—let's go right to my *worst* trait—is the mistaken belief that I can influence events way more than I really can." She could actually picture the Indian now, ruddy hand clutched around wooden cigars.

Stuart lifted a floorboard and looked down at the heads of the keel bolts. "Is this about Paul?" If the bolts pulled through neglected, rotten wood, the keel would plummet to the bottom and the force of the sail would capsize the boat, with the possibility of Natalie trailing bubbles from her lungs all the way to the bottom.

"Of course it is. I can see right away that Evelyn's going to forgive him, and it's just no good."

"But you're not Evelyn."

"I don't need to be. I'm the only one in this family who is consistently on to Paul. Not even you see him as he is." This, given the liberties she still permitted Paul, gave her a special tingle.

"It's not that, Nat. It's just that we spend so much time thinking about him. I'm not fooled by Paul; I'm indifferent to him. You have to accept things about people you don't like or there'd be no one to talk to." Stuart had a bit of trouble understanding why he was delivering such a mendacious gloss on his actual dislike of Paul Crusoe. He'd have to go into that at a later date. Perhaps it was simply his instinct to hold large issues at bay while he enjoyed his small pleasures, like sailing and refinishing furniture. Besides, Natalie tired him with the acuteness of her observations. He once told her that she should be like a good skier and, instead of fighting every turn of the hill, give some time to gliding. But Natalie was not a skier and despised all figures of speech based on sport. "Have you ever actually seen a cigar-store Indian?" she inquired. He had no idea how to field this non sequitur.

It was as though this hearty, uncomplicated man (attributes Natalie associated with victims) was drawn only to her big dark eyes, her pretty, worried face, her slight figure devoid of muscle tone.

Stuart didn't concern himself too much with the testiness of Natalie's relations with Paul. It was his observation that often women who experienced fits of inexplicable resentment toward other men had actually been to bed with them. Paul was so extraordinarily swift to seduce or corrupt women that the whole process was rendered negligible. A friend of Stuart's had seen Paul entering the Super 8 Motel with his cold-sober probation officer, if that could be believed, the very night of Whitelaw's funeral. Furthermore, Evelyn had told Natalie that Paul had asked *her* to meet him there and she had declined. The very notion made both sisters indignant, for different reasons, but Stuart was astounded that his brother-in-law would go to such lengths to economize on a room deposit. In this, Stuart was obtuse.

The sun in the cockpit was so comfortable that what they intended to be a moment of sunbathing turned into a serious nap. The aspens in the draw that led to the lake, old stream courses that once fed a live river, were turning a yellow patchwork among the cedars and red bursts among the serviceberries, plum thickets and chokecherries. Natalie was first to awaken and was startled by the grass shore so close to them. Winter is coming, she thought. She touched Stuart to rouse him.

"We must've needed that," he said as he looked first at the beach, then up the column of the mast to the windex pointing into the light breeze coming down the hills.

"What's going to become of the bottling plant?"

"Oh, good God." Stuart held the cap of her knee delicately between thumb and forefinger. "Let's walk on the beach," he said. Natalie took this suggestion in as though it contained a hidden catch.

"Will we need sunblock?"

He took out the plastic tube and gently applied sunblock to Natalie's upturned face, then put some on his own. Natalie raised her eyes to an airliner high above them. She seemed suspicious of that too. "Where's *that* thing going?"

Stuart said, "Are you hungry?"

"What's in there?"

"Sandwiches and stuff."

"What kind of sandwiches?"

"Are you okay?"

"I'm a little sad. But I'm fine."

They took a walk. From the uplands, they could look back down at their boat rocking gently in the clear water, shelving steep over cold stones, the sun standing around the sleek shapes of the outlined deck. The next range of hills took them out of sight of the water, but the bowl of wild lupine, asters and phlox still surviving the late season seemed like a lake. They could sit on tussocks of bluestem and watch the wild deer grazing beyond the curve of sky. To the west were the Elkhorn Mountains, whose foothills sheltered ancient hunting parties returning from a broad valley that was now a lake. Natalie said, "He stole the best years of my sister's life. There are people who just use others up. Life is short, and I can't just stand by."

"You're going to have to," said Stuart, getting an odd feeling in the pit of his stomach. There was something entirely too avid about Natalie's concern.

She caught the shortness of his reply and fell silent, looking gloomily out upon the natural world. What use was it?

Stuart began to unpack their lunch. As he looked at the meal he had made, he felt hurt. He didn't really know why. Natalie gave him a hug, then sat back and gazed at him.

"Well," he said, "I hope you have an appetite."

"What's the matter?"

"I don't know."

"Tell me."

He didn't want it pulled out of him, but he couldn't help himself. "Maybe . . . maybe it's that we spend our whole time analyzing everyone else's lives. It doesn't leave much room for our own." Natalie was not at all affected by this remark. It may have been that this wasn't really what was bothering Stuart, but it kept them quiet. So they ate their lunches and watched the clouds build up toward Helena. Summer was gone.

They made love on an arrangement of their clothes. It was meant to happen in a slow, afternoonish way, but an unforeseen urgency arose from somewhere and they spent themselves abruptly. He wondered who on earth he was thinking of. But it had a good effect in restoring Natalie's spirits. She said, "There's no real reason for us to get dressed. We can keep walking without our clothes. It's warm."

"It's a public place."

"So, where's the public?"

"They're here in spirit."

"I'm not bothered by the spirit of the public seeing my naked buns. It's only the public in person that's a problem."

"Natalie, just get dressed."

"I'm clogged."

"Aw gee, Nat—"

"Stuart, Stuart."

"Stuart who loves you."

"Yes, I believe that. I always have, and shouldn't that be enough? Shouldn't it be plenty?"

"It should be all we ever need, Nat. But we just think too damn much."

"You mean *I* think too damn much, and I disagree. You heap simple feller, Stuart." The cigar-store Indian had re-appeared; she would have to get a grip on herself.

Stuart knew that this was headed straight to some version of the one-thing-led-to-another speech, in which from the moment they fell in love, they'd followed their weaknesses until they lived under the oligarchy of the bottling plant; and in which they'd failed to find the strength to resist the temptations thrown their way by Whitelaw.

Natalie sprawled on her back. "What were we doing with all our energy, smart Stuart, when we should have been planning our lives?"

Stuart didn't answer, because now in their weariness they could have the time-filled lovemaking they'd desired. He embraced Natalie again and with some difficulty she managed to bestir herself. "I'm enjoying you," she said once

he'd begun. "I'm enjoying you now." When they were finished, they lay back on the deep grass, and Natalie found
herself really watching the clouds, seeing their passage and
imagining their destinies. It was with a rare lightness of
spirit that she resolved to stop seeing Paul at least until she
could dump Stuart. It would be like the release of the white
doves at the opening of the Olympics.

When Evelyn wondered how she had befouled herself with
so unsuitable a marriage, she imagined it was her abrupt
immersion in a carnal world. The widely experienced Paul
hardly thought of anything else. She might have been
moved as well by her father's enthusiasm for Paul welded in
business talk, duck blinds and the national rodeo finals, an
annual trip that left the two under the weather for a week
after their return. Evelyn and her mother never inquired
even when one of these trips resulted in an amateurish
attempt at blackmail by a phone voice named "Nancy." She
also reminded herself that Paul was not always as he was
now; he'd had surgery on one of these Las Vegas trips and
had come back changed. Still, those were good times to stay
out at the ranch, and often her mother went too. Evelyn
was only slightly baffled by the friendship that had grown
between her mother and Bill. And she was amused at the
curiously sharp views her mother had about how Bill
should be running things, which she expressed to him with
what Evelyn considered unseemly familiarity.
    Evelyn's freedom from Paul was expensive, as she
reminded herself regularly. Natalie and Stuart said less and
less, despite being financially chained to Paul and a business that was already declining in value. According to

Melvin Blaylock, the lawyer who'd attended the funeral, the day would come when the bottling plant was worth *nothing*. "You really should sell it yesterday," he said, his tiny features remarkably without animation under the war-like crown of his peculiar hair.

"But that requires that Paul and I reconcile," Evelyn told him. "And we dislike each other."

At this, Melvin Blaylock raised a finger. "It's your money," he said.

"I don't think so," she beamed.

Actually, Natalie did remark, once, "God, we *would* have a lot of money."

Evelyn cringed at the force of the remark, and it rarely came up again.

Evelyn drove past the grain elevator and pulled in by the old wool dock to the feed store. She bought some sacked oats, a hundred pounds of birdseed and a half ton of cattle minerals, and headed toward home, the truck lower on its springs, listening once again to Townes Van Zandt on her CD player, thinking as she heard about the *federales* once again how much she would have liked to figure in some terrific myth like "Pancho and Lefty." She didn't even know what had become of her dream to move off into an unbounded grassland—a veldt!—where human life would arise and expire in the general great sweep of things like a spark that glows then dies. Maybe holding the ranch together with Bill Champion could be enough.

Clanging over the cattle guard, she passed Bill's little frame house behind the orchard and saw his sleeping horses switching flies, and only shifting slightly at the passing of the truck, heads, rumps, prop work of legs, all asleep in the sunshine. Kingbirds spaced themselves along a stretch of barbed wire, while a crowd of young starlings raced the truck before swarming off into a chokecherry thicket whose leaves had curled from frost. When she passed the last hill on which their pinwheel brand was marked with white rocks, her house stood in an angle of warm shadow, an insignificant shape under the chambered upper stories of the black river cottonwoods. While the cooling engine ticked under its hood, she tried to take in her happiness and decided it might consist of nothing more than living by herself. Sometimes it was loneliness, sometimes freedom.

She quickly carried her groceries inside, throwing open a few windows, then resumed her trip to Bill's house, made distant by his discards: metal drums he planned to cut up to hold stock salt and range minerals, tires, sprayer tanks, a set of bedsprings, defunct farm machinery, feed sacks, old batteries, a broken wheelbarrow and a camper top that had lost its windows. Evelyn stopped at Bill's house, where even more of his horses—Who, Scram and Matador—observed her before going back to eating, pulling hay through the bars of a steel feeder, and she recalled her father's frequent exclamation, "Good God, he's got another horse!" Bill didn't answer her calls, and so she assumed he would be down around the barn. She unloaded his groceries in the kitchen and started thinking about Paul again because a package of ground round had reminded her out of the blue that Paul's hero was Ray M. Kroc, the founder of McDonald's. "Life is dog eat dog and rat eat rat" was his favorite Kroc quote, not exactly Emersonian in spirit. "If my competition was drowning, I'd put a hose in their mouth." Paul used to say that hamburger was where the rubber met the road in the cattle business, and that Ray M. Kroc was the ultimate trail boss.

From the kitchen she could see her own unmade bed and loved the innocence of its disarray, rumpled on one side, taut on the other. She thought with near glee of waking early and alone, birdsong coming through the window and no reason to make the bed. She went back outside and walked toward the barn. This would be a fine day, one of the last, to work her young colt, Cree.

Standing in the bad light of the barn under the hay mow, with saddle stands back in between the disused draft horse stanchions, Evelyn searched through the bridles that seemed, in her view, to be festooned from too few pegs, so that in hunting through for the short shanked Kelly Brothers grazer, all she could find were snaffles, Argentine bits, a cable tie-down, offside billet straps, cinchas with broken strings, detached go-betweens, old steel stirrups that Bill said were cold enough in winter to "freeze the nuts off a riding plow," a coppermouth John Israel, a gag bit, an Easy Stop, a knockoff of a Garcia spade, boot tops made into saddlebags and a chain twitch with a handle from a World War II foxhole shovel. Just when it seemed hopeless, Bill walked by and said, "That colt of yours has dug him quite a hole." Pigeons flew out from under the roof of the barn, wings colliding with the eaves like broken fan belts.

"If you'd of left my stuff alone, I'd have him saddled."

"Red Wolf's been in there."

"Right. You feel like turning some cattle back for me?"

Evelyn carried her saddle and blanket out to the colt, who had indeed pawed up a considerable mess. She brushed him and handled him a little, but Cree shied back when she threw the blanket up near the base of his neck and slid it down into place to make his coat lay flat. She kept the off-side stirrup on her own side when she put the saddle up because he looked like he was getting ready to fly back. Cree was coming good, but he was quick to spook. When Evelyn was on his back, she still couldn't open gates and if someone handed her anything, he was liable to bolt. As she pulled the latigo, she felt behind the cinch ring to make sure it didn't roll up some skin and pinch him. Then she fastened his girth and led him around a bit until he quit the little skittering toe dance and let her bridle him. He kept his teeth closed at first until she gently slid her thumb up against the base of his tongue. Evelyn pulled his nose next to her, went around and did the same on the other side, then led him a few feet from the nearest thing it would hurt to be bucked off against and stood up in the near stirrup, feeling him line his body up straight to take the weight, and swung aboard, discovering all over again that it was the very best place to be, and they jogged toward the cotton-woods where Bill and his kelpie dog, Cow Patty, were bringing in some black-bred heifers from a stand of reed canary grass where they had nearly disappeared. From Cree's purposeful little shuffle she could tell the young horse had already happily seen the cattle and felt as if he might have business with them. The scattered glimpses of shifting cattle began to solidify under the movements of Bill and his dog, until a small black mass moved gradually toward the overhead gate of the pen. Then a piece of irrigation dam flapped up from one ditch, and Cree bolted gustily for forty feet before stopping and staring it down. Evelyn nudged him with her spur, and he reluctantly started off where the last of the cattle were skipping past Patty, who lay on her belly at the gate. With her intent black-and-brown face, she seemed to be counting them in.

Evelyn followed the cattle into the pen and swung the gate shut behind her. The heifers had quickly gathered around a bale of hay in the center, and Bill was off to one side on his spavined, thoroughpinned old cow horse Avalanche, leaning one elbow on his saddle horn and his face in his hand. Evelyn walked several circles, jogged, long-trotted for a few minutes and eased into a lope. The first thirty or forty saddles, Cree was wont to bog his head when he broke out to gallop, but those days were gone, and he could lope out smooth now from a walk or any other gait and change leads just with a weight shift in the stirrups. He packed his head with his face enough forward that at morning or evening Evelyn could see the light through the walls of his nostrils as if he had fire around his face. He felt good in the broken-mouth bit she now suspected Bill had tricked her into, for she could see the Kelly Brothers in the mouth of old Avalanche, who generally went around in a US Cavalry bit whose shanks had been mended with a pair of harrow tines.

Cree loved to work cattle but was also thoroughly afraid of them. When he was a green colt, Evelyn took him to the sale yard to be around cattle in the winter. The state livestock inspector scared some steers he was trying to clip to check their brands, and they ran right over poor Cree, who skinned up his legs trying to climb over a Powder River panel. He was a nicely made colt with a butt that was closed right down to the back of his knee with muscle, feet set nicely under him and a pretty slope to his shoulder and withers. He had tight, round hoofs at the end of moderately sloped pasterns nicely domed around the frog that took a size-aught shoe and never split out a nail or chipped when he was barefoot, but left a rounded, nearly burnished edge. Evelyn liked to step back from him after he was saddled. He looked like such a little cow horse, though he wasn't so little and at three, tipped a thousand pounds on the Fairbanks Morse cattle scale whose wiggling floor and clanging weights gave him new doubts about the state of the world.

Cree kept one eye on the dreaded cattle, and when one or another picked its head up to look at him, its face dusted with alfalfa particles, he gained speed. Evelyn just sat deeper and let him run it out. When at last the edge seemed to be off, she slumped down and let him stop.

"I think that ring-eye'd look at your colt," Bill said.

"Don't see a ring-eye."

"It's just rubbed off around her left eye, got a little ridge of hair between her shoulders, mud two inches up her left ankle, frosted ear tip and low headset to her tail, peeled brand. Between the flattop and the bonnet."

"Oh, yup, got her." Evelyn twisted in her saddle to study this particular heifer. She saw what Bill liked, something in the way she glanced at the horse from her place by the hay bale, gentle and alert. Evelyn walked her horse toward the cattle, and they began swinging to the far side of the hay to better watch the horse. With all these faces looking at him, Cree seemed lighter on the ground. One high-headed, slant-eyed yearling took this moment to lope around them, and it was all Evelyn could do to keep her colt from bolting for the gate. Despite Cree's intermittent losses of nerve, Evelyn was able to separate a heifer. Once the yearling was driven off by itself and the herd was well behind him,

Cree's confidence returned. The cow ran to the left and he followed easily with her, then stopped as though chilled. When the cow headed the other way, he rolled smoothly through his hocks, turned around and rated her speed. At this point, deciding she was in earnest about returning to the herd, the cow ran straight at the colt and made a series of wild dodges that carried Evelyn around the pen, running, stopping, sliding as though on skates, feeling all the while the ambition rise within her shy young horse as he discovered new ability at every jump. When the cow gave up, she reached down to pat his neck, then rode him away. The cow went back to feeding. "That will do," said Evelyn, lifting the gate latch from her saddle and swinging it aside.

"Good," said Bill.

They rode through a big pink patch of cheatgrass, and detoured around some lilacs that indicated a vanished homestead cabin while Evelyn awaited the inevitable comment.

"He was great," said Bill Champion.

"But what?"

"It could be you're riding him a little tighter with your left leg, I dunno, seems like it's a little easier for him to go the other way. I'm not saying it's so, I'm saying think about it. Maybe you're not turning your own head as good that way and he's feeling it especially when that cow gets a little bit behind your left shoulder. I was sure pleased you let that cow pull you from place to place, seems like you were a little ahead of him with your spurs last time, just a hair. Also, when he gets to feeling doubtful, go on ahead and just drive up to your cow and see if you can't sink the hook that much more. I noticed once or twice you did that, he started to melt real pretty like he was a hundred percent ready for anything she wanted to throw at him."

"What if you're wrong about my left leg?"

"I could be, I sure could be. In that case you're gonna have to bump him from the other side and make him give you that rib. Either way he has to bend identical either direction or he's gonna get beat by that cow the first turn around or the hundredth. It's there. But don't get me wrong, you got you a good scald on your colt today."

Natalie had an interest in cooking that was unshared by her sister, Evelyn, despite the same patient training in a household that tried without success to be conventional. Oddly, Natalie disliked cooking while Evelyn—with a lifelong history of fallen cakes, loaves and soufflés, overcooked meats, congealed sauces and mushy vegetables—enjoyed it tremendously and was a scourge to her guests. She also loved to eat, especially food that had been prepared by other people. So, when she was invited to lunch by Natalie, despite a feeling of indeterminate dread, she accepted, arriving early and standing in the brisk new fall air in front of the tiny house that Stuart had built for them, the tiniest bungalow in a book of home plans, now surrounded by orderly evergreens and a small bed of flowers. She had taken this pause like some forensic diner to identify specific familiar food items—cold veal, gnocchi salad and, she thought, pumpkin soup—that she could already smell from the partially opened kitchen window. Natalie's refrigerator, unlike the stark cold box in Evelyn's house, would be bursting with cheese rinds, five kinds of mustard, melon parts scattered over five shelves, identical milk cartons at different degrees of fullness, cooked chicken halves, bits of meat wrapped in foil for possible dog visits, browning parsley, cellophane and cardboard boxes no longer containing garlic, Italian jug wine as well as pyramids of root vegetables from the back garden she disliked as cordially as cooking. It all seemed to stand for the wish she had for a life rich in people, for social luxury instead of a gruesome snack box for Stuart and herself.

Evelyn walked into a hallway so abbreviated her eye was at the level of the fifth or sixth step of a steep staircase, and a mere pivot revealed the living room, whose little brick fireplace had, upon its mantel, a photograph of their provider, Sunny Jim Whitelaw, with his accustomed scowl. There was a compact bookcase with a series of "chicken soup" books, some form of chicken soup for everyone and everything, except for the chicken itself which, in Evelyn's view, most needed consolation. "We're eating out on the porch!" came Natalie's voice from the kitchen, and there Evelyn found a table laid, a white cloth, a plate of large tomato slices and Spanish onions in malt vinegar, tall goblets next to a wrapped bottle of Fumé. Evelyn sat down and looked at the low glare of cold sun beyond the winterized confines of the porch, frost-curled green ash leaves scratching at the glass. Evelyn lifted a goblet with its satisfying knock of ice and water within and thought how pleasant this was and how close to success many unsuccessful lives were, and how rare were genuinely sordid existences outside books and movies. Her sister and Stuart were an unsuccessful couple, not as Evelyn and Paul had been, but because Natalie was obsessed by what she perceived to be the hidden advantages of others. While Stuart was gentle and kind, Paul claimed he was simple enough to hide his own Easter eggs. Stuart's remark at her father's death— "That's the best news I've had in years"—made Evelyn think there might be another side to him.

With a great exhalation of breath, Natalie swept in, balancing the meal on one hand and gesturing with the other for Evelyn to remain seated. Evelyn was pleased to see the anticipated tureen of pumpkin soup, but instead of gnocchi, she found sharply seasoned raviolis stuffed with pork.

"I wouldn't do this if I didn't love you," said Natalie, sitting down in a disgusted heap. She found a kind of primness about Evelyn as she waited to be served.

"It's beautiful, Nat. I don't know how you manage."

"What do you eat out there on the ranch, corn beef and cabbage?"

"Various stuff, not that."

"You cook for Bill regularly?"

"Not regularly."

"How's his health?"

"He's hanging right in there."

Natalie spread her napkin in her lap. "When Dad sent you for riding lessons, I don't think he ever figured you were never coming back."

"Must have been the horses."

"Well, whatever. Anyway, it was Mama always drove you out there, not Dad."

"She liked to talk to Bill."

"She *really* liked to talk to Bill."

"I don't think there was anything to it, particularly," Evelyn said.

"Maybe, maybe not. But she sure liked driving you out there."

Evelyn thought she'd let this one drop. But it was remarkable that anything that ever happened to her or Natalie was known almost instantaneously by Bill, however many miles away. And he was forever frustrated that Natalie couldn't be made to take an interest in the ranch. He must have learned that from Alice Whitelaw. Perhaps, a friendship existed, and if so, fine.

"This was Daddy's favorite soup, but not for now, for summer. How is it?"

"Really good."

"You'd eat anything," Natalie said, looking into the tureen as though daring its contents to be imperfect.

"I wish I could cook like this, but my mind goes shooting ahead and things catch fire."

A car passed by pursued by a column of disturbed leaves, and Evelyn felt something odd about the two of them sitting together as though all the elements that had accounted for them were lifted momentarily and they would now bear the gravity of being the only excuse for their own lives.

"I'm in love with Frank Sinatra," said Natalie, starting "I've Got You Under My Skin" with the touch of a button, "and I'm afraid of winter." Wind-borne clouds were darkening the sky, and she was obliged to turn on the brass overhead lights, reconditioned salvage from an extinct ranch house in Black Eagle. Stuart gathered odds and ends from junk shops in such odd places as Box Elder and Medicine Lake and Opportunity. Evelyn remembered his pulling up in front of the house with a mountain of junk on a fifth-wheel lowboy, looking contented. "Thousand feet of straight grain Doug fir tongue-and-groove from Hungry Horse!"

"Old Blue Eyes," said Evelyn.

"Funny you'd know that."

"One of Bill's horses, crop-out paint, he looks nuts."

"How about 'Der Bingle' for Bing Crosby?"

They were at some sort of dead-end, and Evelyn looked around blankly. Stuart had really made a comfortable little house, though he baffled Evelyn in other ways with facial expressions that seemed to lie behind a scrim, like the faces of people on television whose identities were being protected; and he was so remarkably sexless that she could imagine him coming along before the age of anatomically correct dolls, a curious smoothness not without its appeal. Evelyn noted that Natalie's intense concentration on her food would provide an excellent backdrop for difficult conversation offered in the form of mere incidentals. As here it came: "You won't be offended, Evelyn, if I state that Paul is no Daddy." She paused to make room for the reply that did not come. "He doesn't understand the first thing about that business. You know Stuart speaks with the utmost kindness of other people, and even he says that Paul is completely lost. When employees go off and leave their pensions behind, something has gone badly wrong."

"I'm sure there's a problem with the transition. Daddy never budged." Sunny Jim actually had said, "Budge and you die," something he might have gotten from Bill. At any rate, there was this whole culture of budging and not budging that Evelyn couldn't follow.

"It isn't that *at all*, Evie. Paul is cruel and he's inconsistent and he doesn't know how to run the plant."

"Of course he's cruel. Prison made him cruel. That's how he is now, but he wasn't always. In any case, Nat, you need to stay away from him."

Natalie seemed to discover in her soup something so minuscule and annoying, it could be retrieved only with the very tip of her spoon. She then placed the spoon next to her bowl and placed the tip of her right forefinger on its handle. "Whatever could you mean?"

"If you don't know, then I sure don't."

"Well, I *don't* know."

"Then *neither do I.*"

Evelyn looked at her sister. When they were young, she had had an astigmatism that she outgrew and Natalie had had braces and a retainer for her very prominent teeth. They sometimes called each other "Buck Teeth" and "Four Eyes" and now those times seemed to be coming back. On the verge of tears, each had begun to feel ugly and powerless again.

Natalie snuffled, "I made a key lime pie!" She went to the kitchen and brought it out, a beautiful thing, light and golden at the edges. She sank her knife into it, served them both, then sat, suddenly making herself very still.

"Pie okay?"

"Wonderful."

"That's a real one," Natalie said tragically, "made with condensed milk."

"What'd you do for limes?"

"Just Spanish limes from the store, but they'll do. Now. Ev. Listen. Stuart, good Stuart, no big future, right?"

"I don't—"

"No, come on, I should know. This is it!" She gestured

around the little Craftsman knockoff, so suggestive of modest, happy family life. It had been built during a difficult period in their marriage, and Natalie's unfortunate habit of discussing those problems with anyone who would listen had given their marriage a poor reputation that persisted even in better times. In fact, during the era when all of Paul's strengths were a display of lewd aggression and intrigue, Evelyn found herself longing for just such a do-it-yourselfer. But Natalie's inclusive gesture, her "this is it," effectively dramatized the distance between what she dreamed and what she had. Evelyn knew too well where this was headed.

"I cannot go back to Paul."

"We'll starve."

"It will be honorable starvation."

"Surely there could be some accommodation with the terms—"

There was a clangor of the heating that might've implicated Stuart's skills as a plumber. That and the wind-borne leaf storm in the small yard gave the house a precarious feel.

"I don't know how Dad could have done this to us."

"I loved Dad!"

"*So did I*. But it wasn't easy and *please*, Evie, don't be a *bitch*, it wasn't easy to watch him make such a husk out of Mama!" Natalie was holding her hair out from her head with both hands: a Medean tableau that would have seemed insincere except that it was done with such mad force that it made Evelyn watch her steps carefully.

"Nat, look, this is getting to be a scene. Such a nice lunch, so perfectly prepared, as if I were a guest of honor! But is there no way we can *discuss* this?"

"'*Discuss*'?" Natalie asked, quarreling with the very word.

"How do you think I like being called a bitch?"

That stopped her for a moment. Down came the hands, through the thick, crazy hair that only slowly subsided. If only we were wounded celebrities, Evelyn thought, who could set out on a healing retreat away from this pain. Supervised by recovery specialists, we could safely call each other bitch and request that our sister stay out of our estranged husband's bed without the customary repercussions.

"Bitch is a terrible word, isn't it?"

"Lucy was a bitch," said Natalie, and suddenly both women were weeping. When they were girls, they shared a Labrador retriever named Lucy, whom their father would not allow in the house. Twenty years previous, on Christmas Eve, the then old and silver-muzzled Lucy froze to death under the wreath on the front door. Natalie's heart broke as much for her father as for Lucy, whereas Evelyn concluded he was just one of life's nasty surprises and treated him with unyielding distance. "She's a cold one," Sunny Jim later said of Evelyn, only a little chagrined by the feeling that the oldest girl had his number, and completely unaware of the agony he produced in her.

Evelyn loved Natalie's food and so did Paul, who owned a sensitive palate among other refinements including prairie architecture, Porsches and Eames furniture. He spotted Art Deco details on buildings, radios and furniture; and for a while was besotted by Bakelite. Sharing his quest for esoteric collectibles, Natalie was once able to discover what a short leap it was from Bakelite to sordid motels on the interstate and the subsequent raw and bankrupt carnival.

"I love you, Evie, and I don't want you to do what's not right."

"I love you too, Nat."

"Now," Natalie sobbed, "we shall simply have to downsize."

"My God!" Evelyn snapped. "What do you expect?"

Natalie flung her face up, awash with tears, damp hair tangled at her temples. "I'll tell you what *I'd* do. I'd drum up some fucking *white marriage*, some illusion to get the rest of us living like *human beings*."

"What about my life?" Evelyn shouted.

"What about it? Does *mine* have to disappear while you review what makes *you* comfortable?"

Evelyn stood and said, "Thank you for a lovely lunch."

Natalie bowed her head and did not look up when her sister departed. After a decent interval and a deep breath, she consulted her watch, then gave a small sigh.

It was time to go to town.

When Evelyn called her mother to explain she had to pick up some medicine for Bill and would be a few minutes late, Alice said with perfect sincerity, "Bill comes first."

Why was she always so utterly solicitous on his account, Evelyn wondered, standing in line at the pharmacist's window while the two men in front of her had a conversation she couldn't help overhearing. ". . . pulled it out and cleaned it up. Maybe I knocked a hole in it, put the acid to it and then . . . damned if I know. It don't look dirty but it is. I went on ahead and clamped it but then it dropped several amps. Must be dirty . . ." Men were always talking like this: you couldn't understand a thing they were saying.

Once she'd paid for the prescription, Evelyn started up the icy sidewalk toward her car. Coming from the opposite direction was a dandyish male wavering in the poor light of a fall afternoon. Before the figure finally emerged into deep focus, Evelyn felt something of an anxious chill. It was Paul, of course.

"Hello, Evelyn," he said levelly.

She busied herself tying a better knot in the green silk scarf she'd wound around her neck. "Paul. I'm afraid I didn't recognize you at first."

He smiled. "So, Evelyn, why don't we ever see you down at the plant? Those are your vital interests."

"It's never really fascinated me, Paul."

"But it's on-the-job training for the new CEO, and I've got all these dependents!"

"How do you stand it?"

His smile seemed unevenly distributed on his face. "It's a living."

"I picture a ship without a rudder."

"Oh? We've already been approached by a broker out of Atlanta, Joel Kram, old southern family. He made a fortune with a caffeine-laced dairy product called Kreem, then lost half of it defending himself in lawsuits. He used stock footage of Martin Luther King's famous speech in his ads and dubbed in the word 'Kreem' for 'dream.'"

"Do we have to meet Mr. Kram?" Evelyn's arms hung straight at her sides, and she was unafraid.

"I tell you he's real. I'll tape a Dun and Bradstreet to his face so you can read his balance sheet while speaking to him."

Evelyn was tired of listening to him. "I hope you do

something. From what I hear, you're running it into the ground." Then she walked away, skin crawling at this brush of his wings. She was entirely uncertain if she was widening the distance.

"Paul has offered to lend me his luggage for my trip," Alice said, standing stocking-footed in the carpet beside neat piles of her travel clothing. "Isn't that nice?"

"You've got your own luggage," said Evelyn, somewhat shortly.

"Paul says it's inadequate."

"He does, does he? Well, Paul loves his luggage in an immoderate way. It's some kind of English aluminum stuff, like aircraft material. He had a briefcase made out of the same thing, looked like robot luggage or something."

"It's very rugged. And, Evelyn, I *am* going to Alaska."

"Mother, I don't think it's necessary to pack as if this were an expedition. I read the brochure, and it's all a safe and pleasant illusion. If you don't want to meet the natives—"

"On *National Geographic* they tossed people up in the air with a blanket!"

"—you can tough it out with a manicure and a facial."

"Speaking of which, you look a fright."

"We've been worming cattle."

"You and Bill?"

"Yes."

"Is he well?"

"You can't hurt him with a crowbar."

"A beautiful man on a horse."

"What's that?"

"Bill Champion," said her mother, "rides well." Then she moved quickly downstairs to the kitchen.

"Yes, but so did you," Evelyn called, following behind.

"Long ago, angel, long ago."

"I bet it's still there." She swept toast crumbs from the counter into her palm and slapped her hands together over the sink. "Bill said you were right there, right in the middle of it."

"That's very kind, but I don't quite know how he thinks he knows."

"Bill knows everything. Said, 'Alice was a queen.'"

"Oh, my!"

"Mother, your face is red! That's just the cutest thing!" Evelyn was elated that her mother was sufficiently undefeated by her father's death to venture a blush. She picked up the swatter and nailed a fly against the window, fearful that as various intrusions began, this house would become like one of the hulks one saw along old roads. "I can't believe all the health claims on these tea bags."

Once in the living room, and while the tea steeped, Alice Whitelaw said, "You realize I had nothing to do with your father's estate planning."

"Of course I do, Mother. I don't argue with it anyway. If you aren't free to plan your own estate, I guess you're never free." She recognized her own perverse chipperness. Her hands were in her lap.

"Your father felt very strongly about the sanctity of marriage. He desperately wanted to see yours restored. And he was very fond of Paul."

"Sanctity?"

"That will do, Evelyn."

"Reconciling with Paul for the purpose of liberating assets? I don't know."

"Only I suppose if the rest of us should fall on hard times. Natalie nearly reduced to groveling as it is."

Evelyn felt sick. "Mother, aren't you worried about being with that many strangers? It's not such an easy time for you, you know. But *Alaska*—"

"Right now, Evie, it is so very hard to be among familiar things. Of course I dread being with all those unknown faces, but if I can get over *that*, maybe I can begin to handle the rest of my life. Sometimes people get on these cruises and it's all widows. And they have a refrigerated compartment for people who die en route."

"Ugh!"

"Under normal circumstances, Alaska would seem just awful, but I need a change."

Evelyn had come to the house hoping to talk her mother out of plans that, with Paul's deluxe luggage, promised to be unstoppable. She found her courage touching, even though she knew the risk was real: a boatload of party animals hoping to meet the Eskimos; whale watchers with expectations aroused by Disney Studios; drifting, affluent boozers with alluring staterooms. She also felt a childish fear that her mother might return indifferent to her previous life and, especially, her own daughters. In fact, should her mother find real consolation, Evelyn would be, for all practical purposes, an orphan. She was ashamed of this thought that wouldn't go away. Detachment. That's what her mother wanted; and if her reaction to widowhood was a solitary vacation, shouldn't she and Natalie simply admire her readiness? And be happy when she didn't come home in the ship's refrigerator?

"Mother, I never realized you were interested in Alaska."

"Well, I haven't been *un*interested in Alaska."

"But I don't see any books or any—"

"As I said, it's not an abiding interest," Alice said patiently.

"Why not the Caribbean is I guess what I'm trying to say?"

"Can't you just picture those types?"

"It's practically winter up there. This doesn't seem like the time of year to go that far north. Anyway, my thought would be to have some purpose in mind."

"For what?"

"For the *cruise*."

"Darling, I would appreciate it if you addressed me less sharply. I *do* have a purpose in mind, and that is to *collect* myself."

"Which *I* say could be done more comfortably in the Caribbean."

"Evelyn, I don't *wish* to go to the Caribbean. I don't *wish* to be cheek by jowl with the characters who are drawn to beaches and loud clothes, and that music which is just beating on things."

"And what about people who're *drawn* to Alaska, in their plaid shirts and down-filled whatever. . . ." Evelyn was too exercised to go on.

Her mother gazed at her in long affectionate thought. She smiled. "Are you asking if I am hoping to meet someone?"

"I'm not ruling it out."

"Evelyn, I don't like it when you girls are devious. And no, that is not why I'm going. I'm very fragile just now, and I need a change. If I should find myself shipboard with

excitable, harmless people or ninnies, I would be in fright-
ening distress."

"I understand."

"You *don't* understand. I have spent forty years under a
certain roof."

"Perfectly aware of the outer world," said Evelyn, meaning to speak volumes with this suggestion whose impact
was not easily seen.

"Perhaps."

Upstairs, the piles of Alice Whitelaw's clothing had
seemed like the breastworks of a fort.

Evelyn rode up on a crippled bull standing out in a field of
frost-killed mule's ear and mullein, one swollen foot tipped
up behind.

They'd left Bill's house early after a coyote breakfast,
which Bill defined as "a piss and a look around." She
remembered that before leaving he'd stood staring at his
woodpile in thought, then gone back inside for some vet
supplies he put in the saddlebags on his bay gelding. "That
motley-face bull's got foul foot," she told him, and together
they went back to the bull. Bill took down his lariat, moved
his cigarette from the corner of his mouth to the front,
cracked a kitchen match into flame with a thumbnail,
cupped it around the tip, took a deep inhale of smoke and
roped the bull. After tightening his loop, he let the lariat
hang while Evelyn swung her rope and threw a trapping
loop in front of the bull's back legs. Bill winked through the
smoke in approval, wrapped his lariat around the saddle
horn and rode off slowly, rope tightening until it pulled the
bull forward and his back feet tripped Evelyn's loop and he

was roped. Bill rode forward, looking over his shoulder as the bull slowly toppled onto its side. While his horse kept the rope tight, he half-hitched his lariat on the horn and dismounted; the bull watched his approach with a rolling white eye, slammed its head on the ground and gave up.

Bill knelt and touched the swollen foot, feeling around the joint. "Not quite to the tendon sheath," he said, "but the toes's all swollen apart." He held the syringe up to the sky and filled it from a short white jug. "Poor fella," he said, "abandoned like bones at a barbecue."

"Is that LA200?"

"Nope, plain ole oxytetracycline. Don't treat these and it infects a whole pasture. Red Wolf wouldn't like that." He swept the flies from the indentation along the spine and gave the bull his injection in the hip. "We're gonna have to do this several times," he said. "Funny deal, dry year like this. Supposed to bring sulfa boluses, and didn't. Forgot to, I guess."

Evelyn watched him peel back an eyelid and feel under the jaw of the increasingly relaxed bull. She'd watched him closely since her childhood. Now Bill Champion was old, but straight and lean and, when the narrow slits of his eyelids so revealed, the owner of the bluest ice blue eyes. He always had his hands all over his animals, and when something caught him by surprise like this foot rot, he seemed to doubt his own care. Likewise, he watched Evelyn continuously. Today he told her to shorten her reins, sit straight in her saddle, get her heels down in the stirrups and look to where she wanted to go before directing her horse there. "Sometimes they can tell just from your eyes."

Now they gathered more cattle for shipment. Bill liked to leave as soon as you could "tell a cow from a bush," so it was still dark when they trotted out of the corrals. They were desperately trying to beat the first real winter storm, after which shipping and pregnancy testing would become infinitely more laborious and wretched. One day, Bill alarmed Evelyn by leaving his good bay gelding behind in favor of a green colt—"He needs the experience"—which blew up five minutes into the work, dropping his head between his forelegs, then squalling and bucking through wind-bent junipers. Bill managed to ride him to a standstill, and the drive went on. Evelyn rode her reliable baldfaced bay, Crackerjack, and kept her canvas coat unbuttoned from the exertion. Her horse surveyed his land through a forelock that fell over his eyes. "That colt made you ride pretty good," said Evelyn, who seemed even taller wearing spurs and chink chaps, her hair pinned up under a Miami Heat ball cap.

Bill had a sour look on his face, and a band of old sweat ran halfway to the crown of his hat. "I was all over him like a cheap suit." This urgent race with the weather helped Evelyn forget that this was the most depressing day of her year, the separation of the calves from the cows and the shipment of the calves to faraway feedlots.

Evelyn rode along behind the herd, absently untangling Crackerjack's mane with her free hand, reins slung loose from the other, and looked mournfully at the gamboling calves. Several times, an old cow who'd been through this before wheeled around to challenge her horse before losing conviction and joining the herd headed downhill to a certain future.

Wednesday morning it started snowing before sunup; they sorted off the calves amidst the deafening bawl of the cows. When they had divided the steer calves from the heifers into two pens, a rank cow with a single twisted horn grown close to her skull knocked a panel over and they had to sort them again. The big double-decker tractor trailers came down the long lane and circled, one backing up to the chute and the other standing by. Bill had positioned the chute so the early sun wouldn't be in the cattle's eyes when they loaded them. The brand inspector—a small man with iron gray hair, a green State of Montana jacket and worn-out cowboy boots—arrived around eight with a bag of doughnuts and a thermos of coffee, and they commenced the business of weighing the calves, taking them onto the wobbly old scale in drafts of tens and twelves. Evelyn stood with the cattle buyer, resplendent in bright Nocona boots and 40X Resistol with the latest crease, as they slid the weights around, taking turns but each watching the other's hands until the brand inspector came inside and wrote in his book. Bill strode about with a white fiberglass pole, moving the calves here and there as needed as each scale load of confused calves was emptied into adjoining pens and the entire calf crop had been weighed. There was a cloud of steam above the shack, and a stormy sky building overhead in ledges of gray. Evelyn looked at one black calf, curled up on the ground trying to sleep, as if pretending none of this was happening. The buyer woke him with the toe of his boot, and he jumped up and scrambled into the trailer.

By the time all two hundred had gone up the aluminum ramps into various chambers against the roar of the cows and the steady rumble of diesels, Evelyn was covered with manure and had a heavy heart. The truckers stripped off their coveralls and climbed into their cabs in clean clothes. The dark wall that had been ascending in the western sky had overtaken them and it began to snow. Bill paid the brand inspector for his services and, holding the weight tickets between his fingers, raised his leathery face to Evelyn, studied her for a moment and said, "We had a good year."

The bawling of the cattle made conversation impossible. Evelyn tipped her head toward the noise, her excuse for cutting it short. Bill bumped her on the shoulder with an open hand, then turned to make his round of gates and latches, to nail up stray planks on the alleyway that led to the squeeze chute where tomorrow it would be determined which cows had started a new calf for next year. The old dry cows with numerous calves behind them over the long years would be slaughtered. Evelyn was going dancing tonight; tonight she would dance this all away.

She drove off in her little car, its floor a jumble of vaccine bottles, paper coffee cups, baler twine and hair elastics. She drove down the mountain foothills and then, still north of the modest skyline of the city, she turned east toward the stockyards. She followed a semi loaded with round bales until she'd passed the corrals, then parked in front of the café, an encouraging place where cattlemen and hippies could be found sitting at the Formica counter listening to Otis Redding under a sign for Black Cat Stove Polish. Various bits of advice were posted, including *No promises about eggs "over" or "scrambled."* And *If you have a fork, you don't need a spoon to stir your coffee.* And one really caught her attention: *Kill or remove ants on counter.* Here was a spot for Red Wolf, she thought, then added, Now *I'm* doing it. A young man tried unsuccessfully to catch her glance, but without returning it she realized the time for such things was not so far away.

She saw how hard it was snowing and tried to imagine that the calves were better off in the trucks. She ate her breakfast in silence, then drove downtown in weather so lowering the streetlights seemed decapitated. This was when you could discover if your preparations for winter were adequate, and if you were ready for the restrictions of movement and light that were about to be upon you. The snow was blowing up against the front of a travel agency, obscuring the words "holiday" and "foreign currency" on its sign.

With an almost military sense of purpose she made her way through several shortcuts, from which occasional pedestrians appeared or disappeared, coats and scarves drawn across their faces. Her friends Violet and Claire, ambitious beauties, had a small shop on Main Street, Just the Two of Us, that, despite its high prices, Evelyn loved for its rarified sense of exotic couture right next door to an old saddle shop whose owner was their landlord. Evelyn doted on the interior of this silly boutique with its endless chalk white walls and racks of clothes in an arrangement impossible to understand. The owners looked out over their treasures in conspicuous separation from the big old-fashioned cash register to which they hoped to repair often enough to avoid eviction by the saddle maker, who, at the first of the month, came sniffing around for his check. Claire—lips pursed and breathing through her nose in concentration—held a dress abstractly to Evelyn's shoulders. "Thank goodness," Violet said in her surprisingly deep voice, "you don't have a big bosom. Big bosoms make good clothes look stupid. Big bosoms are basically *rural*."

Evelyn stood in manure-covered boots, the dress hand-pinned to the shoulders of her ripped, blue-plaid, snap-button cowboy shirt.

"I hadn't heard that," she said, spotting something else entirely, a black dress whose cut in back Evelyn thought might moderate her overly defined shoulder muscles, something about its little straps, their closeness to the neck, the perfect seams curving toward the hips like arrows, the detailing! She pointed. "That one, I think, if it fits."

"There goes my suggestion," Claire said with a pretended pout, letting the dress she'd held against Evelyn fall over her arm.

"I just have hunches." Evelyn held the weightless thing at arm's length before her. After cowboy shirts, jeans and boots, it looked exciting. "I could get somewhere in this," she said. Claire and Violet stared at this odd remark as Evelyn took the dress back to the changing room. What kind of coat would it take in weather like this? Certainly her Carhartt stockman's coat, stained with veterinary products, was not it. Tonight, she'd find out. A bearded man in a stadium coat was watching Violet and Claire present various items—scarves, a chain purse, a makeup kit, blouses, a beaded top—with ferocious coquetry and a stream of commentary as to their merits. Evelyn changed into the pretty black dress and by bouncing on the balls of her feet made it fall down over herself and into place with reassuring emphasis. Admiring herself in the mirror, she drew the dress up high on her thighs and said to the mirror, and its imaginary occupant, "Will that do?" Tonight she would dance in feral vigilance. She'd find some guy and forget the poor calves, went the plan.

Claire turned to Evelyn, her blue eyes piercing beneath her peachy eye shadow and a new no-nonsense look. She said, "And?"

"I like it," said Evelyn.

The bearded man seized this opportunity to slip away, the door to the street swinging shut behind him.

"You should. *So* killer." Claire started replacing the goods that were evidently wasted on the departed shopper. "I love the big cough as he goes, like ill health prevented his buying something. . . . What'd the calves weigh?"

"They weighed like lead."

"Turn any back?"

"We locoed eight."

Claire made a clucking sound and said, "You can feed 'em out of that, but it takes a couple of months. I had twenty one year and by April they looked like show calves. We took them to Billings Livestock and sold the shit out of them."

Together they moved to the ornate cash register, which stood in nostalgic disuse next to the electronic box for processing credit cards. Violet, despite her blazing makeup and avant-garde clothes, managed to sound wistful. "When the federal government let the meatpackers concentrate, they ruined it for the little producer. That's why *we* moved into town. P.S. I don't miss the wind. But Evelyn, I wish you would let your nails grow." Her brow was furrowed.

"There's no time to grow my nails. I've got to get me a little *tonight*. I haven't had it in such a long time."

Violet looked worried.

"I see a lot of guys, Evelyn. You want a loaner?"

"Uh, no. You miss a bunch if you don't find 'em yourself."

The bar was beyond the city limits, in an industrial-looking building, where a large number of cars and pickup trucks were parked in the snow with little sign of life around them except a desultory shoving match between two bearded men wearing baseball caps. Nothing came of it beyond flattening a circle of snow beneath their feet.

Evelyn was soon inside dancing and tossing down drinks between partners, amidst shouts of "Party hearty! It's beer thirty!" She danced with a ponytailed man wearing hospital scrubs who wouldn't speak to her, then a college student in a lumberjack shirt and with a smooth empty face, then a rather clean-cut youngster in khaki pants and a blue chambray shirt who described himself, with startling precision, as "a Reno-trained slot machine consultant." Apart from the disorienting blaze of lights and electrified music, and the disturbing spectacle of the lead singer's stalking movements up and down the stage at either end of which were snow-filled windows, there was a rather peaceful anonymity, and the black dress continued to thrill her.

She took note of her new partner with the detachment of an anthropologist, his nice quality of having no more than smoothed his blond hair back after his shower; she absolutely loved that he seemed afraid to speak to her. He was a handsome and perhaps uncomplicated unit. When humans are raised for meat, Kansas feedlots will give this guy all the grain he can eat. He had plunged his hands into his pockets in a particularly hopeless gesture when he asked her to dance, and yet he was very becoming. All Evelyn's green lights were on as she hung round his strong young neck. "What is your name?" she asked.

"I'm Evan."

She was mad for this shy politeness, incongruously coupled with his newly palpable arousal. This was getting good, though whether it would cure the dolor of the morning's shipping remained to be seen. The waves of alcoholic euphoria were sure helping. Evelyn was determined, no matter how many drinks she had, not to tell him how attractive he was. That always blew up in your face. That made scumbags out of Boy Scouts!

"My name is quite close to yours, Evan. Mine is Evelyn."

As she said this, she felt the room grow distant and time awkwardly slow. She couldn't for the moment understand why saying her own name aloud made her loneliness so evident that it nearly choked her. Now all funny thoughts had fled. She looked at her young dance partner and wondered if he yet understood that all the cures for loneliness failed, that it was a chronic state and that anything used to anesthetize it turned into its own problem. Yes, she thought, we'll spare Evan that.

The lead singer came rushing across the stage, bent back from the waist, madly waving a handkerchief, his mouth a distorted trumpet. A sort of codpiece slid halfway down one thigh as angry quarter notes from the guitarist drove him back to the microphone screeching, "Don't need no, Don't got no—!" while he raped the stand that held it up. This provided an awkward background that Evelyn suddenly thought was funny. At that same moment, when the front door opened and snow flew in, the singer took time out from his throes to actually frown at the weather.

That did it. Evelyn doubled in laughter. Indeed, Evan had to hold her up, even as she recognized this as hysteria and a ghastly form of release. But it was contagious: the dancing stopped. Right after the fraught singer had concluded several pacts with the devil, the air went out of the room. The lead guitarist peered through the lights furtively. The drummer's blurred arms no longer seemed part of him as he stole furtive glances at the audience. Evelyn's hysteria was a conquering force. The singer seemed strangely platitudinous when, so soon after his arrangements with Satan, he demanded of the crowd, "You want to try this? Anybody like to get up here and show us how good they are?" An unshaven brute in the audience, beer bottle brandished by its neck, his hat on backward, informed the singer that he was "crazier than a shithouse rat."

Evelyn had to get out of here right then. "I need some fresh air," she said to Evan.

His mouth dropped open an instant before he caught himself and tried to look wise and in control. It was *adorable*. This had every chance of being several hours of true love, an inoculation that could last the entire winter.

"I got a car," he said.

"I'll bet you do, Evan."

It was a perfect old Cadillac Coupe de Ville, astonishingly spacious. The foot of snow on the windshield seemed to cast its own pale light on the interior. She unexpectedly began asking herself what she was doing here, with things rather going around and love somewhat less easy to reference. Evan no longer seemed afraid of her, and she was not sure she liked that. The idea of a sudden new Evan was not in the cards. The stillness of his gaze struck her as predatory. "Like the car?"

She watched him to see if anything in his expression might help her answer his question. "I do like it, Evan. It feels big, almost like a boat."

Evan weighed his words, his face barely moving as he spoke. "I like it because it don't have an electronic ignition."

Evelyn felt challenged to understand Evan's remark.

"I'm afraid I don't know anything about those electric things."

"Well, you ought to know about *that* one." Evan seemed riveted.

"It's too late now," she said, thinking to add, "to learn auto mechanics," but she was unwilling to chance anything clever. She had to see where this was going since the unblinking face of the newly confident Evan now made her want to get out of the car. She thought she'd better humor him. "Perhaps you could fill me in on this ignition business, in your own words, of course."

"You know about the New World Order?" He was unzipping his fly.

She frowned at this behavior, and he stopped. "Is it like the United Nations?" she asked hopefully. Oh boy, she thought, here come the black helicopters.

"It's way worse."

"Uh, in what way, Evan?"

"They want to turn us into slaves." He was matter-of-fact about this.

"You don't say. But Evan, what about the auto mechanics you promised to explain?" Everything seemed to have gone to his eyes. She had a fleeting thought that if she were suicidal, this would be her man. "Didn't you promise?"

Evan watched and waited her out.

"The New World Order is gonna use satellites to turn off all the electronic ignitions. They're gonna enslave all the white males who own recent-model cars." Evelyn widened her eyes to suggest that she hadn't realized this automotive feature was available. "Then they plan to use Gurkhas to round us up and put us in concentration camps located in Kansas. It's common knowledge."

Kansas? Evelyn remembered that was where her calves were going.

"But Evan, why do they want to do this to . . . white males?" She was thinking about what great instincts she had, heading for the parking lot with this turkey.

Finally Evan's face moved: he smiled. He had something to share with Evelyn. He told her very evenly, "They want to subject us to maritime law."

Evelyn had to admit that even she didn't even see that one coming. Still, she was reluctant to ask picky questions like, Isn't that the law of the sea? Instead, she said, "Evan, I'm going back inside to dance. This is my reward for a long day. When I dance, I don't think about these larger issues."

His hand encircled her wrist, gently at first. "You don't even like the band."

"That's true. But it's still more or less music."

"You pretended you wanted to spend *the night* with me." She saw two couples angling through the parked cars toward the entrance, hunched up against the latest dusting of snow. One of the men gazed lovingly at his companion, a rosy cheeked brunette. As Evelyn pulled her arm back, Evan tightened his grip and looked as if he was about to accuse her of treason. "Admit you like it nasty."

"No, Evan, I do not admit I 'like it nasty.' But Evan, one thing I do great is scream. Know what I mean? I can get you into the clink even without maritime law. So let go of my arm or you're going to be one of those white males headed for slavery in Kansas. I know Gurkhas in high places."

The grip did loosen. Evelyn was surprised by his compliance. She opened her door, snow falling into her lap. The interior light flashed over Evan. His role as spotter of mega-trends bent on the elimination of his kind was evaporating fast, leaving a disoriented hayseed. Evelyn was now in control of the situation but didn't feel the time for compassion had quite arrived. "Evan, you need a new car." Evan flinched at these words.

"Have a look around," she said. "Take a chance. Buy one with that funny ignition. You'll be in the same boat with the rest of us. And now this old single gal is going to vote with her feet." The snow blowing into the Cadillac seemed to emphasize his forlorn state, and nearly obliterated the view of the bar, which no longer seemed a haven. She stopped instead and turned to her car.

The engine started, but the wipers seemed overwhelmed by the snow. And now, she thought, for some drunk driving. She pulled onto the highway, heading northwest—toward what? The Missouri River? Maybe a cozy bar a thousand feet lower? Asylum? Maybe no snow, and a chance to reconfirm the existence of sky behind this ominous cover of white. Sometimes these squalls came in so low you could push toward White Sulphur Springs and be under the stars inside twenty minutes. Though it was rarely necessary more than once a year, you could drink all night with strangers.

She found herself driving on a dirt road through frozen wheat stubble at about the time the dashboard clock showed two a.m. Now every bar was closed. She mused upon the dreadful events that seemed to pile up after closing time on winter nights: schnapps in to-go cups, jumper cables, brutal groping and slurred affections, horrible radio music that was suddenly "great." Every new season bore something macabre on the wind, with people clubbed, pushed out of cars, people *murdered*. Not everyone could

handle last call when they were already facing winter. Nor
lonely escapes on empty roads and lost highways.

Evelyn drove at a steady pace as the wind changed the
shapes of snow in her headlights. A deer stepped onto the
road from the barrow pit, its eyes bright as platinum. She
hit the brakes and the car simply shifted its angle and traveled in a frictionless drift toward the deer that stepped out
of the way, its amazed face showing briefly in her window
as she slid past and off the road into the ditch. The engine
quit. Everything she'd been watching was swallowed by
darkness. The engine ticked and cooled in the quiet.

She had no trouble restarting the engine, but the headlights wavered as though losing electricity. When she put
the car in gear, the drive wheel spun so freely it failed to dis-
turb the stillness of the vehicle. And when she opened the
door to get out, it collided with the side of the ditch bank.
She opened the opposite door and the wind ripped it out of
her hands, snow whirling inside wildly until she pulled it
shut. In her fear she tried the radio, finding only a station
on which someone was ranting. She turned it off.

But the motor ran, the heater ran, and there was a reassuring vibration in the car, a feeling, like life, that seemed
to hold the piling snow at bay. She held her hand up to the
rearview mirror and felt that hope was confirmed by its
reflection. There was no food in the glovebox, just the
owner's manual and, somehow, an old issue of *The Watch
Tower*. There was enough gas to run till sunup. Things
could be worse. She felt an odd need to seem to be occu-
pied. The radio, again, was no help, no more than a steady
hiss, and when she shut it off, the knob came loose in her
hand: she put it in the glovebox with the Jehovah's Witness

tract, quite formally promising herself not to let this get to her. Instead, she elected to concern herself with whether Bill had fed Cree, Jailbait, Scram, Lady Luck and Cracker-jack. Of course he had. He'd made a small pile of alfalfa away from the other horses, because Crackerjack was timid, and then had piled the cob and rolled oats in the middle. After tiptoeing up to dine, Crackerjack would watch all around himself between mouthfuls and, once the food was finished, would paw at the ground with his speckled right foot to make certain he hadn't missed a single flake. It wasn't cold enough to freeze the creek, so there was as yet no need to spud a hole in the ice for the horses to drink. But the cows, that was another story. She knew they were searching everywhere in the storm for their calves; they would search for days and never find them. Each cow believed that just one small further effort, one more step, and her calf would appear. Evelyn looked down at herself, half curled up on the seat in her little black dress and the black coat in which she'd wound herself: she looked like a calf herself. She tried to smile at this thought. Perhaps she could sleep.

The chugging of an old vehicle could be made out over the sound of her car. She twisted around and in the distance could discern two uneven cones of headlights bouncing up the dirt road in her direction. The vehicle was moving slowly and the good light penetrated in a straight line toward her like an arrow while the weaker one wobbled its light across the ground. As it came closer, she could make out the dark mass of an old sedan behind it and, buttoning her coat, decided to take a chance. She got out of the car on the low side and clambered up the bank onto the roadway. She held her arms straight out from her sides, raising and lowering them in what she thought was a universal request for assistance. Then the car slowed down and stopped, the animated, snow-filled beam of good light shining off into the distance.

The driver's door opened and a huge man got out, a dark beard against a torn military coat, a billed cap pulled low. For some reason he didn't speak, didn't ask what her problem was. She listened to her own overly detailed description of the deer coming onto the road and grew acutely aware of ice she now felt under her feet and the odd patience with which the man let her speak. The three other doors of the car slowly began opening, and she could see men getting out. "I don't think this will be necessary," she said, without quite understanding what she meant. "Not required," she added with a dismissive wave of her hand, then turned and hurried through the drifts into the night. She didn't look back until she was out of breath, when she could see the interior lights of her car and the shapes of men going through it. In another few yards, the snow obscured them.

Evelyn was walking away from the river. She knew that by walking away from a river you could be walking into nowhere. But at the moment, walking of any kind seemed entirely positive and the snow was at her back, the only way she could see through it at all though it didn't prevent her from colliding with a fence. The wire was too tight to crawl through, so she felt along until she reached a brace post and climbed over. To be inside the fence was a relief. Pioneers coming through Indian country often wept when they saw fences. But she was beginning to get cold and would have to find something to break the wind. The first prospect of shelter was a slight ridge, but the snow had piled up just beyond it and the lee was insufficient; this was a possible place to die and therefore would not do just now. She felt quite level-headed in acknowledging that she was unprepared for death. Even if her mind was in ribbons, she wanted to go on.

The strap broke on one of her shoes. They offered little protection, but she now had to shuffle on one foot to keep from losing it and, from time to time, lost it anyway. The snow was melting in her hair and running down her neck, and she wondered if she hadn't been better off following the fence, or if perhaps she should have trusted those men. Nothing in her route suggested a destination unless it was sunrise still three hours off, if she could last. It was heartening to plan to meet some point in time when meeting some point on earth seemed unattainable. She realized how cold she had gotten when the thought crossed her mind, What difference does it make? She was traveling toward sunrise and sunrise was traveling toward her. Either they met or they didn't. Nothing else mattered. She and sunrise were old friends, no?

Evelyn sat at the base of a juniper tree acknowledging that it was poor shelter and that while she was certainly not giving up, it was time to await an idea. That was all that was missing. Noting that the broken shoe was gone, she was vaguely surprised that she hadn't noticed any pain or coldness in that foot. Perhaps, she thought, it was simply more courageous than the other foot. Maybe it was tired of sharing. Lately, people were always offering to "share" with you, usually something entirely unwelcome, occasionally a nasty surprise. Her heart went out to the warmer foot for keeping its own counsel. Overhead, the slumped contours of the juniper were sagging with snow. The shredded bark against her back seemed protective. Then something strange happened: the wind stopped, leaving an apprehensive quiet.

Her head was down on her chest and the snow piled upon herself when she heard a tentative lowing which gathered into a broad, inquiring volume. Evelyn stared hard toward the rumble of deep voices, the spinning whiteness of the snow. At length, the first black faces began to appear, massing in front of her, crowding for room, then around her, each different from the next. In her black dress and loose coat, she curled on the ground before them. The circle tightened until she felt their heat.

Was this the warm outer room of death? Evelyn was wrapped in several army blankets, her head turned against a gray-and-white-striped ticking pillow. The shade of the bedside lamp had pine trees appliquéd to panels of imitation buckskin, the seams laced not with rawhide but shoelaces. The room smelled of cold wood, and beyond the uncurtained window the flat winter light contained no detail. Evelyn ran her hands over herself and discovered that she was in the same black dress, then noticed pants and an old blue sweater folded over a chair, it seemed, for her use. Some of the tension went out of her body, and she was aware of a sound outside.

Evelyn looked down into a yard enclosed by a shelter belt of caragana and evergreens, grown tangled together and unkempt, banked by graying snow, fastened here and there by debris that seemed to have blown from the general refuse of the house into the nearest thing that stopped the wind:

newspapers, binder twine, plastic grocery store bags. Wrapped in one of the blankets, she started as a figure appeared below her dragging a length of wood and adding it to a rick of logs and branches. An empty flagpole stood to one side, its ropes slapping in a steady wind. The figure was a man, encumbered by heavy clothing and a navy blue hat whose earflaps were drawn alongside his face, and for as long as she watched, he continued to drag wood from out of her sight into the square steadily formed by the logs. What is he building? A shelter? Nothing about this procedure changed, and in its repetition was something grim that Evelyn wished to see no more of. She turned from the window and looked at the clothes on the chair, reluctant to put them on. When she dropped the blanket from her shoulders, she regarded the previously fashionable black dress as some annoying slut suit and unhesitatingly rid herself of it and replaced it with the baggy, warm and clean clothing on the chair. She balled up the dress tightly and put it on the chair, where it began to expand; she compressed it again and pressed it between the rungs. She was ready to be seen, should there be anyone to see her.

Her door was locked. She went back to the window and thought at first to signal to the figure below but saw that there were two people dragging pieces of wood to what was now a considerable pile. The carcass of a huge, leafless cottonwood hung over the yard and the patterns of human activity below, patterns Evelyn could not begin to understand. Maybe the tree would come to life in the spring, but this did not appear likely. It looked dead, and its black trunk was textured in the seams of its bark by the flying snow that made crooked vertical lines almost up to the crown, where it turned black once again, perhaps above driven flakes, and was composed entirely of the frantic shapes of the leafless limbs. Somehow these arboreal corpses kept returning to life.

There was nothing in the room to read except an old Norwegian Bible next to the rustic lamp. Evelyn glanced at it and then made the bed, crossing from one side to the other to pull the gray blanket until it was quite as tight as a drum. She plucked out the corner of the pillow so that everything was perfectly symmetrical and turned to the dresser and washstand where she could see herself, her face somewhat interrupted by a fading BIG BROTHER AND THE HOLDING COMPANY decal. A key lay on the dresser and when she moved it, she saw that its shape had discolored the wood beneath it in its own dark shape. There was a keyhole in the top drawer, but the key did not fit the lock. The drawer opened perfectly well without it and inside were advertising materials for a Packard automobile, a coin from Mexico and a flat carpenter's pencil advertising a lumber company in Miles City.

A nice room but nevertheless she was locked inside it. Possibly this was a mistake that would painfully embarrass her gracious hosts. Or maybe she was enslaved.

Evelyn pulled a chair up beside the window, where initials were carved into the sill. Ice had formed around the upper pane in a smooth bluish arc suggesting the window of a church. The square of logs and branches had not gone further, and the people were no longer present. Into this emptiness appeared a dog whose face was divided black and white almost precisely down the middle. He had a tail that curved high over his back, and he sped around the yard sniffing the ground intently before departing from Evelyn's view. She had begun to remember the cows, the ones in flight across the country in cattle trucks and the ones that circled her . . . when? Last night. Last night, after she'd run off the road, after the truck with the men had come up, the flash of light on opening doors. She had a great conviction that she'd been right to flee, though the flight and the sense of being overtaken by driven clouds of stinging snow, and then it all just not so gradually stopped. She had slept in a circle of cows and now she was here. Her anxiety had subsided and, hearing footsteps ascending the stairs, she became hungry, as if whoever was coming knew she needed food.

Evelyn watched for the door to open. She stood well away from it, in front of the window, which she was imagining as an exit without expecting to need it. When the door did open, she immediately recognized one of the figures from the snowy yard, a rather short and stocky woman, with a nose in the exact center of her face, bristly hair and a small round mouth. Her face was red, probably from the cold, and she had a very direct gaze. "Well, you're up," she said.

"Yes. Thank you."

"And are you rested?" she demanded.

"I am, yes."

"I'm Esther."

"How do you do; I'm Evelyn."

"You're just lucky to be alive," the woman said. "If Torvald hadn't gone out with his bale feeder, you'd of froze. You was near froze as it is. Most of the time Torvald just spikes a round bale, cuts the strings and rolls it down a hill about a mile away. But the weather got so fearful he says he's worried about the cows and goes out with the feeder, only this time the block heater come unplugged and the hydraulics was kaflooie. Had to use a can of ether—smell it clear to the house—and I'm thinkin' Torvald was liable to blow hisself up. Took half the night, but lucky for you, you wasn't clear froze yet, no more froze than Torvald. Well, how'd did you get there?"

"I went into the ditch. I was looking for help."

"Should've stayed with your outfit and waited for help to come along."

Evelyn decided not to say what it was that put her to flight and thought it was better and shorter to let Esther assume that she was foolish enough to try to cross a snowfield at night in search of rescue. No explanation for fighting a blizzard in a party dress seemed adequate. She was comfortable now and hungry and the old clothes were warm.

"I'd better feed you," said Esther.

"Oh, that's not necessary at all," said Evelyn. "If I could impose on you for a lift into town, I'll grab something there."

"Impossible. We're snowed in."

"Oh."

"We been waitin' for this. We been hopin'."

"To be snowed in?"

"You bet. Oh, you bet." Esther went out the door. "Your food is ready when you are." Evelyn thought about the couple in the yard, and marveled that there were people who actually longed to be snowed in, for whom there was never enough isolation.

Evelyn stepped tentatively out onto a landing that she could not remember and that produced an unsettling blank in her memory, which must have begun in the snowfield. Never before had she "passed out," and the very notion made her queasy; too many friends had awakened to find some lummox toiling away over their bodies. Nevertheless, she went down the stairs she must have gone up, and on a table at the bottom found a meal prepared for her of bread and eggs and a drink, a cold liquid which referred to oranges. Esther began putting food on the table, nothing that looked particularly familiar.

"I wonder," Evelyn said, "—this is very nice, *mm*—if I could borrow the phone?"

Esther was frowning before she'd even heard the question.

"No phone," she said firmly. Evelyn couldn't tell whether that meant there *was* no phone or that she couldn't use it. Esther then pointed to the meat that was part of the breakfast array with subdued glee. "Moose," she said. Moose 'n' eggs, thought Evelyn. I must pray for an airlift.

The room where Evelyn sat had on one side a small kitchen and, on the other, a passageway in whose yellow, angled glow appeared a large, strangely dressed and rather shambling man, with a kind of boardinghouse anonymity and hardly a glance her way. Perhaps he, too, was snowed in. While Evelyn contemplated these things, picked at her eggs and considered creative disposal of the moose, Esther set another place beside her with a comparable meal. When Evelyn raised an inquiring and smiling gaze, Esther spat out the words, "Our son Donald!"

Donald strode into the room, a great big man with a remarkably bushy gray beard and piercing black eyebrows.

"Hullo!" he said, sitting down with such force that Evelyn was afraid his chair would break. Except that his hair was in curlers, he looked like any other rancher. Peering closely at his breakfast, he offered a great paw in Evelyn's direction. "I apologize for appearing before you *déshabillé*. Normally I am zipped up in my coveralls by now and making myself useful to Papa. But we are snowed in. And this is the weekend, when I do as I please especially on these exciting Saturday nights! Chores done, cows are asleep, sheep askew and th—"

"Donald, that'll do!" This rough voice came from the kitchen but did not belong to Esther. Donald's face compressed and his eyes narrowed as he took this in with unyielding fatalism.

Evelyn craned to see where the voice came from. "Is it true we're snowed in?"

"Boy howdy."

"And the phone?"

"Not available at this time."

"Oh," said Evelyn. "And what are you building in the yard, a cabin?"

"That's a bonfire for Grandpa."

In the doorway appeared an older man with high cheekbones and small, close-set eyes, a coarse and energetic character who identified himself as Torvald Aadfield. Donald raised his dark eyebrows, darker than the wide fan of beard, and oddly peaked just over the bridge of his nose, giving the impression that he had never seen his father before or else had seen him but was struggling to remember anything specific about him. Mr. Aadland caught this and nodded privately, suggesting that Donald was grimly incorrigible.

"We're snowed in," he said.

"See?" said Donald.

"How's the moose?" Torvald asked. "Very good for you. Prepared it myself. With a seven mag."

"Walking food doesn't have a long life around Dad," Donald said.

"I remember the lean times," his father said. "Montana's a boom-and-bust economy. "

Evelyn swung her head from one speaker to another without making a contribution. Her feigned affability did little to conceal her discomfort.

"During one of those busts," said Donald, "I went to San Francisco for a Mott the Hoople concert. Spent six hungry months in the Haight, then almost two years in a cross-dressers' review, very big with the tourists in a tourist's town. I dreamed of saving enough to buy my own ranch. I thought I could hoof my way into the cattle business!"

"You're in the cattle business," said Torvald.

"Yes," sighed Donald, "but one that can never grow. I have happy memories of those days, the gorgeous outfits so full of meaning, staying up all night with my disturbed friends, racing to the sea in the foggy morning, lumbering along in our frocks and smelling like a gym, past the Penguin's Prayer sculpture, breaking out on Ocean Beach at dawn to storm the surfers in their wetsuits. Do I miss those days? What do you think!" He looked at his father but continued speaking to Evelyn. "He buys cheap bulls, won't fertilize, irrigates with a shovel and doesn't sprinkle. . . . " Donald was agitated. The plastic cylinders festooning his head knocked against one another.

Evelyn couldn't make out whether this was some old

routine between the two men or something specifically for her.

Donald now was storming around so that the noise of his sandals on the floor and against the furniture was a dismaying backdrop to his remarks. "He won't take a cheap Farm Home Loan or sign up with the Great Plains Program."

Torvald was shrinking with truculence and embarrassment.

"He won't use gated pipe because he likes to see me out there dragging mud-covered canvas, soaking wet in a cold wind. He won't buy a calf table when—"

"Donald's a great roper," his mother added. "We wouldn't want to miss that—"

"He's got Mom flanking calves like she was in a rodeo. *And tonight*, to save a few bucks, he's gonna cremate my grandpa."

The older people winced to have this stated so boldly.

It was a good while before Torvald spoke. "Snowed in, has to be done," he said complacently. "Lady, I don't know what your plan was out there in my pasture, but if them cows had come to their feed like always, I'd of never found you atall."

"I'm very grateful. Really, there is a telephone, isn't there?"

"Line's down," he barked, the last word on that subject.

"Home cremation's illegal as hell," Donald noted, "but like the man said, we're snowed in and even minor calamity can help boom-and-busters economize. Lucky you weren't on your feet when Dad found you. He might've had you popped for trespassing."

"I *am* a strong proponent of private property rights," Torvald said, and left the room at the sight of his wife passing the doorway, pointedly ignoring the activity in the dining room but shouting as she went, *"Torvald, fill the bird feeder!"*

"Donald," he said, "we've got work to do." He seemed mildly elated by this information and, rising from his chair, clapped his calloused hands together. The men left the table apparently without a thought of what Evelyn might do with herself, though it was obvious her job was to wait for the storm to pass. From a nearby room, old psychedelic music suddenly boomed. Mr. Aadfield passed the kitchen doorway, shaking his head contemptuously. Evelyn heard him go out, and shortly thereafter Donald appeared in insulated coveralls, a housebound Bohemian artifact transformed now into a rather conventional farmer. He had a war-surplus campaign coat over his arm and was gesturing for Evelyn to follow him quickly. As she crossed the kitchen behind him, he draped the coat over her shoulders and opened a narrow door into a cold storage room, reaching familiarly around the inside wall to turn on the light switch.

"You're safe with me," Donald said, leading her into a room piled high with crates and rough shelves that stored canned foods. "My wan and ambiguous sexuality wouldn't offend a gnat. And I love having a houseguest." He went straight to the far corner, where he began removing burlap feed sacks from something leaning there, something that proved to be a corpse, rigid from cold storage. Having revealed it, Donald stepped back and bent slightly forward, hands clasped together in fascination. "Grandpa," he said, with purring delight.

"I've never seen a dead person before." Fleetingly, she wondered about her father, but he'd been boxed. "Is that a costume?"

"That's his uniform from the Norwegian Navy."

The corpse was balanced in the corner of the concrete walls, a small old man dressed in a pristine navy blue suit complete with epaulets. "Rescued from a Norwegian light-ship that got torpedoed by a German sub. Thirty years later he was a county commissioner in Montana *and the uniform still fits*." Rubbing his capacious stomach ruefully, Donald said, "If Grandpa's genes were what they're cracked up to be, I'd be still in the chorus line. Instead I spend my days on the wrong end of a number-three irrigating shovel or hitting the zerk fittings on Dad's front-end loader with a half-frozen grease gun!" His sob, Evelyn knew, was not genuine. Her eyes were fastened on this peculiar effigy. It was certainly not a person. Nor was it remotely horrifying, though it did produce a strong sense of the ridiculous, perhaps due to a uniform right out of Gilbert and Sullivan.

Evelyn asked cautiously, "What's he doing here?"

"Oh, boy," sighed Donald. "'What's he doing here?' Well, Evelyn, we're going to do a home burial with Gramps, a home cremation. My parents felt very *oppressed* by Grand-dad and promised themselves they wouldn't spend two cents burying him. They told him so to his face. They said, 'Granddad, you've been very cheap and mean. You never fed your cows in the winter. When you die, we're not going to spend two cents burying you. We're not buying you a headstone, and we're not notifying your hometown newspaper in Trondhjem.' My mother and father might be hard, but they're not unkind. When Grandpa said he preferred cremation, my father said, 'You buy the matches,' and it was kind of a family joke—you know, a Norwegian family joke that's not at all funny. Anyway, Grandpa bought a box of kitchen matches, and my folks still have them after about ten years. Tonight the old fellow goes up in smoke, which, given certain laws, is why we had to wait until we were snowed in to do it. We can't get out and, except for you, they can't get in, even if they see smoke.

"My mother really tried to reach out to him, but it was all lost on Grandpa. Everyone on the place was half starved while he paid into a pension plan through the Odd Fellows. And he had a high-dollar pinky ring, which was totally inappropriate to begin with, and which he swallowed once he knew the end was at hand. Said we'd only use it to buy train tickets out. These were all more or less jokes, but serious enough that he actually did swallow the ring. My folks and I are just unwilling to go in and get it, even though it's pretty obvious we could use the money. Now—" he rapped his knuckles on the corpse's stomach "—you'd have to use a chisel or tire tool or some damn thing."

Evelyn, shivering from the cold, couldn't quite keep her eyes off the corpse, and was tempted to blame it for everything. Donald said he was uncomfortable having it lean up against the wall like cordwood and put it in a small wagon, towing it around the room looking for a better place. "I remember when the damn thing was jumping around barking orders," he said. He looked through the room for a place to park the wagon. "My dreams change every day," Donald was saying. "For years I've also had a great interest in going to Mars. It seems more and more possible. If I hang on to my share of Grandpa's pension and invest it wisely, I could be on one of the first trips. When I heard they'd found evidence of water there, I thought, *Whoa*, I could have it all: *a hot tub on Mars!* Here, this is good, I think. . . ." He lifted the corpse out of the wagon and stood it in an upended metal stock tank, where it took on the aspect of a roadside shrine down in Mexico.

Evelyn tried to see the merits of hot tubbing on Mars, the plains of the Red Planet all around and the troubled, complicated Earth hanging on the far edge of the void. Donald had put her in a strange mood.

Donald, meanwhile, was gazing reflectively at his grandfather. "I'm sort of orchestrating the funeral tonight. There will be modest pageantry and some music. If only he could talk, eh? I can guarantee you he'd say we were doing everything all wrong."

Viewed from the Red Planet, of course, casual wounding within families would seem trivial.

"What kind of music?"

"I have some bitchin' tunes." He reached deep into his beard in thought, his eyes moving slowly from side to side.

"So much snow," said Evelyn. "If only you had a phone. Is he going to stay propped up okay? A few flowers would make a big difference." She was losing her grip.

Evelyn sat at the kitchen table with a pile of old magazines, never quite taking her eyes off the weather. She had inquired about all the distances—to the county road, to town, across the fields, to the interstate highway—and finally Mrs. Aadfield, at the stove with a towel over her shoulder, told her she would just have to accept her predicament and that it was unlikely to last more than another night.

Evelyn was looking at the meat on a platter atop the stove.

"That's not that moose, is it?"

"No, and I'd offer you some TV but Donald backed over the dish with the swather and the reception ain't so good. Sometimes it skips off the stratosphere and we get Red Deer, Alberta. Dad watches it anyway, just for the movement. Says it helps his eyes."

Evelyn said, "Can't I make something?"

"Like what?"

"I don't know, a pie?"

"What're you gonna make it out of?"

"You got any apples?"

In fact, they had a cellar full, and once Evelyn had them piled on the table, she abandoned herself to peeling them while she tried to remember how to make pie crust. None of these people knew what a terrible cook she was, and she wanted to bask in their not finding out. At the critical moment, Esther removed a box from the freezer and handed it to her: a brown generic box that said PIE CRUST, and inside were perhaps thirty crusts in a stack. "Jeez," said Evelyn, "how do you get them apart?"

Eventually, Torvald and Donald reappeared in the kitchen. Esther suggested that being indoors, which they obviously craved, was a luxury to which they were not yet entitled. Nevertheless, they stood shoulder to shoulder pounding their hands together, then pulled off their insulated coveralls, stamping up and down, and seeming to become smaller as clothes piled around their feet.

"Everybody fed," said Donald, reminding Evelyn that a herd of cows was often referred to by ranchers as "everybody." "That old brockle-faced, crooked-horned, prolapsed,

swinging-bagged, broken-mouthed, spavined whore chased
Dad and me up on the wagon again, one of us ever trips
we're gonna be toast."

"She's going to town," said Aadfield sternly. "I've had
enough."

"Must be three foot out there," said Donald to Evelyn,
turning his palms up hopelessly.

"Can't you go to the shop and build something?" asked
Mrs. Aadfield in a tone of exasperation.

"No, Ma, we can't. The propane line is froze, and we
can't get heat to it."

Donald led Evelyn to the living room, which bore no
intuitive relationship to the rest of the house insofar as it
was necessary to pass through two obscure doors to reach
it. A small fireplace with a Heat-O-Lator insert was surmounted by the inevitable bugling elk against an over-
wrought tangerine sunrise; and it had been a long time
since Evelyn had spotted tassels on furniture. A badly
stuffed and moth-eaten bobcat was poised midpounce over
a thoroughly dilapidated grouse, a tableau that proved to
be a centerpiece for the windowless wall where hung various family pictures, including several of Donald as a rodeo
star in pre–cross-dresser days and Grandpa in the Norwegian Navy. There was also a rather glaring colored portrait
of Diana, Princess of Wales.

Donald simply wanted to talk, and Evelyn found herself
touched by surprising trustfulness. He wished to know
where she lived. "Mostly in Bozeman," she said, "but also
on our ranch—well, sort of ours—helping out."

There was a long and comfortable silence before Donald
spoke.

"Well, uh—?"

"What was I doing out in your pasture in the middle of the night?"

"Yes," he said solemnly, eyes seeming to drift for a moment, but then his face lit up. "Is it a fun answer?"

Evelyn looked vaguely at the ceiling, really thinking this over. Then she described the men getting out of the old sedan and her sense of foreboding, her instinct that she would have just one narrow opportunity to avoid the fate they held in their hands. "They were sort of uh, uh, *looming*." But no, that wasn't it so much as the differing speeds at which their faces were lit up by the headlights. As she went over this in her mind, it was suddenly very clear that she'd been right, that if she hadn't run something very terrible might have happened.

Donald nodded. "Those might've been ordinary men," he said, "believing all women in the world are just a bunch of Lorena Bobbitts. Probably just regular fellas leading decent lives, but when you get them together there's always this one other fella—who you can't see, you can't even see, but he's there all right and it's no telling what he's liable to do." Evelyn sat very straight as he spoke.

A chinook wind began to blow in early afternoon, sowing panic among the Aadfields as the temperature steadily climbed and melted snow began to run from the gutters. The roads would soon be passable, and any mission of seeing Grandpa off would be subject to the interfering visits of neighbors. Thriving on this emergency, Donald announced, "We've got to make our move."

Evelyn, reading a front-page story in the *Livingston Enterprise* about the advance of Africanized bees north from Texas estimated to arrive here in about thirty years, noted that his parents were immobilized.

Donald looked from one to the other in moderate disgust. "Let's put an end to this," he said to them. "That old man is gone. He ruined our lives. He—"

"*Donald*—"

"He ruined *your* lives. What can you say of a man whose last words were 'I stood up for my water rights'? And when I left for San Francisco thirty-five years ago, he said, 'Don't come back, you no-good fairy.' He never had a kind word for you, either. So, I say let's burn the evidence."

Torvald spoke. "Donald, you're going to have to light the match. I can't do it."

"*Me?*"

Evelyn looked up and said, "I really shouldn't be here."

The silence in the kitchen was extraordinary, and Evelyn retreated to the classified section. "Nordic Track. Lo mileage. Illness forces sale." She read on, in an effort to beat back the sadness invading the room, about available babysitters, archery sets, pop-up campers, sporting goods, help wanted, pet grooming, firewood, swing sets—until that, too, finally became unbearable. She put the paper down and said, in a remarkably flat tone, "I'll do it. Then, can I go?"

Donald leaned close to Evelyn, his beard rustling dryly against her ear, and whispered, "Atta girl, you get out there and set fire to that stiff."

Evelyn pointedly ignored the rest of the arrangements, though she was impressed with the Aadfields' renewed vigor. And when Donald wheeled a hand dolly through the kitchen, she began to feel something of a chill. It was a windy dusk and quickly turning dark when their preparations were finished and Donald, with a look of significance and gratitude, placed the box of kitchen matches on the table. Evelyn looked at them and thought that she would have no trouble with this task at all. She picked them up and asked, "Now?" The Aadfields nodded eagerly, and Evelyn found herself touched by their childlike unanimity. She put on the coveralls handed her by Torvald and went outside and into whirling air that was taking the snow from the roofs. She was oddly excited simply to be out of the house.

The heap of wood was a jumble in the darkness, but as her eyes adjusted she could see a mass of carefully crumpled newspapers at its base. The cadaver was in there somewhere, but for now it was just tinder and firewood. Her hair kept blowing over her face, and she reached behind and shoved it under the heavy collar. Now she could see the faces in the windows, one each in three different windows. She knelt by the paper, but the first match failed so abruptly that she looked to see how many remained in the box. It had been made clear to her that not any old match would do, and she had to get the job done with one somehow associated with the penny-pinching of the deceased. She had been struck by the helplessness of the faces in the windows—not the competent, if peculiar, household that had rescued her, but three cripples waiting for the fire they could never have started without her. This would be no problem once she got a match lit, which she did by making a great shelter of her own body and then carefully setting a bit of paper alight, and then another, until a cheerful glow blossomed at the base of the pile. She stood up and her hair blew free again and whipped around her face as the little fire spread into a general blaze as the wood finally began to burn, steadily and then with spontaneous speed until the entire pile became a globe of light etched by limbs and branches and revealing, with increasing clarity like the tiny figure in a fertilized egg, the corpse at first blue in its uniform, then black against the intensity of light and at last, as Evelyn retreated from the heat, waving its limbs about as though signaling from a Norwegian lightship to a cold outer dark. It had become little more than a silhouette, and at that moment, thinking of her father and his own accumulation of hope and pain, Evelyn knelt down and wept as the inferno illuminated the angled streaks of snow overhead.

After a while, she gathered herself and saw, in one lighted window, Esther, cradling a steel bowl, whisking a meringue with terrific energy; in another, Torvald was watching television with his fingers in his ears. On the second floor, a window was flung open almost at the level of the flames, and psychedelic music filled the air; Donald leaned out, his hands on the sill, and shouted, "Captain Beefheart! I love Captain Beefheart!"

As the bottles teetered along their track from the jet tank that filled them, they passed under a smaller machine that capped and sped them toward further automation in a humming, tinkling chorale of sound until they reappeared concealed in cases and moving at right angles to their first appearance, at which point they were borne out of sight and headed for the multipacker. Along the array of activities were gauges and instruments, and reading them, clipboard in hand, was a young woman named Annie Elvstrom from Two Dot, Montana. She was twenty, a shy beauty with a high clear forehead and chestnut hair drawn back in a tie, one of a large family that had starved out ranching.

Paul visited Annie Elvstrom several times, starting conversations that went nowhere as Miss Elvstrom, glistening with high fructose corn sweetener from the machines, seemed frozen at the very sight of him. She behaved as though she'd seen someone from another world, and afterward needed a few moments to resume her tasks. Because he had given her several chances, more than she deserved, Paul entertained firing her.

She meanwhile directed her questions to Stuart, at first because the other workers claimed he was the only person who really understood all the plant's operations, then because his gentle manner had emboldened her to speak just a little. Once, when a steel roller in the conveyor track jammed and bottles shattered around her legs, Stuart was there to shut the line down. Kneeling at her feet, he gathered the broken glass until it was safe for her to move. She thought Stuart was the most beautiful man she had ever seen. Knowing he was already married to the daughter of the august founder, whose very name glowed over the plant in yards of neon tube, Annie Elvstrom nonetheless wished Stuart would presume a little during their friendly chats; the smallest insinuation would have been welcome. It's impossible to imagine her reaction had she learned Stuart had already named his sailboat after her.

From his office high above the floor, Paul concluded that Miss Elvstrom was gaga over Stuart, and that this would be an excellent time to have a smallish discussion with him.

Stuart was summoned by means of a loudspeaker. The bottle-washing foreman he'd been talking to, a small gray-haired man with forearms like Popeye's, said to Stuart in solemn tones, "There's a fuckin' afoot."

When Stuart entered the office and sat down, Paul was writing on a notepad—"I am collecting my thoughts," Paul said before looking up into the slightly anxious eyes of Stuart, whose long, gullible face suggested impending flight.

Paul was aware of the fact that since the death of his father-in-law and his own installation as the new boss, Stuart had been entirely too forthcoming in expressing his reservations about the future of the company. Hearing this, Paul vowed to "kick his ass," and had done lots of homework in preparing for this deed.

"Stuart." There was no sense that Paul had ever seen him before.

"Good morning, Paul."

"Beautiful, uh, day." Paul glanced at the window to discern if this was in fact true, then he pointed in case Stuart didn't know where it was to be found.

"It certainly is."

"Stuart, I want you to look into some water-management services we could offer, some franchise we might consider. . . ." He could make out the impact of this preface on his clueless brother-in-law. Yet it took people like this to make headway in places like up on the High Line, say, where anything but the outright monosyllabic produced xenophobic hysteria.

"You mean like—"

"So we're not *stifled* in this his*toric* building by the spirit of our father-in-law, now dead and only maybe in heaven." This whiff of kinship made them both uncomfortable.

"I'm not sure I know what you're thinking about."

Neither, of course, did Paul, but it was Stuart who looked disoriented. Less-than-idolatrous discussions of

Jim Whitelaw were at best experimental in this new post-mortem world, and at worst an insufferable deviation. The idea of discussing Sunny Jim's place in the afterlife was disconcerting.

Paul raised his voice. "*I already told you.* Water-management services as it is understood by most Americans: various forms of conditioned water that we can sell without doing the R and D ourselves. Like with water softeners. We put the widget in the home, sell them the salts for the rest of the life of the operating unit, then sell them another unit. How far are you getting with this, Stuart?"

"I'll look into it," he said quietly.

Paul knew that with Stuart, he could really raise the pitch, even let a bit of it be heard down on the floor where Miss You-Know-Who stood by. It wouldn't be a speck on the regular blistering old Whitelaw regularly doled out to this beaten man. He had concluded that further heapings of the assigned tasks might abet Stuart's sense of disadvantage.

"You know, we could do need analysis right in their homes and charge for that too. *All* the water around here is too hard—a whole population with itching scalps, flaking skin, mineralized pipes; half of Montana scratching their asses trying to get on with their lives. It's not right. I've seen our elected representatives back there in Washington scratching their asses on national TV, so half of America thinks we're uncouth, when it's really just a water-quality issue. But there's a big opportunity out there for you, Stuart, especially vis-à-vis a guy with a twenty-year-old profit-sharing plan. So look into it, Stuart. *You're fully vested.*"

"I will, Paul. I know I am, my whole fu—"

"Lot of outfits like us supposed to be bottling plants, and they're nothing but prisoners of some empire. You can tell our customers all about Coca-Cola products but you're still a prisoner—" Paul paused at the startled look the word produced on Stuart's face "—watching some behemoth ('What are the chances this guy knows what a behemoth is?') eating your goddamn margins. Sure, I'm worried about sales, but I'm *more* worried about profitability." With these types, you go straight to the rules of the game and stay out of some value-driven mess where their opinions could have merit. Paul was beginning to believe this himself and vowed to rant more in the future. This was a complicated business, and Paul had no idea what was going on. Even the Coca-Cola concentrate—arriving in separate shipments from Atlanta and Puerto Rico, to guard its secret recipe—added to his anxiety, though in bolder times he dreamed of cracking the code.

"I'm constantly concerned with profitability, Paul." Paul, who thought Stuart's little show of gumption was a scream, fanned this show of spirit away. He pursed his lips and stared up into a corner of the room where there was nothing to look at. This lull ended when his gaze came spinning down like a bird of prey. "What, for example, do you say when you call on someone who was just visited by the dipshit from Pepsi? What do you say?" This seemingly cruel redirection was actually a sop enabling Stuart to show the colors a bit and recover a shred of dignity. Paul knew he wasn't smart enough to credit him with this kindness, but it would be fun to see him on his feet for once, at least for a few strides. Breathe some life back into him. Not much use having a shell out there pushing some dubious product when real conviction was required.

Old Stuart was off and running. "I explain that our sugar content and carbonization differs. I tell them that Pepsi is flatter. I tell them Coke is more orange based, while Pepsi's more of a lemon flavor." He concluded in a tone of quiet reason, "I tell them Coke is cocaine free, but that the caffeine's still there."

Suddenly Paul was contemplative, his handsome face and great brown eyes at rest. "You know there's every reason to fear glass bottles are going to be phased out. You need to make it clear that aluminum recycling is iffy *as hell* and that the best interests of their communities are served by returnable glass bottles. Glass bottles hold carbonization and flavor better than anything. Also, on the Coke front, your customers need to be reminded that Coca-Cola is *more* American than apple pie." Here Paul began to speak in a stentorian tone that would've done Lincoln proud. "Dr. John Smith Pemberton first made this elixir in his *backyard* in 1886, and the world has been drinking it ever since. Forget the *expansions*—Minute Maid, Fanta, Sprite, all those peripherals. Stuart, please try and forget them. You need to sell the old original, and you need to sell it out of glass bottles."

"I tell them we combined with Tri-Star to form Columbia Pictures!" Stuart cried, causing a brief but unsettling quiet.

"No, Stuart, *please*, they don't need that, Stuart, they mustn't hear it. They do not need Hollywood. They need a time-honored cold drink in a glass bottle. But look, the headline for today is water-management services, the sort of slam dunk you can do on the weekend across your neighbor's fence while you're roasting weenies on the barbecue. Tell the one about how the problem isn't keeping his wife out of your yard but keeping *your* yard out of *his* wife! It's an old one, but the old ones are the good ones, aren't they, Stuart? I think they are. And you can make stuff up, too. Tell them Pepsi gets its water out of the cyanide leach fields from abandoned mines."

"Uh, I'm going to dig into it today, Paul. Services basically."

"Good, Stuart. And look, I know this takes some getting used to, but what are we going to do? Jim Whitelaw is dead." Paul felt strangely soiled by his own performance.

"I realize."

"And *puhleeze* don't pretend you miss him."

"I did respect him though, Paul."

Paul clenched his forearms to his rib cage. "*I* bet you got a *million* more where that one came from."

Now Stuart was rising from his seat, shaky and undefiant. Paul found his search for an appropriate facial expression semi-risible; it was like Stuart came in a shoebox full of spare parts. With a slight frown of ostensible concern, Paul urged him to pull himself together.

"I can't, Paul," Stuart said. "I never expected to be treated this way. I should've prepared myself better."

He didn't know how he found her here, nor how he managed to get her to share a bench with him, though she maintained a certain distance by pushing her hands deep into the pockets of her winter coat and withdrawing her neck into its collar so that the only actual flesh of Evelyn on display was the bridge of her nose, her eyes and the portion of forehead that showed below her Irish wool cap. Paul—coat open, gloveless—seemed warmed by his not inconsiderable charm. "Why don't you just call off the divorce? That satisfies everything."

"God knows there's plenty of pressure on me. Why can't you at least get a bit of money out to my mother?" Her eyes still followed the dogs, the Frisbees. "And Nat could use a boost."

"I don't make those choices. These distributions are based on profits."

"What happened to the profits?"

"They're going down," said Paul glumly.

"Why? Don't you know how to run the place?"

"Of course I do. But there are market forces I can't control, and our sector is getting hammered everywhere."

"*Sector*? Paul, you just make stuff up. What if I did stay married to you—let's just say I did—all that happens is I inherit Dad's equity in the ranch. In other words, no difference. You keep appealing to my greed, and it's not working. Why be so tiresome?"

"You may not get any money, but it would enable us to sell the company and cash out your mother and your sister. *Your mother and your sister.*" Evelyn decided not to comment on this appeal to family values. "I don't see Bill living forever, and that land's worth a fortune. Someday you'll sell it and—*ta da*—you're in San Juan Capistrano shaded up under a California oak, a margarita in one hand, a Palm Pilot with stock quotes in the other, just waiting for the fucking *swallows* to return."

"You make a romantic case for liquidation, but in my version Bill gets to a hundred and I live in peace out there at least until menopause, at which point your plan might start making sense. But say all this happens. Where are you?"

"The usual place, trying to get back into your good graces. Natalie says I can use the spare bedroom once Stuart gathers up his sea boots and boogies. Then I'd have to look around for something to do, pretty good at selling myself."

"You'll need a fresh audience."

"Could be, but what's for you to think about is this company, which, despite its quantifiable value to others, seems to be caught in bad undertow. And, frankly, are you selling enough cows to support your mother? Not to mention the various treatment bills lying ahead for Natalie, given her deepening despondency—i.e., more than pissed *and* gone back to stealing, just for instance?"

After a moment's thought, Evelyn said, "This is an absolute curse."

"Maybe so, but I didn't put it on you. Your father did. Remember, I'm not the devil."

"You just work for him."

"Really? I wonder why. The pay sucks."

The doors were all closing. Paul's mother called her that same night, undoubtedly tipped off by him to some perceived weakening. And knowing he would report to her probably kept Paul from going crazy. She claimed to be correcting papers but was, in fact, stinking drunk. "You're not sufficiently aware of the value of continuity," Mrs. Crusoe began in general garrulity, "or other long-run values that make your apparent need for some dreamed-of bliss shrink by comparison. Marriage is like the devoted study of a long, sacred document. Think of the Bible! Think of the Koran! What's that other one? Where all parties are raised to sacramental heights by the dedication of their lives."

Evelyn's attempts to interrupt were unavailing. She actually put the phone aside for as long as it took to put a few dishes in the sink. When she picked it up again, Mrs. Crusoe was winding down and growing confused. Finally, she demanded, "Who *is* this? With *whom* am I speaking?"

Natalie stood outside fastening her coat and determining if she'd left any lights on. The wind cut into her cheek while she took in the tidiness of the bungalow with both faint distaste and some alertness to maintenance issues. She recalled putting its little rectangle of a garden to bed as though it had been an act of complicity with seasonal forces that wished to make her colorless. She understood that she had to work this particular fear. She knew it was not reasonable when Stuart asked if they could move the boat from Canyon Ferry to Flathead Lake, and she'd replied that it made her want to kill herself. And it mattered less than it should have when Stuart made his little puzzle-face and tried to cheer her by describing the huckleberries west of the Continental Divide and the summer theater and shopping opportunities around Bigfork. Foolishness of this sort had once landed her in a karaoke joint lip-synching Tammy Wynette to gales of laughter and a booby-prize free pizza. Natalie was a Vassar graduate, and at the time this had seemed a very long fall indeed.

She was heartened by the surge of her Mustang as it pulled inexorably through the snow in front of her house, while a westbound train called through the storm. An old man with earflaps on his hat came down the sidewalk towing a sled with two bags of groceries beneath the bony outlines of snow-laden trees. A hundred fifteen thousand miles, and the Mustang still pulled like a Georgia mule. The weather report on the radio revealed a desperate picture from across Montana and through the Dakotas, sweeping south beyond Medicine Bow and threatening the faux-Indian village of the Denver airport; fatal strandings lay ahead, chained-up ghost ships on the interstate, and Natalie felt a commensurate desperation to be around people instead of standing at the kitchen window and watching the birdbath in her backyard turn into a colossal ice cream cone. With considerable irritation, she pictured Evelyn's insouciance out there on the ranch, soldiering on when the shit hit the fan. That much virtue could choke a hog.

She pulled up in front of Just the Two of Us and parked between a motorcycle and a florist's van, its ice-plastered corsage rapidly disappearing in the blast. The day her father died, Natalie had been busted for shoplifting a tortoiseshell comb in Jan's, the in spot for out-of-towners, faculty wives and bureaucrats; the news made the papers, but her mortification failed to preclude visits to other shops, despite Jan's small-scale but successful prosecution. Never done it before. Now she stole entirely from Just the Two of Us and because she was also a good "paying" customer, she felt a complex emotional game of cat-and-mouse whenever she prowled their aisles. She had had several allusive chats with Violet and Claire, leaving them with a somewhat cloudy view of her as an interesting person suffering an illness, and this, combined with normal competitive feelings, made them hate "the old sluts" at Jan's for being too stiff to accommodate her small awkwardness. Plus, Natalie was a *nice person.* Never did she suggest to Violet or Claire that they were wasting the best years of their lives showing the wives of yokels how to accessorize or how to avoid looking a fright when Mr. Right appeared on the horizon. Nevertheless, Natalie thought that Evelyn rather overrated this duo simply because they'd grown up on ranches.

All of which seemed beside the point as Natalie entrusted herself to the store, knocking snow from her sleeves and breathing this perfumed comfort beyond the cold solace of the hearth, amid the scents and soaps and bibelots, under the beautiful tin ceiling of a former Dodge Garage which threw a gentle light on the stacks of blouses, sweaters, scarves and hosiery.

"Don't say anything nice about this weather," Natalie cautioned the two proprietors who stood shoulder to shoulder at this challenging appearance.

"We won't," said one or the other. These were mountain geishas, indistinguishable but for Violet's hatchet jaw and Claire's close-set eyes, which showed equal concern when listening or sorting rubber bands.

"Don't worry about me," said Natalie, "I'm just going to poke around." The exchange of glances at the level of supper-club theater gave Natalie the sense the jig was up, and she cast a longing glance at the sensuous rows of merchandise.

Remembering dear, dopey Stuart coming to the police station to pick her up, she had the teeniest frisson that an involuntary joyride awaited her; but the tolerance of the shopgirls had the effect of tempering desire. She knew that wrong numbers floated from the murk of troubled selves.

"Girls, stick with me while I shop. I don't want to have a slip." And she didn't. Violet and Claire, too, were disappointed at this lapse in Natalie's dark wishes, reducing them all to spectators in a mountain storm. Now they went to the front window and commented on pedestrians. The motorcyclist was beating the snow from the seat of his machine with his hat. Across the street, ice fog had created rows of bodiless faces. All you could read of the movie marquee was a fragment—*FESTI*—and a steady, throbbing light was the little that showed of what perhaps was an arrest in progress.

"Come on in and buy something!" Claire shouted through the glass.

"You look like an asshole!" Violet cried out to a bundled-up passerby.

"This is like being locked in an elevator," said Natalie quite sensibly.

"No shit," Claire commented sadly. "Why don't you steal something."

"I'm not in the mood. You steal something."

"We can't; they do inventory."

"Then steal from the cash register."

"You're pretty naive," said Violet, looking at Claire. Both ignored the ringing phone and Natalie suddenly felt anxious. She thought of the bulbs of perennials asleep in her garden, wondering how they were doing in this terrible cold. She thought next of Stuart's unwavering sense of duty and loyalty. Then she thought she might cry but elected to postpone it.

In the opinion of his father-in-law, whose greatest praise for anyone was "reminds me of myself at that age," Paul was a ball of fire. For years, he had barreled around the

State of Montana in a white Ford Crown Victoria, dry cleaning hanging in the backseat, calling on every conceivable customer of their bottled products. And he bragged to his own father-in-law that the towns he visited were chock-full of cheating housewives.

"But where is your *expense* report?" Sunny Jim demanded.

"My *what*?"

"Your *expense* report. You must submit an *expense* report complete with receipts, after every trip. Where is it?"

"Mr. Peabody's coal train done hauled it away."

"What in the hell's the matter with you, son?"

"I hate it when you're sore. You've got a face that could stop a clock."

This appealed to Sunny Jim Whitelaw but not at first.

It was Paul's capacity for unstinting companionship that endeared him to Sunny Jim Whitelaw, whose business acumen and family leadership were matched by another life entirely, that of an unwearying old goat. For this, he needed company, and it illustrated his remarkable ingenuity that he chose Paul to accompany his carousals.

On one such jaunt, before Paul had hit on the bright idea of trading jail time for corporate glory, he had traveled with Whitelaw to Las Vegas for a bottlers' convention, evidence of which, in the form of brochures and industry newsletters, was strewn in Mother Whitelaw's path. Paul had long acted as beard to Whitelaw's secret life, a simple enough arrangement except that he increasingly associated his confidentiality with raises to which he felt entitled, an association Whitelaw indulgently called blackmail while plotting, without so revealing, a severe reprisal. For this secret reason, Sunny Jim had invited a guest on this trip, a business acquaintance named C. R. Majub, whom he described as a "very, very, very old friend."

At first, they saw little of Majub; he was ailing and he was also a hockey fan. If any sort of game at all was on television, Majub was absent; if the Montreal Canadiens were playing, he took the phone off the hook, piled pillows under his door to remove extraneous noise and drank Crown Royal from a bathroom glass. "You can't believe a towelhead could love hockey so much!" Whitelaw exclaimed, then added, more thoughtfully, "but he'll show you how to get rich, so long as you don't care how you make it." From the beginning, Majub cheerfully exuded mystery and secret knowledge, and he was one of the few people whom Paul had ever instinctively feared. Majub's attentiveness was like the savoring of a cannibal.

Sundown seemed prolonged on the eve of their arrival, and it was not quite dark by the time Sunny Jim attached a mercenary showgirl named JoAnne to his arm, a high-kicking hooker with muscular hands. Paul, straggling along like a remora following an old shark, tried to make small talk, citing Evelyn's love of her horses and cows, and causing JoAnne to moan tragically at the recollection of her North Dakota yesteryears. For obvious reasons, the two men kept separate rooms, the latter a suite where Whitelaw could entertain. Indeed, he entertained so many that Paul began to wonder just what demons drove his father-in-law; it was hardly a moral judgment, since Paul sometimes did some entertaining himself. At such occasions C. R. Majub often appeared, a precise and well-dressed man of forty with a flat midwestern voice. Majub, it developed, was an Ohio Bengali, and too ill to entirely indulge the technical investment questions in speculations as to "where our economy is headed" that so absorbed Whitelaw. Majub seemed to be in Las Vegas looking for a cure, though when Paul asked if it was to see a doctor, Whitelaw said, "Not exactly!" and laughed uproariously. Majub saw no humor in this and continued sizing Paul up. Whitelaw beamed upon his sick friend. Trying to curry his favor, Paul told him, once Whitelaw had left the room, "His teeth are loose but he still wants sex."

Whitelaw enjoyed Paul's prying nature and was willing to feed him tidbits about Majub on the rare occasions when the whores were elsewhere. He was, it seemed, a successful broker of businesses who'd helped Sunny Jim acquire, with leverage, several—"semi-mom-and-pop"—going concerns in the Midwest, including a sign company, a foundry and a Dunkin' Donuts. During a steep and unforeseen downturn, in which the offspring threatened to eat the parent company, Majub saved Whitelaw's bacon by "spinning the subsidiaries *way* offshore."

"This guy knows from loyal," Sunny Jim said. "He's on the business end of loyal. P.S. I owe him." As he almost never acknowledged debt, Paul figured this was merely a figure of speech.

Paul's only private exposure consisted of a single drink at the hotel bar where Majub acknowledged that he was not well; but when Paul asked what he was doing about it, he merely shrugged and said, "Waiting." The brown rascal's Perrier made Paul's Budweiser seem the epitome of vice, and Paul was further discomfited by the silence of Majub, a quality that—being unattainable by Paul—he always rather admired. At length, Majub turned to him wearily and said, "Sunny Jim isn't going to be around forever," then handed Paul a card that read *C. J. Majub, bro-*

ker and, after finishing his Perrier at a swallow, added, "I make companies get bigger or I make them get smaller. Best of all, I make them go away."

That night, chatting blearily with his father-in-law in the latter's suite, Paul showed him his latest plan for a promotion, which consisted of a fistful of Polaroids with which the girl from North Dakota had provided him for five cool century notes. Whitelaw didn't show a bit of annoyance at the connection between these pictures and his son-in-law's economic well-being, and Paul could hardly have known that he himself was about to go on the black market. Sunny Jim took possession of the Polaroids with inexplicable gratitude and, resting a heavy paw on Paul's shoulder, said, "I just like getting my ashes hauled." Then he announced he was tired and wished to go to sleep. But for a nightcap, he recommended the Capitol, in Henderson, where Paul could use his credit by just identifying himself as his son-in-law. After giving him directions and begging Paul's indulgence, the old fellow rolled over and closed his eyes.

The Capitol was next door to Seizer's Palace, an agency specializing in repossessing unpaid-for goods. Its motto, emblazoned on poured concrete walls, reminded Paul of a book he'd once read. "Render unto Seizer, that which is Seizer's." The cabby who'd dropped him there said the women wouldn't be prostitutes, but they'd be close. The Capitol had white columns fastened directly to its stucco facade and its discreet entrance promised high jinks. Overhead, the sound of arriving and departing airliners was constant; the night air smelled of jet fuel, and desert clouds were lit repeatedly, at heartbeat intervals, by strobes and beacons from the city. The persistence of odd-hour life gave the town a kind of fluorescent alpenglow.

Late as it was, it was early for this bar. A few people were drinking, their belongings scattered in front of them, purses, wallets, cigarettes. When Paul established his relationship with Whitelaw to the bartender, he was rewarded with a significant nod. Down at the end of the bar, two women were talking to each other in a manner that disinvited interruption, yet they perked after this exchange. Their dress suggested that they were on their way home from work rather than out for the evening, but before Paul could even order a drink, he found himself accompanied by one of them, a young, dark-eyed, humorous-looking girl with mid-length auburn hair parted casually at the middle. "Next, I buy you a drink," said Paul.

"As you wish. I can afford it."

"Really? Then why don't you buy *me* a drink?"

"You got credit here, sport."

"How'd you know that?"

"A little birdy told me."

Not long afterward, when things seemed to have slowed to a crawl, Paul asked a question whose answer he was not destined to hear. "What's there to fucking *do* in this town?"

He woke up in a bathtub full of ice, a row of new stitches like a parade of ants across his abdomen; on a chair beside him, a portable phone rested atop a note: "*Call 911 for post-operative care. And remember, your health comes first!*" Even before the immediate pain of surgery, he was aware of an odd, sweeping tingling that soon turned into horror. Looking at the faintly puckered slit across his stomach, the neat dimpling of the stitches, he pounced on an oversight of his abductors: Since he didn't *know* where he was, how could he tell Emergency? His clothes were neatly folded and the hopsacking jacket, whose wheaty hue had seemed so lighthearted and summery in the Vegas night, was draped carefully on a hanger embossed with *"Courtesy Hotel."* Paul climbed out of the tub and dried and dressed himself, sitting down several times in a recliner by the window where he tried to form some impression from his view of telephone wires and languorous side-street traffic. He was on the second floor, he concluded, of an out-of-the-way hotel perhaps called the Courtesy, and, judging by the traffic, well away from any significant artery. Still, there was some reassurance in daylight, but it was short-lived and Paul found himself in misery again. The clock radio went off and Latino music filled the room.

When the macabre mystery of his surgery came sweeping back, he rose and started for the door, a general sickliness sweeping over him, combined with a stab of guilt as he saw himself explaining to Evelyn how he'd been drinking with some girl, but he'd been drugged! Right! Unlike the kidnappers of a dictator or industrialist, his didn't want money or power. They wanted one of his insides and he didn't yet know which one, though they hadn't gotten anything he couldn't do without because here he was lacing his cordovans, lightheaded with fear, in a dull glare from the window. A shiver began in his colon and rose to the back of his throat. He emitted a small, peculiar sound, like the mewing of a kitten.

Paul opened the door, then turned the lock so it wouldn't close in case he had to get back inside. The doorknob was wet from his own hand. He started down the stairs, worrying remotely about passing out and gripping the steel railing with both hands. An old cleaning lady holding vacuum cleaner parts watched him from the landing, sizing him up as if he were something she could use.

Once he had attained the lobby, Paul had to sit down even before he could say a word. The desk clerk looked at him indifferently and, after an ensuing quiet, said, "You missed checkout," pointing at a sign on the counter with a ballpoint pen. Paul declined to state that he didn't know who'd checked him *in* and instead just stared without energy at the desk clerk, at the tomato-colored coat, the thin, slicked-back hair, and the horn-rimmed glasses that spanned the man's cheeks. Reaching across his chest with his right hand, Paul clasped his wallet and pulled it out. The rushing creeps abated at the discovery of his own picture on his driver's license.

He looked at the desk clerk, held up his driver's license and said, "This is me. I need an ambulance."

"Oh?"

"They . . . they . . . cut me open."

"Who's that?"

"*Please*—" At which point, he lost consciousness.

When the emergency team asked what happened to Paul, the desk clerk replied distantly, "Somebody went to town on him."

He did in fact wake up in the hospital, thinking nothing quite brings out the good Samaritan like an unconscious body at the front desk. Simply because most people there were at work, the hospital seemed to peacefully imply that all was normal. And Paul soon learned that the procedure by which he had lost a kidney was one of high professionalism, the wound was clean, and he heard several admiring remarks about the surgery.

Paul could have taken it hard and learned nothing from the experience, but in the end his lesson was one that only people like Sunny Jim Whitelaw could give, people free of confusion and self-doubt who looked at the rest of humanity as perhaps the astronauts do. But Paul's full control of his fate would not arrive until he figured out what to do with the dead motorcyclist.

At Firestone, the young man with the two-tone goatee who said it would be at least an hour before her snow tires were installed clearly enjoyed making this statement. It was dark, but Evelyn was tired of being cooped up all day at home and wished, even in this terrible weather, she could be out on the ranch. So, instead of waiting around, she walked up to see Natalie, mentally preparing herself to be patient as Natalie seemed more than usually erratic. But the house was empty, so Evelyn headed back downtown, thinking she might get a cup of tea someplace. Then, when she passed a house belonging to the last of her father's many doctors, Randy DeRozier, the door opened abruptly and Randy leaned his whole good-looking self through, including the great big blue eyes previously approved by the sisters. "Evelyn! How *are* you?" he called. They'd not spoken since her father's death, and she was surprised that his look of concern seemed somewhat overlearned, given that he and his wife, Juanita, were friends of the whole Whitelaw family.

"Just fine, Randy."

"'Cause if you're not, let me know."

"Is there something you take for it?"

"Evelyn, come on in for a moment." He took a tentative step onto the snowy porch. "You need a break from the cold." There were already globes of cold, hazy light around the streetlamps, and it would be nice to duck in somewhere close by until the car was ready. She could hear tire chains clanking away one street over and the weirdly clear whistle of a train north of town. Hastening into his front hall, she noticed how youthful Dr. Randy was, in college sweats and bare feet. He could have been fifty, but he cultivated a scrubbed, boyish dishevelment. She was less comfortable with the open inspection he gave her while helping with her coat.

"I have a surprise for you," he said, leading her toward the Poggenpohl futuristic kitchen with its granite counters and deep black double sink. Next to it was a beautiful wet bar, bird's-eye maple and stainless steel with little circular lights above like the cabin of a yacht.

"Where's Juanita?" she asked. Juanita was a great girl, an Oklahoman with a powerful contralto voice who reminded Evelyn of tornadoes. On at least two occasions that Evelyn knew of, Juanita had slugged people who richly deserved it, including a fantastically pompous state legislator.

"That's my surprise!"

"What do you mean?"

"No Juanita." He dropped lime slices into two glasses and repeated, "*No* Juanita."

"It's time for *Larry King Live*!" Evelyn said quite irrationally.

"Come on, Evelyn. Take a moment here: she left me."

His own vainglorious disbelief in this helped Evelyn decide that silence was the best policy, silence without any comforting grins or the doctor was going to launch himself onto her before the two lovely drinks he'd just made were consumed. He touched a button activating the audio system and said at the first notes, "Pavane for a Deceased Infanta."

She took a sip of her very strong vodka and tonic, which Dr. Randy had correctly remembered was nearly the only thing she ever drank. This one was a shade high-test.

They moved into the study and sat on a black, flowered sofa, where Evelyn registered a welcome feeling of nothingness or serene detachment, of letting it all go, that didn't last ten seconds.

"And Paul's out too?"

"Yup, regular grief workshop for the two of us, eh Randy?"

"Maybe Juanita'll be coming back."

"I'm sure she will."

"Evelyn, you don't know a thing about this."

"I can spot a man in a hurry."

"You're a hard woman, Evelyn," he said, slipping his arm around her.

She'd made the mistake of putting her drink down. Now he was trying to kiss her, his neck straining against her forearm. "Randy? *Randy*! Stop this."

He sat straight up, shoulders square, folded his hands in his lap and gazed around the floor, then said, "I have to make a call." He went into the next room, and she could soon tell, from the sharp bursts and long silences, that he was talking to Juanita. Still, she couldn't quite see the right way to walk straight out of here to her snow tires. She'd actually been up for a bit of this, had there been any way of skipping all the posturing. When the conversation in the next room stopped and Randy failed to return, Evelyn found herself searching for him, despite a feeling of queasiness. She discovered Dr. Randy in his den having changed into starched pearl gray pajamas with red piping, and sitting in a bay window, his handsome face profiled against the falling snow.

When Evelyn told him how sickening she found his performance, Randy turned his big pretty eyes toward her and his lips retracted from surprisingly small teeth. "So puke," he said.

Evelyn rued the vodka on her breath as she pawed around in the closet for her coat. She flung open the front door, glad to be in the light-shot whirlwind of snow. Glancing back at Dr. DeRozier in his pajamas, fighting the door shut against the wind, she levitated her way toward Firestone, thinking, This is weather!

Surely this storm would paralyze the city. The great yellow plows were flashing lights in every direction, the powdery, weightless snow pouring from one side of the blade, burying cars and blocking alleys, leaving ghosts of diesel fuel in midair. As Evelyn lay in bed, she felt the luxury of stolen time as the burden of human planning was absolved by weather. Surely the intensity of this storm, with all its fury retained during long passage from the Gulf of Alaska, would have to abate. Because she was remembering her life with Paul, Evelyn began to weep, abandoning herself in this isolation to choking sobs, remembering two things: the breadth of his back and Mexico, somewhere near San Felipe, in low desert far to the south, when he had done something to the car. It looked as if it had tractor tires and you practically needed a ladder to get in it, but they'd parked right out on the sand next to the Sea of Cortez where Evelyn sunbathed in the most provocative bikini, one you couldn't wear just anywhere, though their sense of reckless liberty was such that they made love in any patch of sand free of vinagaroons or sidewinders, the bikini generally dangling from the thorns of the nearest cat's claw bush.

They'd hiked on a night as bright as blue day, and discovered a tiny owl occupying a hole in the arm of a tall cactus that stood above a trail where gaunt-ribbed Corriente cattle walked oblivious around them, horns rattling in the narrow passage.

Her love there had unfurled in agitated, unrecognizable cries, and she had no hope of getting a grip on herself. She trusted Paul and was fascinated by his sauntering style, judging him in his bleached-out Waylon T-shirt and canvas shorts held up by twine to be free of the usual claims that clipped the wings of most young men. She also understood that women suffering hypnosis by criminals or mama's boys was nothing new. Good-looking, quick-witted, a soul rented to darkness, Paul had everything.

Evelyn had first met him at her parents' house one nice night in May. Though she was in a rush to get back to the ranch, he seduced her on her walk to, and finally inside of, her car; it was that kind of abandonment, from the beginning. She didn't even know what he did aside from turning up in Bozeman on a "fact-finding mission" for some agency. He'd met her father at a local association concerned with treason in national life, and the two became immediate friends despite their great difference in age. Had it not been for Sunny Jim Whitelaw's success in conveying the glamour

of the entrepreneur's life, Paul might have satisfied his
mother's dreams and gone to graduate school.

Though sex probably caused her marriage, Evelyn had
tolerated so many cautious suitors that she failed to notice
that Paul's admirable lack of self-pity was actually part of a
cold and predatory nature. The marriage also improved her
relationship with her father, something she'd longed for
since childhood. Sunny Jim was happily fascinated by the
unerring way Paul homed in on the bottle company and
wasn't so much surprised when Paul began stealing as he
was enchanted by the impertinence. With disarming hon-
esty, he told Paul he would recoup his losses by selling his
vital organs, if these thefts should recur. His son-in-law, of
course, didn't believe him.

Whitelaw never backed away from his passionate approval
of the marriage. Even when Paul was in prison, he kept him
in control of numerous accounts. It was the opinion of
Sunny Jim that here was a man's man, one with real value to a
fellow with a few skeletons in his own closet. They shared a
lack of sense of humor and a conviction that the general
population was crippled by the need to see only what it
wanted to see. They both loved the Shakespeare-in-the-Park
program and referred to their secret girlfriends as strumpets
or jades. Sunny Jim was so swept by the feeling of youth
restored that he sometimes described his marital endeavors
with Alice in bed, racking his mind for high points and rare
instances of pleasure. Paul found this, as he later confided to
Evelyn, "icky," though he was amiably wowed by the old
man's profound indecency. Once, when Sunny Jim told him
he thought Alice loved someone else more than him, though
he never said who, Paul was touched. He assumed it was
God, or her gynecologist.

The light of day revealed a cavalcade of shadows on a still landscape of snow. The city was out of order. Evelyn dead-bolted her front door and pulled the phone cord from the wall. In the bathroom mirror, she seemed such a haggard preview of her own old age that she waved to herself, then went into the bedroom where she reflected on her fate in walking past Dr. Randy's house. She pictured him washing their cocktail glasses, and she recalled his ludicrous appearance in the front door, pajamas flapping in the gale. These reminders of her freedom gave her the peace to sleep.

In the deep snow outside, the plow was as quiet as a sailing ship.

Evelyn got up, made coffee and plugged in the phone; it was the middle of the afternoon. While she was on the back porch refilling her bird feeder and before the coffee was done, the phone rang. It was, of all people, Dr. Edith Crusoe, who was in town and wished to see her, "oh so briefly." Evelyn complied as cordially as she could and got off the phone, trying not to start thinking about something to which she could hardly look forward. Though Paul's mother had little interest in the fortunes of her son's marriage, separation, divorce or any other aspect of his domestic arrangements, she was keenly interested that he get on in life; therefore, she felt his present malaise was something she ought to do something about. That, and she so stated, was why she had driven all the way over from Missoula solely to meet with Evelyn. She'd raised Paul with the belief that he needed only the broadest views to get through life in the West; these included nativism, appropriate settlement and the dizzying romance of low rainfall. It went right over his head. He only thought about such large themes when he was smoking reefer or had the flu.

Evelyn found her erstwhile mother-in-law in the lobby of the Holiday Inn, reading a large, old book with a Dewey-decimal sticker on the back. Her coat and green canvas purse were piled in front of her, and she wore low-heeled pumps, a pleated blue wool skirt and a shawl-collared red sweater with coins for buttons. Evelyn took this all in, faintly hoping for some sartorial concord; but in her baggy but clean pants, Sorel felt packs and down jacket she was clearly of another mind.

As Evelyn arrived, Dr. Crusoe put down the book and accusingly wagged a travel prospectus published by the state. "Skiing, snowmobiling, lake sailing, trout fishing, you name it. Clearly the locals think the water will last for-ever. This mess began with the last Homestead Act and won't end until desertification turns the West into a vast parking lot for sport-utility vehicles." She stood at her con-siderable height. "These are happy times for anyone un-troubled by the extinction of wildlife and the destruction of the countryside. I know you invited me for coffee, but what chance might I have for substituting a highball? I have already determined the presence of an adequate 'nightery' on the grounds."

"Sure, that's fine."

"Do you still drink?"

"You bet." They headed for the lounge, which already enlivened by five plastered individuals piecing together "Luck Be a Lady" over the piano. Judging by the fervor of the lyrics, "luck" was the only word that gave them any confidence. They did far better with "Love and Marriage," positively roaring the phrase "goes together like a horse and carriage." The songbirds greeted Evelyn by name as she cringed past, leading Dr. Crusoe to a distant table while giving the waitress a small nod.

"It's a gift to be able to just have fun and let time pass without a quarrel," Paul's mother said, beaming at the boozers around the piano.

Evelyn knew her to be an old bar fly, but it was interesting to see her in action, generating accompanying theories.

"The lush life, a peaceful part of America." She ducked her head into her collar out of delight with this remark.

"Are you still teaching, Edith?"

"*What?*"

"Are you still actually teaching?"

"Good God, let me have a drink first."

The waitress took their order, anxiously glancing over at the group by the piano, which included two car dealers, a CPA and a chiropractor the other three swore by. The latter had the pianist by the back of the neck, and it looked as if he'd get satisfactory playing out of him or else work him till he did. The pianist, now coerced into the moronic anthem "My Way," looked frail, even ill, behind his wire-rimmed glasses. Evelyn indicated his plight to Dr. Crusoe, who commented, "It's Jung's wounded prince. If he can't play alone or in that cerebral jazz quartet he dreams about, he doesn't want to play at all. But his talent is small and those men need music to bolster them on their more vigorous quest."

Evelyn wanted to kick her in her big butt. "Car sales, tax returns, lower back pain?"

"Fine!" said Dr. Crusoe. "Work must be done." Flushed with her third highball, she bobbed an ice cube with her forefinger. "To answer your question, I'm still teaching, and of course that consists now and forevermore of my award-winning, oft-recorded seminar on rainfall, What Comes Down, Must Go Up." She let out a whoop and gulped from her highball. When she replaced the glass on the table, she looked straight at Evelyn without seeing her. Evelyn felt the gaze go through and past her. She waited as the hooch made the long drop. Dr. Crusoe's lips parted slowly at the desired effect.

Evelyn said, "Was there a special reason you wished to see me?"

Mrs. Crusoe was staring off into a dark, empty corner. "I'm never sorry when politicians die," she said.

"Right . . ."

"Oh yes, dear, there was a reason, and naturally I escape into prevarication where my interference might be unwelcome. First of all, I never extended my sympathy to you on the death of your father."

"Thank you."

"And are you recovered?"

"Yes and no."

"'Yes and no'?"

"Well, we were never sure he liked us."

"Liked you! Of course he liked you; he was your father."

"Somehow this was different."

"Really? I don't see how. I met your father. A commanding presence. And normal in every way. I despise it when your age group extracts some poor old male from the culture that made him, all the things he survived, only to conclude he was a brute. It's banal."

"Like I say, this must've been different. He *was* a brute."

"And Natalie believes this too?"

"No, but she's been hurt by it."

"Oh, crap."

"He never smiled once."

"That's fact masquerading as theory."

"We were very wrapped up in him, but I don't think he ever really saw us."

"Did you," asked Dr. Crusoe with a magisterial lifting of her whole person, "give him anything to see?"

Evelyn inspected her thumbnail, then looked off.

"Go to hell, Edith."

Paul's mother rotated slightly from the waist, lifting her arm high over her head and wiggling her hand fervidly. Fearing immediate attack, Evelyn failed to realize Dr. Crusoe was merely ordering another drink. "When the time comes," she said, "I shall go uncomplainingly." Once again, she shook the tourist brochure. "If, as is here claimed, this is heaven, then I intend to go trippingly to the alternative you have just suggested." The defeated pianist was now rendering "Thanks for the Memories," and it was clear that Dr. Crusoe would have preferred being in the chorus. "Evelyn, let me get to my point. I'm here to ask if there is *anything* I can say to make you consider reconciling with Paul." She tilted her head and peered down into her drink with one eye like a parrot.

"No."

"I find that a most troubling reply."

"Edith, you ought to realize how painful this has been for everyone."

"There must've been some basis for the original attraction. There must be some respect due for the time invested. Upon every relationship reside the claims of others: we do not live in a vacuum. It is an economic universe, and you are bankrupting a family. You are only hurting yourself, and revenge, Evelyn, is a diminishing motive."

In the background, the pianist was banging out "The Mexican Hat Dance" while the four businessmen took turns jumping up and down on what was once his appealing fedora.

"A marriage can be reduced to an arm's-length contract, should the benefits to all outweigh the limitations of appearance for one."

Evelyn had had enough. "Mrs. Crusoe, I am entirely aware of two things. Academic salaries are not what they should be, and Paul has always been a most dutiful son."

"Not a *cent* of child support did I once receive," the woman hissed. "Thirty-one stitches as a result of his birth and a *gruesome* convalescence."

"Shouldn't you have told him who his father was? He never knew."

"An arid-lands botanist, a scofflaw, a premature ejaculator!"

"Aw gee," she said as Dr. Crusoe lurched to her feet. Evelyn had long worried about the effect of ending Paul's checks to his mother; she saw now that it was profound, and that earlier wailings as to the possible termination of a January research project in sun-drenched Tucson were but the tip of the iceberg.

"And may I say," Dr. Crusoe spat, "that you have painted yourself into a very narrow corner, young woman. Belligerent self-sufficiency is on no one's list of virtues. But perhaps, you are a *pioneer*."

"I've had as much of you as I can stand," Evelyn said. "I really have." And with that she left the room. The group around the piano importuned her to return for the good times, but she pretended to be stone deaf.

The desk clerk was refilling a bowl of complimentary red-and-white mints. A television monitor revealed, in bluish light, corridors and exits and empty spaces around the laundry room, pop and ice machines; it was like an art movie, not a soul in sight, great reviews in New York. Worried, she stole back to surreptitiously observe Paul's mother, who seemed to be explaining something quite grave to the bleary faces around the piano. Finally, the men rose to their feet, facing forward in a line, the pianist gloomily poising hands over the keyboard. Dr. Crusoe took her place at the end of the line, hands on the hips of chubby Martin Jelks, and when a vaguely Latin tune emerged from the piano, "Cherry Pink and Apple Blossom White," a primitive conga line began to snake between the Formica tables with festive grunts invoking the ghost of Perez Prado.

Out in the cold and starless night, Evelyn smiled ruefully at the old broad's self-sufficiency. She might have deserved better luck, but Evelyn gave up immediately on trying to find the roots of Paul's feral nature in her high spirits. Besides, Evelyn admitted, Edith was not without appeal, a good soul really.

The meeting with Edith seemed a turning point, the last straw that helped her realize that she stood in the way of her own family's happiness. Three unhappy days later, Evelyn withdrew her suit for divorce, wearing the same clothes she'd worn in the park, slumped in a metal folding chair at the edge of the Justice of the Peace's desk. Paul was with her, having decided to promote this as a romantic occasion. Papers were pushed toward her, she signed them and pushed them back. The Justice of the Peace, a middle-aged woman in a dark green pantsuit, hair tucked into red plastic combs, kept looking back and forth, focusing on the contrast between Paul's dark suit, blue shirt and vivid paisley tie, and Evelyn's crumpled costume. She must be pregnant, Justice of the Peace concluded, but at least we have a proud papa!

The next morning, house finches, magpies, two kinds of chickadees and a belligerent Canada jay awaited her. When the phone rang, she put down the bag of seed, held her bathrobe around her waist, went back inside to answer it.

"Sis," Natalie said abruptly, "I needed to fax some papers to Mama from the state tax people. And I called Mountain Travel for a number on the cruise ship in Alaska. They sort of *laughed in my face* when I said the word 'Alaska.' In fact, they said, 'Look out your window.' Anyway, long story short, Mama didn't *go* to Alaska."

"*What*?" Evelyn was pouring hot water over her coffee grounds.

"You heard me."

"Where is she, Nat?"

"She's on a cruise, very sensibly, in the South Pacific."

"I don't believe this!"

"It's not easy. Any thoughts?"

"Just one: How did we ever believe 'Alaska'?"

Evelyn cut two pieces of sourdough toast diagonally, got out a jar of black Oxford marmalade and set them all on the small table in the kitchen, then sat pondering Natalie's news until she became aware of someone at the front door. By tilting her chair back, she saw the shape of a face in the oval glass and called, "Yes?" in a particularly unwelcoming tone. These questions about what was becoming of her family and this latest anomaly about her mother were like the weights that hold divers underwater.

Thrust into the slight opening of the doorway was the cold reddened face of Dr. Randy. "Terribly sorry," he said, face surrounded by down-filled nylon and surmounted by a tam-o'-shanter.

Evelyn said through a mouthful of toast, "You were lonely."

"I won't even ask if you can forgive me. I'm just sorry. I have no excuses."

"You're forgiven. Now close the door, it's making a draft."

She called Natalie back in hopes of amplifying the information, but Natalie had other interests. "Stuart and I," she said, "have decided it was time to get on with our lives."

"Why am I not surprised?" said Evelyn. She'd been down this road too many times. Alaska, at least, was new.

"I don't know, Evelyn, why aren't you?"

"We've heard a good bit of the preliminaries."

"In the future," said Natalie, "I'll make a greater effort to hold your attention."

This was cooling down quickly, and Evelyn thought it best to get off the phone.

Stuart, meanwhile, had heard nothing of getting on with their lives. And he wasn't nearly as thick as Natalie or anyone else thought; it was a mistake to take his disinclination for conflict as weakness. When he declined to embrace Paul's more dubious ventures, Paul wrongly concluded that Stuart was "plodding."

Paul also had decided that Natalie and Stuart weren't getting along and would at odd times intrude upon them.

He did this breezily, coming into their house with beaming detachment not unlike a minister's and often speaking of higher values no one imagined he was aware of or took seriously. Sometimes as he spoke he held both of their hands in his own, a deed that filled Natalie with such disgust. Given the details of her intimacy with him, she marveled at the perversity of these counseling sessions, whereas Stuart, sitting there at the refectory table, seemed warmed when Paul addressed him particularly. "The union of a man and a woman," he intoned, "is smiled upon by God only to the extent that their faith in each other is unsoiled. Loyalty is God's particular blessing upon a marriage."

Now that his own marriage was effectively in escrow, Paul moved quickly to the trust documents themselves, which specified the conditions that permitted the sale of the company and found that a broker had already been appointed, as though Sunny Jim had reached out from beyond death to extend one final arrangement. He called the broker, C. R. Majub, at his office. Majub had at this time a beautiful British accent, lived in Atlanta and described himself as a specialist in selling companies related to packaging. It was ten years since they'd met in Las Vegas, and Paul tried strenuously to place him, certain there had been a previous meeting. Majub examined the trust document and finally stated that it was the first time he'd seen a will function as a lien. He emphasized that there was some ground for optimism, since "never was a trust that couldn't be busted," a hope Natalie seized upon as though it were already an accomplishment. Thinking of their possible liberation from the bottling plant, she said, "I'm excited for you, Stuart. I always thought Dad and Paul made too much of your small earnings."

"Golly, I guess I just got used to it. I have other rewards. Maybe they're known only to me. What was it Emerson said? 'It's amazing how much you can accomplish if you don't care who gets the credit.'"

"Ralph *Waldo* Emerson?"

"Yes."

"I thought he knew better than that."

"What do you mean, Nat? Do you know who I'm talking about?"

"I saw a special about him."

"Really, about Emerson?"

"I think it was. I'd have to see it again. I never forget a face."

"I can't imagine them having a special on Emerson—"

"Well, maybe they didn't, for Christ sake, Stuart. But whoever it was, it's childish to expect people not to want credit for the things they do."

"Sure, Nat."

"Now what? We're hurt?"

Stuart shook his head no and began to busy himself with small tasks around the house, while Natalie imagined how it might be after this fork in the road, given of course that Mr. Majub had the mother-wit to make good on his statements. Natalie decided to find some way of meeting with this Bengali.

A pillow doubled under her head, Evelyn watched the streaming night clouds outside her window, a cold new moon illuminating their apparent speed. She was thinking of girlhood stories wherein the dead inhabited a paradise beyond the stars; and later, near-death stories that seemed to validate this outward voyage her entire species longed for. Were they all there, Dante, Torquemada, Lincoln, even Elvis? She felt ill with worry that at the very end of her great escape into starry darkness, Paul would still be in full pursuit. Perhaps these thoughts were just precursors of sleep or part of a troubling enchantment. Her father was speaking. "My mother once told me, 'They say if you break a mirror it's seven years' bad luck.' She broke one on her wedding night and told me I was her first bad luck." Why had she never forgotten this conversation?

"Evelyn," he asked, "have you ever wondered if I was happy?"

"I suppose I must have."

"Would you like to hear a surprise? I am. I'm happy."

"Dad, you should show your happiness. You should smile more."

"I've heard that all my life."

"Mama says you smile in your sleep."

"That's gastric. People smile to get others to agree with them. It's pitiful. If they had any guts or leadership, they wouldn't care."

Evelyn wondered why her father gave such awful advice.

"And Paul," said Sunny Jim.

"Yes?"

"I like this guy."

"I know you do."

"I've been waiting for this guy."

The light had not come on for Sunny Jim with her previous boyfriends, not Fred Casey, the Yale-educated forester; neither Drew Bolt, a doctor of remarkable innocence; nor Aaron Coulter, the star of the National Finals Rodeo and heir to the vast Diamond J southeast of Winifred; and obviously not the several jejune drips with whom she fornicated through her junior and senior years in college. This refraining light had come on in only one case and for a man some saw as a career criminal in the making, but whom Sunny Jim considered his ideal successor, this son of an eccentric history professor and a teenaged juvenile delinquent she was counseling under a university-sponsored community outreach program in Boulder. Only much later would Edith upgrade his biography to "arid-lands botanist." By that time, Paul had decided to pay his father a visit.

Southern Rockies Investigative Services—once engaged by Whitelaw Bottling—had provided him with a street map of Gillette, Wyoming, and the address of Richard "Doc" Sanders, presently living on disability from Badlands Coal Company. Paul billed their somewhat expensive investigative services per prior arrangement to Whitelaw Bottling.

Paul knocked on the front door, peering inconspicuously into an interior lit only by quietly explosive flashes from a television that was out of sight. Backlit by this intermittent blue light, a figure emerged in the hallway, Paul thinking, "Oh God, this must be *my old man*." He decided to begin with stroke after stroke of untruths and he felt an odd electrical sensation at his hairline.

"Yes?" Sanders said with thorough suspicion. He was short, and Paul quickly and gratefully calculated the genetics of height contributed by his mother. He was less excited by the thinning hair, and instinctively touched the crown of his own head. Doc Sanders's teeth were blindingly white, and he was unrealistic about his figure, for Paul could see that the top of his newish pants were far from buttonable.

Obviously Sanders viewed his own son as a Badlands detective and reached a hand to the small of his back with a helpless-looking wince.

"Mr. Sanders?"

"You're lookin' at him."

"Paul Whitelaw, Badlands Coal. I come in?"

"I'm afraid the house is a mess."

"You ought to see my place!" Meant to put his father at ease, his remark had the opposite effect. Doc Sanders apparently did not wish to imagine Paul's place, and his lips were flattening with cold wrath.

"Pull my comp and you, me and the State of Wyoming are back in court!" he bayed from a face that was turning several new colors.

"No, sir, Mr. Sanders," Paul blurted through the screen. "You have misunderstood me *completely*. I'm here to reconfirm for Badlands that one of our most cherished employees is getting along as well as can be hoped, given the sacrifice he has made to our corporation. We contribute to workmen's compensation not because we *have* to but because, like all Wyoming coal companies, our employees are our first priority."

Sanders's look suggested that he'd never seen so much airborne shit in his life, a quick signal to Paul to dial it down ASAP. "Of course I'm kidding, aren't I? You can see that, can't you? Most coal companies are happiest when their people leave their blood in the pit, squeeze 'em till there's not a drop left, right? We're somewhat different, maybe not a lot. But we're satisfied in your case, and frankly have no interest in disallowing your claim. We've got plenty of other workers we can crush in your absence."

"We better get us a beer," Sanders said. He left Paul standing in the small living room facing a soundless talk show on which a striding, vigorous woman with a microphone and furrowed brow faced a row of seated people, all of them crumpled, some weeping bitterly but with enough vitality to watch their hostess cautiously. In a moment, Doc was back with two cold cans of Grain Belt. Bending from the waist, he probed for the channel changer and the television screen shrank to a blue dot and disappeared.

"So, how's the back?"

"Aw, I can hardly move."

Holding up his beer, Paul said, "Badlands will support you for*ever*." Sanders, bright-eyed as a ferret, weighed these welcome but not entirely trustworthy words. "We're committed to our family of workers from the *e*rection to the *re*surrection." Both men erupted with artificial laughter, and then Paul resumed his debriefing of Sanders, many of whose features he could reluctantly acknowledge from his many hours in the mirror. "When'd you come up from Colorado?"

"'Bout seventeen years ago. You found that out, eh? With Badlands all that time."

Paul could see now that he'd confused weariness with age. Sanders wasn't so old, and Paul imagined rejuvenating him, dress him up a little and put him in a BMfuckinW.

"We was old settlers in the Boulder area. The college pushed us out."

Flannel jacket with an easy drape, pleats across the protruding belly, cuffless but with a break over oxblood loafers. Hardly know it was him. With chuckling complicity, Paul decided to introduce some family lore with his next inquiry.

"Weren't you some kind of juvenile delinquent?" This Paul could see was outside what might have been in the employee records of Badlands Coal, and a flash of confused suspicion crossed Sanders's face.

"A vagrant," he said sharply, as if defining a highly evolved category.

"And there was a little group of you."

"They was three or four little groups of us."

"With a counselor."

"Yeah."

Sanders was freezing up, so Paul hoisted his empty. "Spare another cold one?"

"Yeah," Sanders said, watching closely and getting to his feet.

"Gotta keep the li'l buzz goin'."

"Right."

Once they were resupplied, Paul said, "I actually went to school down there. Had a history prof name of Crusoe, Edith Crusoe, did some of this counseling you're talking about. Ever run up onto her?"

"What'd she look like?"

"Tall."

"Real wild, kinky hair?"

"Yes, at that time."

"She have humongous tits?"

"Well . . ."

"If we're talking about the same professor, she had some bodacious knockers on her. What's the matter with you? You smell somethin' bad?"

"No honestly, Richard, I'm a big fan of humongous knockers myself." Paul's upper lip pressed fretfully into the lower, and he acquired something close to a look of prissiness. "Yes, Professor Crusoe was *substantially endowed*."

"Well, spit it out, son. Is it too hot for you in here? I can turn it down."

"No, no, more than comfortable. But thank you, Richard, I—"

"Anyway, back to them knockers: I knowed 'em good. I was just a kid, but when I spotted them I was harder than Chinese arithmetic, know what I'm saying?"

"Ha, ha!" said Paul, but the laugh was so ghastly it gave Sanders pause. "Got you a little, did you?" croaked Paul.

"You bet your life! I got plenty!"

"Where on earth did you find to go?"

Paul, so close to his moment now, feared that so much as the sound of a fly landing would send Sanders out of his grasp forever, and he urgently wanted to be present at his own beginning.

"We was in her office. She went into the coat closet. I kept hearing the hangers fallin' on the floor. Then she more or less ordered me in there."

"In the closet."

"Yes."

"And you, what?"

"Piled on."

"Piled on. Ha ha! That's *great*," Paul cried from a twisted face. Perhaps, he wasn't enjoying his own conception as much as he'd hoped.

"Hangers just everywhere."

"Whoa, that's too much! What a scene!"

"Yup, them was the days, wettin' the old wick. Big pile of hangers, but I got 'er in all right. Got 'er plumb home."

"Whooee," said Paul, from behind his hand.

Doc Sanders scrutinized him. There was something definitely not right here.

Evelyn met Natalie at Prairie Coffee, where young people in stocking caps were getting coffee to take out and a more sedate group, coatless and hatless, were drinking their coffee over back issues of the *Hungry Horse Times.* The two women took their mugs to a broken-down sofa in front of the gas log fireplace and talked over the happy, inchoate chatter of voices occasionally joined by frigid drafts of air from the front door tainted slightly by exhaust fumes.

"I called the ship," said Natalie ominously.

"And?"

"No reply."

"I guess she just changed her mind, I mean, it's her vacation."

"Don't be naive, Evelyn, not now. We need to speak with her, and above all we need to know when, exactly, she's returning."

"Why?"

"Because Mr. Majub isn't going to wait around forever."

"What's this Mr. Majub have to do with it?"

"Mr. Majub has offered to meet with the whole family to see if he has a mandate to open this trust and liquidate the business."

"It's just so depressing."

"We'll get through all this," said Natalie fixedly. "We're going to be well off, you and me."

"Oh, good."

"At first I thought about moving to a better climate, but I'm not sure about starting over someplace where people don't understand my problems. The idea of being no spring chicken under some palm tree, I just wonder. Plus, with the bottling plant we had status." Evelyn raised her eyebrows. "We might not notice it until it's gone. But now that you've called off the divorce Paul's got Majub involved."

Evelyn's eyes widened. "I had reached the point where I thought it was time to write off our losses."

"I know," said Natalie. "And, Evie, I realize that wasn't easy." She looked vaguely around the room. "Who are these people?"

"They're our fellow Americans," said Evelyn.

"I'm starting to get like old lady Crusoe. This looks like an invasion to me. How's our friend Bill getting along?"

"He's fine, looking after the mares. Cows have a ton of feed where the hay froze before he could get to it. He had to go to Ekalaka for another funeral—a cousin, I think."

"What becomes of him when Mr. Majub sorts out the estate?"

Evelyn declined to comment on what she took to be arrant wishful thinking, Instead she said, "Bill stays."

"Evelyn dear, I hope we'll come into a bundle. There's a lot of stuff I'd like to buy my way out of."

"You think that works?"

"I sure do. It's pathetic when they say the rich aren't happy—"

"Paul's going to haunt us even *if* this Majub succeeds in getting us liquidated."

"I know," said Natalie, suddenly wide-eyed. "I'm scared shitless. I realize it's sick that I need to be comfortably off.

But tell me, Evie: we're for sure coming into a bundle, aren't we?"

Natalie's great faith in serendipity seemed confirmed when Alice Whitelaw returned with no more fanfare than a call indicating when she would arrive at the airport. She'd had to overnight in Denver, she explained over the phone, where all her belongings went astray in an automatic baggage handling system that sent both of her huge Samsonites back to the South Pacific via Los Angeles. If she hadn't had such a helpful companion, she said, she would have lost her mind.

"*What* companion?" hollered Natalie as she and Evelyn pulled up to the curb.

In the crepuscular afternoon light the little airfield, mysterious in descending snow, looked like an outpost. They went inside, pulling off their mittens as they did so and unbuttoning their coats.

"I don't know what companion," said Evelyn, peevishly.

Looking everywhere but at her sister, Natalie said, "I dislike surprises."

From a glass-enclosed corridor, it was possible to watch the arriving passengers come out of the jetway and into the boarding area, then pass through security into the lobby. From here they hoped to get a preview before greeting their mother, for whom they had several questions. Alice was not among the first to file out, as these consisted almost entirely of hurtling recreationists already attired for skiing, snowboarding, ice climbing, a surprising amount of Texas and southern accents. Finally, they saw the top of their mother's head, reasonably sedate but not quite natural blond, the shearling collar of her black coat, the new tan! It was impossible to determine much about the companion at her side as he was wearing a hat with enough brim to suggest a convinced cow man. It was not impossible that they already resented the spring in her step. There was little for them to do now but face the swarm and wait.

What they laid eyes on—and what Natalie later claimed in the most sanguine tones to have foreseen—was their mother beaming through her embarrassment and, at her side, tall, tan, hard-eyed and not remotely uncomfortable, Bill Champion.

Geraldine knew something was changing, though she was unaware that Paul had gotten his wife to call off the divorce. She wasn't happy when he insisted that she must never act as if she knew him, because having a parole officer at all was "incriminating." She sympathized with several of Paul's fears, even if she didn't entirely agree with them, because of the years of mistreatment he'd received at the hands of his wife, who clearly had never understood him or how he'd been maligned and wronged by the system, and who could use a swift kick in the rear of her excessively tight Wranglers. Sometimes Geraldine imagined a fulfilling scene wherein she gangster-slapped Evelyn until she whimpered for mercy.

As she was well short of recognizing that her heart was being broken, Geraldine was reduced to examining her own reports on Paul and was fascinated by how rapidly they evolved from the first, which compliantly reflected the alarming view of the prison officials who believed without any proof that Paul had planned a violent and murderous uprising among the inmates. No one with such small charges against him had ever been accused of so much. She by now had decided that his role in unlocking the secured wing, so the most violent prisoners could get at the snitches, was fabricated in the fevered minds of the guards whose professionalism was thereby placed in doubt, and whose pride was impaired by having been barricaded in the showers for two days. Geraldine alone had come to understand how Paul had been swept up in a maelstrom exacerbated by the deteriorating conditions of the facility. Her letter to the prison board elaborating this view nearly cost her her job; they couldn't know how scrupulously she'd reached her conclusions, discounting much of what she'd learned while she and Paul were drinking or in bed or both at once. If he'd had a few failures, they were pure products of guilelessness. When the prison board cited his wearing a T-shirt illustrated with a Glock handgun and the phrase "Snitches, A Dying Breed" as evidence of his lack of rehabilitation, she was thunderstruck by their gullibility. She had actually forced them to settle for the tepid notation that Paul Crusoe was "a lightning rod for evil."

She devoted her heart to trying to resolve the contradictions of their situation. This was difficult in the sense that Paul didn't seem to want it resolved, seemed to prefer their love sealed in its own compartment. "Like a cured ham!" he'd said in a ghastly explanation she quickly forgave. The progress of their love was a boozy, twilit enterprise in motels along Interstate 90, with wheeling lights, air brakes and clamorous movement of snow-handling equipment the principal accompaniment to their intimacies. If Geraldine tried voicing her wish to take their place in a real community with daily, sunlit duties, he either drifted off absently or crudely groped her. When she overcame the worry that she was growing stupider by the minute, she saw this all as a kind of rough magic despite the occasional inkling that she might not get out of this nameless love with her health intact.

The best part was giving him a monthly grade and making it clear that it was code for his vigor in bed, overlooking the perpetually aggravated expression on his face. "I bet you didn't know it had sides before you met me," he said. After a particularly satisfying night, she described him in her report as "a miracle of rehabilitation," adding the cautionary note she shared with him that it was "a game of inches."

But things now were not going so well, and she'd begun to feel bereavement partly derived from a suspicion that she was being bamboozled. Making love, he told her, was "something women did while guys were hosing them." It was in her own best interest to keep fooling herself, but perhaps now she had an eye out. Once she even caught herself dreaming pleasantly of Paul trussed up like a hog by her friends in the sheriff's department. "Love," he told her confidently, "is never having to say you're indicted."

Evelyn wanted to spend a bit of time with Natalie, because Evelyn was worried about her sister's recent euphoria and unnecessarily high hopes about Mr. Majub. Evelyn could have used a little euphoria herself, but at the moment liquidation mainly meant she could trade in this Jap flivver for some stouter iron.

On the way to pick up her sister, she was stopped at the Northern Pacific crossing while a freight train, its sides obscured by a thousand miles of frozen Dakotan slush, crept behind the striped barriers and flashing lights, west-bound on tracks disappearing into the icy switching yard. She listened to local Montana news on the radio, and it wasn't helping: the move seemed to be to kill the buffalo that roamed out of Yellowstone, kill the wolves wherever found, lower water-quality standards, undermine the laws of the Indian reservations, strip mine the prairie, dry up rivers where pollution was too time-consuming, cut funding for education and health care, and make animal-control poisons more readily available. Evelyn slumped and sighed all at once.

The driver's window of the car in front of her, a battered blue Plymouth Valiant, came down, and a cigarette glowed through the twilight to expire in the snow; the interior was dense with smoke, and the driver was beating out a rhythm on the back of the empty passenger seat. Evelyn turned the dial of her radio until she found the music that matched his tempo: "Achtung Baby." An old woman crossed in front, scarf tied around her face, shin-high boots laced over baggy sweatpants, her arms around a brown paper IGA bag from the top of which projected a bunch of cold wilted celery and a glimpse of bright Wonder Bread packaging. The old woman adopted a sailor's stance as she hobbled cautiously over the corrugations of snow and ice. The frigid air was heavy with exhaust fumes, and in the time it took the train to pass, the yellow lights of houses up on the hill grew hard in the advancing dark. In one front yard, miniature Dutch windmills protruded from the gray snow, a few with blades still twirling. Evelyn feared that when the train passed and the gates opened, she would lose some vital piece of continuity, just as a bubble of air is said to be able to stop the heart, and she would be unable to resume.

Finally the gates opened, and a long-haired brakeman hanging from the caboose looked back down the track from where he'd just come. As the train slowed into the switching yard, the groan of couplings filled the air, and Evelyn pulled across the track to begin ascending the hill. Old Christmas trees at the bottom of a ravine surrounded the remains of a snowmobile. For an instant, life seemed desperate. This year, I'm not going to watch that Super Bowl, she thought and laughed oddly.

When she got to the house, Natalie was ready to go and climbed into the car chattering happily. "I've been doing marriage counseling all morning, Evelyn, so let's go to the pet shop. My friend Andrea, who owns that store, hired a young filmmaker to make a video of her wedding anniversary, and she ran off with him! Then, after she paid Rim Rock a considerable sum for his addiction problems, he lights out for Martha's Vineyard with one of the patients! No, go right on Main Street; turn here. Anyway, he gave her this sob story about wanting to make features but being stuck with weddings and bar mitzvahs and documentaries about endangered species. So Andrea went back to her husband, but he said she'd been tainted by Hollywood! You love that, don't you, Evelyn? The husband does a great job portraying Andrea as a tart in the eyes of Judge Tower, who has no use for dope fiends with video cameras. Long story short, Andrea got cleaned out, but she still hasn't lost her sense of humor. She told me that the times had turned against good-hearted party girls."

They had to park over behind the Baxter Hotel, and Evelyn found herself following her jaywalking sister into whiteouts on snowy sidewalks until they found themselves in the cedar-scented warmth of Pet City, where between rows of birdseed, cat and dog food they found wing-clipped, hand-fed cockatiels circulating in the bottom of a great tub, in beautiful desert colors and a hum of conversational bird voices. Natalie gathered them in handfuls, adorning Evelyn's head and shoulders with birds before selecting some for herself. Three or four dodgey individuals, their crests erect with suspicion, remained in the tub, craning around to see the fate of their fellows.

"You've never looked better," said Natalie.

"I've never *felt* better."

"This is the pretty part. Next, an avalanche of birdshit if anyone startles them. They can't fly, so they express themselves with a big number two."

"Can you believe Mama and Bill Champion?" Evelyn said. The sisters faced each other like two caciques from the Orinoco, heads and shoulders covered with birds.

"No, and I can barely picture the implications."

"Is this a romantic story?"

"I won't be steamrollered by that if it is. We don't have any idea who we are anymore if we've been so ignorant about our own mother, assuming she is our mother; or our father, assuming that was our father. Ouch! The little sonofabitch just bit me!"

An intense clerk in green surgeon's scrubs appeared and impatiently wanted to know if they were going to buy a bird.

"We're unsure," Evelyn said.

"We're just test-driving them," said Natalie. "How're you fixed for hamsters?" When the clerk left without a word, she added, "We check the fish."

Glittering creatures sailed through a bubbling world, a price list fastened to the glass currently being scoured clean by a morose catfish whose industry Natalie found "demented." "You'd be surprised how much company even one fish is," she said, "Just in case you're thinking you might be alone for a long time. For vim and vigor, I always recommend an aquarium. They've proven effective in keeping mature women from jumping at the wrong guys."

Suddenly a look of alarm crossed Natalie's face. With a conspiratorial widening of her eyes, she subtly indicated a new customer with a gesture of her chin. Evelyn saw a rather pretty brunette examining a revolving rack of pet-care pamphlets, and was trying to recognize her when Natalie leaned over and whispered, "That's Paul's parole officer. They're having them a big time. You're only young once," she added, giving a tower of sacked cat food a sardonic hump.

Evelyn handled this revelation with minimal falsehood; at every stop in the pet store, she stole evaluative glances and would have had a lighter heart if Geraldine had been as ugly as a mud fence.

Outside, the snow hit them in the face. The wind abated briefly and the snow descended in clouds. At the car Natalie nearly spoiled everything by saying, "You know, I hope, that Paul really loves you. With all his heart."

"It's sad when someone like Paul elects to go on living."

"He must have his reasons," said Natalie. "Just give him another chance to be a husband."

"Paul does great on the side. It's when he's in the middle of your life that his real deficiencies emerge."

Natalie just looked mournful. "I struggle to make a life with a very strange man, yet I have plenty of bounce left. I want a cockatiel."

"I just wish I could recover the years I spent in the arms of Mr. Rent-a-Dick."

"I wish you could too. Now, who gets to talk to Mama?"

"You take her. I'll talk to Bill."

Evelyn didn't go to the ranch until the snow quit and a low, lead-colored ceiling descended halfway down the Gallatin Range; the Crazies were completely obscured, but the Bridgers stuck clear through the top like Shangri-la. Finding Bill wouldn't be hard. All he had to do was roll out feed with the Hydrabed truck, spooling last summer's hay a half ton at a time. Or if he had cattle in farther pastures, he would haul the bales with the tractor, cut the strings and roll them down the hill. Evelyn liked to be there for that, liked watching the cows form in along the luscious scroll of green, vivid and anomalous against the winter landscape. Once a few calves came, the ravens could begin their late-winter stroll, maintaining a discriminatory air even as they poked about in the afterbirth. As the season progressed, calved-out cows, bags swinging, shadowed by new off-spring, joined the line up behind the truck, several green-headed from crowding the unraveling bounty of alfalfa.

A snow fence protected the last of the road into the house, and a berm of packed and drifted snow rose to the west. The road itself was dry, as were bands of ground in the ranch yard where the spruces blocked the wind. The cows lay down in the afternoon sun behind the shelter belt and a flash of moving water could be seen in the watergap behind them. High above, on a ridge of sagebrush and prickly pear, deer trails spiderwebbed toward the river. All life was submerged, but there.

Evelyn found Bill in the corrals working on a waterer. He had the float out of it and was rewiring the heating element. He knelt on the concrete slab surrounded by tape, screwdrivers, sidecutters and insulated pliers. Knowing Bill, the breaker was still on and he was dodging various shocks while he worked.

"Oh, golly," he said and stood up, not all the way at first, and smacked his hands against each other. His coveralls were unzipped to his chest, and his face was mottled with exertion.

Evelyn reached out and gave his sleeve a little tug.

"Evelyn," he said.

"Who fed while you were gone?"

"I seen to it."

"I could've done that."

This didn't warrant, and perhaps didn't deserve, any reply at all. "Well, you could throw in now, Evelyn. Had a panel go over during the night where I'd put some first-calf heifers that was springin'. Then the waterer boiled over and made just an ice stump here where I had to beat half it off with a tire tool to fix it. Still ain't fixed."

"I should look for those heifers."

"Don't like that sky." It was low and gloomy, and off to the west hung a ragged curtain of something darker.

"How long has this thing with Mama been going on?"

Bill inspected the band inside his hat. Evelyn knew it said Ajax Western, Clayton, New Mexico. "Fifty years," said

Bill. Evelyn found this news dizzying. What else had she not noticed? What else was she wrong about?

She thought for a long moment, then asked, "Who's shod?" She could at least do the work in front of her.

She was going for these heifers; some wouldn't be able to have their calves without help, and the idea of them torn open by their own offspring in a winter storm was terrible. Besides, Bill would head off for them in the dark if something didn't happen now.

"Cree and Scram. Scram's got borium stickers. He'd be better on the ice. Don't even think about taking Cree. He's far too green."

"Fifty years."

"Fifty-one at the end of next month."

Scram, a big claybank gelding with withers like a fighting bull and the rather primitive head of a Civil War cavalry horse, was twelve hundred and thirteen pounds of plain suspicion. No matter how many times he'd seen a saddle or bridle, he snorted like a locomotive all over again. Evelyn once asked if he was a bronc, and Bill said, "He *thinks* he's a bronc." He would stand humped up under the old Connolly saddle, ears backed alongside his head, front feet skittering from side to side and the lead-shank bone tight to the hitching rack. From the time he broke him, Bill said he'd never be a falling-down or rearing-over horse. "Once I seen that, I knowed he's foolin' with me." The few times he blew up, it was all in one place, never bogged his head, never spun. Bill let it run through him, fed him eleven miles of hill and now, he "couldn't buck a straw hat off the saddlehorn." Nevertheless, Evelyn always noticed the concussion of his coal black hooves on the pounded earth when he was trying.

As Evelyn hunted for him in the willow thicket, carrying her halter, she recalled the time Bill roped a bull, and Scram, staring down that straight Plymouth cordage rope, slid eighteen feet through shale before the bull tipped over. But he was no pet; to catch him you had to corner him, and, if he got his pivot foot behind you, he'd whirl and be gone. Once that started, it was best to look for another horse.

Scram watched her approach from his hideout in the golden willows. Through agility, guile and murmurings, Evelyn was able to lay a hand on his shoulder; an electric shiver went out from the spot her fingers touched his skin. Then her hand was over his neck to catch the halter from the far side and lift it into place. "So," she said, "now we make beautiful music together," then led him through the snow to the saddle shed; treading his hot, nervous feet while she saddled him, he reduced the ground to mud. Evelyn brushed away the little pocket of snow in the groove at his croup, then undid the witches' knots in his tail while he gazed about in worry. She gave him an old red-and-gray Navajo that was well molded to him, and when she threw the saddle over his withers, he jumped straight up, then froze when the offside billet fell against his side. He was selling this as the worst hour of his life, especially when Evelyn reached way under to catch the cinch and ran several loops of the latigo through the rigging. She tightened him up all round, ignoring his posturing, slapped the ground seat noisily. When she grabbed the horn and pulled the saddle back and forth to check the fit, he humped up so much the front and rear of the saddle were clear of his hide.

"Oh, my," said Bill to his horse. "The Indian feller got holt of you."

"Do you believe this?"

"I'm more worried about the weather. Find 'em quick and get back. Six, all black-hided." When Scram sighed, Bill cheeked him at the bridle and said, "He's ready."

Evelyn got on, just boot tips in the stirrups until she felt certain the present good-natured prancing didn't become more enthusiastic, and the two of them loped off toward what looked like approaching night. Bill watched them go. Evelyn told herself she was heading even farther away from convenience stores and dealerships, fraud protection, exclusive passwords and travel coupons. She felt free.

A thousand feet of sandstone bluffs used up all the prancing, and the river was winding below them like a silver snake. Evelyn never lifted a rein and immediately had the feeling that Scram knew exactly where the cattle were; once they started toward the crest, she could see fine snow streaming off the lip in the north wind. She tied her scarf around her face and urged Scram up the steep hundred yards that remained, a wall of serviceberry brush forcing a tortuous route. At the top, they were met by terrific space, a thousand-mile prospect of three great mountain ranges under speeding clouds, and the spindly trail of a railroad. Good God, thought Evelyn, six heifers? The wind had pressed the trees around them into a crooked wood of stunted trees, now a haunting, boreal chorus.

Like a trail of water most visible to cattle, there was a pattern in the steadily descending side hill of wild cottonwoods, some broken away by a small avalanche. At the base of a low cliff the wind no longer blew, but snow fell heavily on lichenous rock, a trampled salt trough and a patent mineral feeder with a windvane whose axle made the most plaintive noise. Scurf pea tumbled across the flats, scattering its seeds. The heifers had paused here before moving on

north, slightly shielded from the weather by the falling
away of the country to the east.

It was necessary to turn into the storm along a drift fence
as the ground grew more sloped and shaley. After several
hundred yards, it was a relief to come upon an old sheep-
herders' cairn that she recognized. Only now could she
admit that she'd been turned around. If the sky were clear,
she'd see the Belts from here, but the storm had confined
this place. In the clouds of shifting snow, the breakouts of
light and the groans of winter, Evelyn could hear the cattle
above her in a stand of sere juniper. So she encouraged
Scram to make a climbing curve around the trees to keep
from driving the heifers away into even deeper invisibility.
She wanted them to flee toward home thinking they'd
invented the idea. Scram got right onto the plan, which
turned out to be unavailing as the heifers saw them and
bolted high-headed into the driving gale. To try to gallop
around them when she couldn't see the ground beneath her
required a heart-stopping leap of faith, but Scram knew the
heifers were escaping, and he electrified the tentative touch
of Evelyn's spur into violent acceleration that started
between her knees and rushed back into Scram's lowered
hindquarters. Ledges of brush—just dark shapes—disappeared behind her, an explosive gait that was not interrupted until Scram had jumped over things he alone could
see. She'd forgotten the sting of snow and hard cold wind.
Indeed, she had little idea of anything in this moment of
absolute stillness atop a stopped, heaving horse, until she
gazed around her into the astonished faces of six heifers.
Their final bid for escape was answered by quick floating
turns as Scram sent them ambling home, Evelyn rocking
along to the creak of an old saddle while Scram assumed

his businesslike, shuffling walk. As her eyelashes gathered a cloudy fringe of snow, she turned everything over to her horse; he seemed to know there was a trail here somewhere.

Upon reaching the corrals the heifers bucked and cavorted jubilantly. Why had they been sent away? They were so grateful to be home. Bill closed the gate with a nod as Evelyn noted thin pine smoke from the chimney and considered the warmth inside the house. She wrapped Scram's reins around the pipe rack and unsaddled him quickly; he was still dry under the blanket, and at his paddock, he dropped the bit from his mouth and wheeled to his hay feeder without waiting for a pat.

"Where were they?"

"It's hard to say. I couldn't see a thing, but Scram seemed to know where we were."

"Well, the waterer's fixed. The float was jammed and cross-pin bent. I had to drive it out and make another one."

"Those things are nothing but trouble."

"Beats spuddin' a hole in the ice every time you need to fill a bucket."

"Ice," said Evelyn. "Whose idea was that?"

"Sonja Henie."

"Do you need any help?"

"Don't think so." He couldn't face her. "I don't look for nothin' with the cows. Haven't had to pull the first calf. I might get the neighbor kid to help at night when the heifers start springin' regular. No problem walkin' them heavies in. They been there before." Bill was a great cattle nurse, one with foresight, sorting tasks ahead of time, feeding, calving, grafting a twin to a cow who'd lost her calf, knowing which neighbor had an orphan to spare, salting in the right places, cleaning corrals, controlling flies, branding and doctoring, breaking, weaning, shipping, culling and picking sound replacements or appropriate bulls, holding birth weights and weaning weights in his head for every cow, avoiding panic, anger at the agricultural economy and, worse, the inexorable feeling that he was going backward and living in a country all too happy to watch him drown in a job that probably didn't exist anymore.

She wasn't sure when Bill would finish, so Evelyn went into the house and called Natalie to tell her this would be a good time to drive out for a visit. With that done she set about making dinner, even though she knew it would have to be served to Bill when the cattle had no need of him. She concentrated on his great qualities out of fear that there might be a grievance between him and Natalie and herself.

But for all that, he couldn't quite look Evelyn in the eye when he came inside and perched on the edge of the couch with an anxious, ingratiating look on his face.

"I'm throwing something together. I think it would be a good thing if we went ahead and sat down to supper before long." She thought it would break her heart, seeing the fear in his old face. Once they were inside, he rambled on, scared.

"You see, my grandfather met Theodore Roosevelt at Mingusville, Montana. Roosevelt got him a position running the public stockyards for the Northern Pacific Railroad at Forsythe. Mingusville was changed to Wibaux. He come up the trail and I own his spurs, and the axle holding the cloverleaf rowels has run out the hole to an egg shape and they make a noise like a little Christmas bell, little tinkly kind of a deal just pretty as can be. Went to Wyoming, worked on the Spectacle for Hard Winter Davis, then come here, stoled a horse and got caught in Big Timber, didn't have no jail. So they lowered Dad down a well for three days and it sure enough made him into a solid citizen. Got out and put this ranch together."

Evelyn moved food onto the table. She had taken special pains for this meal, and was noticing, as if for the first time, the faded nasturtium wallpaper. There were certain things that emerged in winter when a house went from shelter to the whole world. It wasn't long before Bill gave in to his need to talk. "Another time, Dad cut off his toe and would have bled to death but he dissolved black powder in his mouth and it stopped the bleeding, he said. When he was a kid he'd have strangled from diphtheria, but his ma put her finger down his throat and cleared the phlegm. Must've been tough, worked for everybody, Briggs and Ellis, the 22, the 79, the Two Dot. Also a outfit name of Jones."

It wasn't until Evelyn was carrying half of a store pie to the table that she had a burst of courage and said, without preamble, "When can we talk about this?"

Bill took a deep breath and exhaled. "We'll get to it," he said.

Then Natalie drove up, and rushed inside pounding her hands together. Once she'd hung up her coat and poured a cup of coffee, she sat down in a deep, upholstered chair, dropping her arms onto its sides to commence a new discussion.

"He says he'll talk," said Evelyn.

In the full heat of August, Bill stood with the smoke tank in his hand, the net over his face and watched the dust cloud of an approaching car. He knew how he must look to its driver, and he wondered who the driver was. He lifted the bottom of the hive and held the spigot underneath and waited until the smoke sped heavily through the sides. The day was cloudy, hot and still as he looked within at the gold and varnished chambers of this myriad larval world, a city whose oozing districts he could slice into or break off, sweet and heavy, with his hands. Bees swarmed around his head, their indignant movement swooning piecemeal into the smoke. It was the young merchant paying him a visit, Sunny Jim Whitelaw, the man who never smiled. He was so handsome it was terrifying.

Alice always got up at five and turned on the kitchen light. If no light showed by five, the neighbors would get wind of it and pass it all over the valley. Sleeping in was a bounty rarely enjoyed, especially in those early days when, short-handed, they fenced alone and hayed alone and a night calver was an unimaginable luxury and in the end they almost starved. But this day, Alice turned the kitchen light on at five and didn't come back to bed. Bill had kept it in mind all day. He had it in mind now. The idea was to sleep till seven. They had two baby girls, Evelyn and Natalie; and Alice, who had rolled with everything that came their way on the ranch, was now consumed by fear that the impoverished family that had forced her out would be obliged to take her back.

This year his hives were out of the flood plain, a supposedly hundred-year flood plain that flooded every three years. The man from soil conservation told him it was a convulsive river, prone to lateral migrations. So Bill moved the hives. It was fine with him if the river had plans for the house, sooner or later. Being master of his own fate was wearing him out.

He was not going to finish this job in time. He couldn't centrifuge this honey and get up to the house before Sunny Jim Whitelaw in his Buick. He set aside the smoking canister and rearranged the broken combs, then abruptly lifted the bee helmet from his head and tossed it aside.

The road took a wide curve around the hill between him and the house, and the hill was too steep to climb swiftly. Bill was a young man who had so much to do on this place, and not enough of it on horseback to suit him, that he no longer felt young. After he came home from the war, he lived and ranched alone and remained for some years a convinced bachelor. The service had not made him a glamorous stranger the way it did a man with money, and he'd married a poor girl from a mile up a dirt road who desperately needed to get out of her house. When the Buick didn't slow down, Bill felt denied a common courtesy.

He would go straight to the house despite that the very distance seemed to be pushing him back, making him aware of his own cloddish footfalls and the glacial emergence of his house from the hillside. The car was parked right in the center of the gate, with two big lilacs above either fender in the summer heat. Parked as though no one else might use the walk, it was a smart, late-model Buick with rear fender skirts and whitewalls, "Treasure State" on its license plate.

Whitelaw, with a cup of fresh coffee in his hand, shifted his shoulder to look back toward the door as Bill entered. Alice stood next to the stove. Whitelaw had coal black hair and an unlit cigarette in the corner of his mouth. The paleness of his eyes gave him a remote quality that Bill thought made him seem here and not here.

Alice looked so small just then in her cotton dress, a nice

one she rarely wore, and she pressed the fingertips of both hands against each other before weighing her words. She removed one hand from this contact and used it to indicate their guest. "Bill, this is Jim Whitelaw. He is going to start a bottling plant."

"There's a big need," Whitelaw said emphatically.

Bill nodded nervously as Alice ran down all the things they were doing on the ranch until Whitelaw raised a hand to quiet her. "Hey," he said, "I completely understand. It's a hard job, even if it *doesn't* pay."

Alice Champion never mentioned the two little girls in the next room, not even that they existed. The main thing seemed to be how beautiful she looked: auburn curls pinned behind her ears, the cotton belt of the dress soft across her stomach.

"Do you live in town?" asked Bill.

"Have to." He flicked the rim of his coffee cup, making it ring. Alice refilled it, the black stream pouring slowly.

When the cup was filled, Alice raised her eyes to Bill's for the first time. He was aware that his mouth was not quite closed. He was about to ask for a cup of coffee for himself.

"I'm going to leave with Jim," she said.

"Oh?" Bill had put all this together, yet he hadn't.

Whitelaw stared down at his hands, trying to seem to share Bill's pain. As yet, no pain accompanied this information.

"You only live once," Whitelaw said with unusual force.

Bill supposed that this was meant to explain their recklessness and considered how this differed from "You're only young once," a phrase he found disturbing, as though youth was something you tried to flag down as it shot past.

"Have you already been unfaithful to me?" he asked Alice.

"Yes," she said. Her mixture of contrition and pride was not quite working, but even Bill understood that this was not the time to choose one over the other. His time for wishful thinking had come to an end. The thought of some carnal turmoil overwhelmed him. He may have still loved her, but he certainly hated her. He couldn't understand how this could be happening to them. She had loved the land absolutely when he hadn't cared. Maybe that changed with the babies. She was the one always discovering eternal values in their lives, and now she was going off with this merchant. Her mouth had become an ugly slash. It would be years before she was more than an effigy, and Bill and Whitelaw would be partners in ranching before that ever happened.

Another thing he could tell was that they were waiting for him to say something they could really get their teeth into. They needed him to get this all out in the air. Standing next to the relaxed and handsome businessman in a house filled with a kind of pearly twilight from its small windows, Bill Champion was able to escape his pain in a feeling of injustice and relief in his contempt. Suddenly hungry, he opened the refrigerator and ate a big green apple so fast that Alice and Whitelaw just stared at him. There were dizzying columns of flies at the screen, and the distant bawling of a calf that had got on the wrong side of the fence from its mother.

Bill finished the apple and thumbed the small black seeds onto the floor. He looked up and thought, The hell with these two, then walked over to the door that opened between the pie safe and the Frigidaire and went into the children's bedroom. He stared in at the two babies, Natalie and Evelyn, two small lumps under the same blanket. "What about these guys?"

"One step at a time," said Whitelaw. "One step at a time."

Bill agreed that this was an ungovernable question. He looked over at Alice, but instead of pain, he saw a kind of blank. Though he couldn't blame her, this look of being stumped on a quiz show was disturbing. He feared that he was going crazy and about to sleepwalk through something terrible.

Just as abruptly, he was tired. Apple pulp filled the spaces between his teeth. He felt the individual weight of his eyes. The flies had gotten worse. When he looked at Whitelaw's nice clothes, all he could think of was moths. And when he thought about the ranch, he knew it wouldn't be beautiful anymore. He'd gotten the beautiful bit from her. He had come to believe that the cattle of America were like a big shareholders' company, and that he had a little share and was part of it. But before Alice, he hadn't seen any beauty. His mother had had him during a blue norther while his father jugged an old cow by lantern light in a path of red osier willows where the critter had gone to die. He thought of his own birth as equivalent to the poor beast's bloody struggle. And then Alice filled him in on the true beauty of birth by having the two girls.

"You're really being damned decent," said Jim Whitelaw, beating his own thigh with his motoring cap.

Bill followed the hat around with his eyes.

"I'm just stumped," he said.

"That's true," said Alice. "He's like this when he can't see what to do." Bill never quite got over this remark, even after trying for thirty years, but on the day itself, the whole situation seemed to be drifting away from him. For one thing, Jim Whitelaw lost his looks. He wanted conflict, and these two were still in love; it made his face look lumpy. He was going to take the girls, all right, but from then on he would be subject to wondering what it was he got.

Nevertheless, the marriage was ruined, and Whitelaw and Alice were united in a much-photographed wedding. But on that day the marriage had a few minutes left, and once Whitelaw drove away, Bill Champion turned back to Alice Champion and, through a world of pain, rubbed his hands together and said, "Let's wake the kids. You get Natalie and I'll get Evelyn."

When they came out of the children's room, Alice cradled Natalie like a real baby and Bill had sleepy little Evelyn under the arms, her bare feet dangling. Bill leaned his face in until the end of his nose touched the end of the little girl's nose.

"Do you want to hear how Daddy put the bees to sleep?"

Natalie glowed with happiness to learn that Sunny Jim wasn't her father. Not that Bill made much sense to her. His taciturnity so annoyed her that she once angrily offered to send him to charm school. Still, this was a profound liberation, and Natalie looked transformed. "Bill, what did you do then?"

"Kept ranching."

"So hard," said Evelyn. "For everyone."

"Bill," Natalie said, "don't worry your little head. We can handle this kind of information. We're *happy* with it."

Bill was still looking downward.

"I doubt it," he said. "It should never have been this way."

There was no penetrating the gloom that had settled upon him. It was only a matter of a very short time when the cattle demanded his attention, and he left the house. Afterward, the sisters tried to make an evening of it, but with new biographies their capacity for casual conversation was impaired. Natalie was virtually ebullient. "I never thought I'd get out from under Dad's shadow," she said, "and it's going to take a while. Basically, I don't get Bill like you do."

"Bill lives the life he was born into. It's his gift."

"I'm sure you're right. It just looks like he's in a rut to me."

"He's not in a rut." Evelyn quickly recognized that this conversation could go wrong as she was already in a disturbed state. She did not want Sunny Jim eradicated entirely. The admiring degree of separation from Bill was gone and, in its place, bafflement that Sunny Jim had so insisted on her spending time here. By the time she'd understood her real relationship to Bill, she'd been around him a long time. Who arranged that?

One effect of this perturbance was that Evelyn suddenly needed to know about Geraldine. She was so compelled to see her, it was as if the wind drove her across the town. Geraldine was wide-eyed with alarm when Evelyn burst into her office. At first, she refused to discuss Paul. Instead she talked about her nephew having rolled her car, speaking to Evelyn with an odd, frantic intimacy.

"Shane's fine, but I wish they'd just totaled the car. Honda Civic. These days, if there's anything left *at all,* they fix 'em. I went over there and watched the estimator fill five single-spaced sheets. Every body panel is toast. Frame's okay, *we think*, and he says the unibody looks all right. But they had to pull the dash, and that gets to be a mess with the AC, the mounts for the steering column, the wipers, the CD changer, and the fan housing is just hanging in midair. And *nobody* knows about the electronics, because of this secret chip that's in there."

Evelyn thought she was going to jump out of her skin. Then, from some kind of subdued rage that also meant to indict Geraldine's professionalism, she demanded to know if reviewing Paul's record was what had attracted her to him.

"Is this a joke?" asked Geraldine.

"I assure you it is not," Evelyn heard herself say.

"Let me tell you something, lady. When I read the prison reports on this guy, I was afraid to be in the same building with him."

Evelyn reluctantly noted the woman's prettiness, and furthermore disliked being addressed as "lady." She also thought that in making Paul seem so fearsome on the basis of some in-house files and reports, this bitch was acting as both judge and jury. Moreover, Evelyn's heart went out to Paul, who must have felt imprisoned by these attempts by state wage slaves to malign him. "What exactly did these reports say?"

"Well, one of them implied he'd taken the fall for your father, and that had made him pretty bitter."

Evelyn recalled that Sunny Jim made numerous general remarks about Paul, the strongest being that he was "incomplete." Evelyn found this a very troubling observa-

tion about her husband. When she finally found the nerve
to ask him to elaborate, Sunny Jim looked grim and then
stated that while Paul had the prettiest swing since Bobby
Jones, his short game left much to be desired.

"Anybody would be bitter just to be *in* prison." Evelyn
said, trying to reference something—she thought, perhaps,
a study how prison actually *created* criminals—but it
wouldn't come. She remembered how having a husband in
the penitentiary had changed her own status. It was an education she intended to remember.

"Paul did well in the general prison population. Plenty of
people were afraid of him, which is surprising for someone
in on fairly small charges. He had a lot of leadership.
Depending on who you believe, it may be that he misused
it. I've got to hand it to Paul, he makes his own trouble."
Geraldine was in full control of the situation.

"This is where it all turns into interpretation." How Evelyn hated the defensiveness she heard in her own voice.

"Okay."

"So, I guess that's it for the facts."

"You could say so. Some very informed people think he
figured out how to burn through the Plexiglas on the guard
shacks to release the secured wing. It cost some lives. But
what do they know?"

Having heard all she could stand, Evelyn abruptly
departed, driving toward home to the sound of hectic, disquieting jazz coming from some low-wattage station on the
High Line, whose host implied he was broadcasting from a
smokey, hip and urban dive—"bebop, fusion, acid jazz"—
instead of this wind-blasted cow town on the Canadian
border. Evelyn gave plenty of room to a Nova in the ditch,

three annoyed young people regarding the car as though it were a bad dog. On the other side of the street were seasonal vehicles, hunting rigs, firewood trucks, covered in deep snow, that people didn't care if they saw until spring anyway. Evelyn remembered one of Paul's favorite pitches about liking women with ideas, and how unwelcome hers had been to him. Approaching her neighborhood seemed increasingly strange: trotting horse wind vanes, ferns crowding snow-covered windows, family names—KUCKER, ORDWAY, GOOLEY emblazoned on signs—amber icicles hanging from roofs bristling with antennas, uncollected newspapers, solitary figures smoking behind windows and watching the street, windowsill figurines, blue glow of TV. It was bewildering.

She couldn't stop thinking about Paul and even remembered loving him, if that's what you wanted to call that lurid abdominal yawning. Worse still, how spiffy and cool he was while making love, a stone-faced officer in some conquering northern army. She never doubted that her craving for him was a vice. She'd had crazy spells, telling people she was a cheerleader for the Calgary Flames, wearing a T-shirt with a snarling Rottweiler over the caption: *I don't dial 911*. She also had an awful feeling her father was presiding, somehow, or conspiring with him. He would sit back and cast a cold eye on old relationships while Paul changed the rules, abandoned former restraints and undertook, far from federal regulations, the ruin of the competition. "Consolidate or die," one or the other of them would say, folding up another mom-and-pop enterprise leaving a handful of shallow-margin bottlers stranded by the demographics, soon to be empty, bat-filled, broken-windowed hulls where winos, glue sniffers and unowned dogs could get out of the wind.

The last thing Geraldine had said to her was, "We'll never really know, will we, Evelyn?" And how confidently she laughed!

"This cruise I've just been on was an absolute eye-opener," Alice exclaimed, "a large group of *average* people who were quite wonderful. It must not have occurred to me that such numbers of people could be completely normal. I thought that half the world was sick, sick, sick. It turns out, if that cruise is any indication, significant numbers of persons are able to be grateful for life and each other's company. They do not wish to humiliate one another for sport. My, did I enjoy learning that!"

Later, Natalie remarked that her mother was "just doing her number." Evelyn found Alice's diction loftier than normal, but said, "She has certainly conquered her grieving!"

Natalie got right to the point. "You want to tell us about him, Mother?"

Alice tried to look at her sternly, eyes grazing past Evelyn's in a kind of warning. Then she looked at the ceiling as though pondering the best answer to Natalie's question, but her mouth collapsed in a goofy, beaming smile. Finally, Alice Whitelaw collected herself.

"Bill Champion and I are together at last. I never thought I'd live to see it."

All the meekness, all the compliance that had defined her life seemed to have evaporated. Her two daughters suddenly felt themselves to be in no position to ask questions.

Nevertheless, Natalie thought she'd try. "Do you think this is realistic, Mother?"

"Don't be asinine." Then she chuckled out of some deep reserve, some private enjoyment. It was all quite unnerving. The songs of humpback whales on the stereo, though scarcely audible, didn't help a bit. Their mother was offering no direct statements whatsoever, and besides seemed transformed by this new daunting will of her own. She talked about anything she felt like talking about, regardless of her two daughters, who'd brought her a Sunday *Denver Post,* coffee and croissants, and now sat there among her plants in mild frustration.

"Everything about my school days is clear," Alice happily proclaimed. "And my childhood is clear. I had a loving father and a very distant mother who always seemed destined for great things, but it stopped there." She declined to mention that they'd lived on the edge of starvation, and that her father was rarely sober. "I was *very* popular in high school. Thank God I was pretty, though it brought so many temptations. I like to think I passed that test, because I failed conspicuously in so many other ways. But everything since school is a blur, a *blur*. Even your fa—, my husband is a blur. Don't you think that when people take over your life, they really stop being people at all? They just become a . . . a situation. Still, I'm living in a whole new world now. I knew it would be and it is. I *have* learned one lesson from my girlhood, though: I'm not good at being alone."

"So what do we do about *that*?" asked Natalie pointedly.

"Only time will tell," said Alice, "but I've noticed a funny thing. There doesn't seem to be a big difference between having your whole life ahead of you and having only a small part of it left. The amount of hope seems the same."

· · · · ·

It may or may not have occasioned the end, though it did give a serviceable signal that things were phenomenally askew. Natalie and Stuart had asked Evelyn to join them for drinks at the Bar and Grill in Livingston, where Stuart would give them the average man's view of the latest developments.

It's true that the big back bar facing into a room of diners had always invited theatrical drinking, but neither of them suspected its effects on Stuart. Both he and Natalie were mildly drunk when Evelyn arrived, but before long Stuart had a jar of jalapeños under one arm and he was strolling among the diners showing them how courageously he could throw down these extremely hot peppers. Evelyn had never seen him so aggressive.

"Wait," said Natalie, "it gets worse."

Stuart had passed beyond the usual offensive ken, and had brought the humped-over drinkers off the bar to demand his removal. By that point, Natalie had renamed him "Shit-for-brains." He returned from his wanderings only long enough for another drink, then resumed by commandeering the dessert cart, wheeling it around while bellowing various sea chanties. "I signed aboard this whaling ship, I made my mark it's true. And I'll serve out the span of time I swore that I would do!"

Several diners began waving for their checks. Chanting rhymes about the capstan and raising the anchor from "Poseidon's floor," he attempted a sailors' jig: arms akimbo, knees pumping, feet causing several of the desserts to fall onto the floor. When he threw his head back for a final

"Way hey, blow the man down!," he lost his footing and, with a bounce, sent the dessert cart on a slow roll toward the toilets and not so much collapsed as gave up in a heap, perhaps struck down by returning self-awareness.

"What happened to Stuart?" Evelyn asked. "I thought he was going to give us sensible advice."

Natalie presently went home, locking the front door behind her. Evelyn lingered outside to watch the northern lights, which hung in tapestries, stripes to the horizon, gradually growing slender as the ribs of an umbrella. She had to smile. She'd never seen Stuart so lovable.

The following day, after Natalie had filed for divorce, Evelyn went to see him. He was alone in the house. "Stuart, what is to become of you?"

"Well, Evelyn . . ."

"Really, I'd like to know."

"I see this as . . . as a chance . . ."

"To do what?" she prompted. "To go home?"

"I thought I was home. Maybe I'll just adopt a baby."

"As a single man, Stuart, I'm not sure you could."

"Oh I bet you could, sure. There are older ones, ones no one wants."

"Is this practical?"

"No, of course it's not."

"But you don't care?"

"I do. Oh, sure . . ."

Evelyn found his lassitude unsettling. As they spoke, Stuart rearranged empty pots on the stove and fixedly observed his backyard from the kitchen window.

"I can't believe how fast they go through that feed," he said. "It's a terrible winter."

A gust of wind kept obscuring the view with flying snow. A paper wrapper passed airborne toward the alley, somehow as full of expression as a ghost.

Stuart gazed at Evelyn, trying to say something. Finally, it came. "I think we learned one thing from last year's Stanley Cup. You can't second-guess the referees and have a game anybody wants to watch. Waiting for overhead cameras to tell us if we can celebrate, why, no fan wants that." Stuart's looked so close to losing it entirely that Evelyn tried to move him to a happier note. "Well, the playoffs are a long way away."

"Never count out the Maple Leafs," he cautioned her. She chose not to tell him of her manic desire to become a cheerleader for the Calgary Flames, because she wasn't sure hockey teams even had cheerleaders.

"The expansion teams are hardly the whole story."

"Stuart, are you all right?"

"No."

"What can I do?"

"Nothing."

"I'd really like to be available to you as your friend forever."

"Yes."

"You know that I've always liked you, don't you?"

"Yes." Stuart was a man in front of a firing squad.

"I won't make you talk. We can continue this when . . . when—"

"When I've absorbed my situation," he said with sudden clarity.

"That's right," said Evelyn, oddly desperate to confirm his discovery. Stuart would absorb things and they would go on from there. He would take in the idea that his dedication of a serious portion of his life to someone he loyally loved was now to be canceled by divorce, and that he must begin to plan how he would get on with his life.

This feeble concept was barely enough to allow Evelyn out the door; his eager nodding was about to break her heart. Stuart had indeed hit bottom, but it would be amazing to watch how far he would bounce.

"We have to deal with one of Daddy's lawyers again, Melvin Blaylock. Why can't we get one of the nice ones? Remember the nice one with the breath mints? This Blaylock was always against us."

"Exactly," said Evelyn. "So fuck him."

"I'm there," Natalie nodded emphatically. "When's this shit supposed to go down?"

"At three o'clock. But which one is Blaylock? Is he the one with the pointed teeth?"

"No, that's Larry Crowley. This one has wiry hair."

"Long earlobes with creases?"

"No, that's Calvin Banning. This one is just wiry hair, no neck and a wet lower lip."

"Of *course.*"

Neither knew why Melvin Blaylock wanted to see them, but they feared bad news. Seated in the conference room at Valley National Bank, they were doodling on complimentary pads. Natalie was making a picture of Melvin Blaylock from memory, and it was surprisingly accurate. Evelyn's horse was a juvenile silhouette.

The only surprisingly thing about Melvin Blaylock, looking as he always had in gloomy worsted, his bald pate

allowing wrinkles of insincere surprise to travel all the
way to the back of his head, was that he was accompanied
by Stuart who, through size and vitality, seemed compara-
tively glamorous. Because of his dramatic black turtleneck
sweater, the central heating was giving him a red face. He
still had his blond hair in bangs, and the big watch that
gave time and tide for both hemispheres was fastened outside the sleeve of the sweater.

"Which of you are we meeting with?" asked Natalie,
exhibiting extreme wariness at the sight of her vigorous
husband.

"You're meeting with Stuart," Blaylock said, closing the
door. "Can I get anybody anything?"

"Then why," Evelyn said, "are you here?"

"Stuart wants to keep the record straight, and—" he lit
up the pause with his smile "—he has hired me to represent
him. *You're* here to preview the impact on the estate. That's
a courtesy for which you can thank Stuart."

It was hard to believe that Stuart had called this meeting.
Having deployed papers in front of himself, he looked, for
the first time since entering the room, at Natalie. "I told
Mel here that nothing you say is true, and Mel told me that
if we go to trial we don't want somebody else controlling
the dialogue, that we want a level playing field. Isn't that
how you put it, Mel, level playing field?"

"Just like that, Stu."

Natalie made an exaggerated slump into her chair and
breathed out through pursed lips while allowing her raised
eyebrows to drop. Evelyn went back to work on the horse.
Melvin Blaylock was thinking how the opening rounds of a
divorce were like the first bowel movement after Thanksgiv-
ing, awful and unforeseen. But it was great having an irate

client, since reasonable ones turn you into a bureaucrat. Stuart's opening salvo was gratifying, though Melvin was glad no extrafamilial witnesses were present, as a large percentage of them would've concluded that Stuart was ready for the booby hatch. He'd need to clip his wings if this thing ended up in court. Also, the sweater would have to go; all you could see were those blond bangs.

Stuart was ready. "It started with a dance, the way you moved your pelvis like a breeding polar bear. I went for it. I slaved for your dad, that goddamned cannibal. I couldn't do what he wanted, not and go on believing I was still a human being. Then I got a pile of wood and bricks and pipes and wires and concrete and shingles and I built a house." He showed them his hands. "I built a house and moved a whore in. Then I moved in with the whore. The old man beat me up on the job, and the whore sold me out every way she knew how. My answer was to work harder so my father-in-law could screw me over and lavish opportunities on Paul. Evelyn, did I ever tell you who I think Paul is?"

Evelyn shook her head infinitesimally.

"Well, let me tell you now, Evelyn, because you're a good person, maybe not quite on the planet but a good person anyway, and you should know: Paul is the Antichrist."

"Ah," said Evelyn. This was one she hadn't thought of.

"That's strong," mused Natalie.

"I wanted a baby, but you wondered how you'd look in a bathing suit. That's understandable, but you didn't want to go swimming. Natalie, when I get done with you, I'm adopting a houseload of little kids from Bulgaria, where they let you have as many as you want, and I'm raising them to college age on *your money*."

"You'll have to get it first, and that comes after *I* get it."

"Oh, you'll get it."

"Thank you, Stuart, I appreciate that."

"I thought, Natalie's going to be fine, Paul's going to be fine, Mama Whitelaw too, even though she abandoned her babies. Evelyn, I hate to put you in the same list with them, but you'll be fine because you take it as it comes. When I asked Natalie where I'd live after we got this behind us, she said she had 'no idea because as far as this house is concerned you're shit out of luck, I've come to like it, corny grows on you.' I had my mother's china—now I don't care about *china*—but I had this china she painted and it's not well done and it's not worth anything, but Natalie, when you told me I couldn't have it because you expected company, I said to myself, 'Let's blow this cunt out of the water—' "

Covering his face with one hand, Melvin raised the other in caution as Evelyn felt herself cringing.

Natalie turned to Blaylock. "Do I have to listen to this?"

"In a word, no. But it makes a nice preview. Stuart has retained counsel, and this is pretty much where he's coming from."

"Will I be able to explain how bored I am by all this?"

"Absolutely. Jurors are unlikely to be moved by it, but you can unburden yourself as you see fit."

Stuart was motionless except for the tears that began to pour down his face. Evelyn spoke to him.

"I am resigned to the fact that your divorce is inevitable," she said, "but I think you both will have to go through the usual channels to get this settled and even so it's very very sad."

"My favorite channel," Blaylock said, "is the one where you take the asset pile and go right down the middle with a cake knife. Stuart, pull yourself together."

Stuart said directly to Evelyn, from an anguished face, "It's not money, I want to get even."

This propelled Melvin Blaylock to his feet. "Stuart, Stuart, Stuart," he said, "money is *how* you get even!"

Choudri Rabindrinath Majub, at precisely 9:15 a.m., strode into Paul's office, his calling card fluttering to the secretary's desk midstride, a vigorous presence. "Ah, good morning," he said, thrusting out his hand and tossing a ratty tan topcoat over what Paul had imagined to be important documents. "C. R. Majub," said the visitor.

"Yes," Paul said levelly. "I know who you are."

"My God, what a climate!" Majub was a small man, a narrow-featured face, his neatly parted hair combed straight to the side from the part. He wore a Scottish tweed jacket, twill trousers and an unstarched white shirt with a broad red-and-brown silk tie covered with tiny horses, and a pair of cordovan shoes that on a normal-sized man—Majub was small—would have weighed six pounds.

"Papers arrived at my hotel—plenty of time, thank you—and reviewing everything—may I sit?—I experienced appropriate shock. Never saw receivables at these proportions! There's a loyal customer base we can continue to look to, but not as panacea for some very startl—"

"Look," said Paul gruffly, "instead of going over this column by column, can you give me sort of an executive summary?" There was a very long silence, long enough to begin hearing sounds from outside the building.

Majub smiled, and Paul tried to remember why this aborigine kept turning up in his life. At the same time, he meant to keep a bit of pressure on Majub. "Why the smile?" he asked.

"I always smile when I conceptualize," Majub said with an even bigger smile.

"Oh," said Paul. "How far'd you get with it?"

"I'm there, baby."

"Would you like to share?"

"Mr. Crusoe, I am a polite man. I aspire to being *infinitely* polite, but I accept that I shall never achieve it."

"The self-improvement craze is sweeping the country. What about my bottling plant?"

Majub's attempt to seem imperturbable was unavailing, given the light that danced in his eyes. "Clearly, you have had great success," he cried, "at running this concern into the ground!"

Paul gazed at him heavily. "You look happy."

"I'm not!" With the flat of his hand, Majub smoothed his tie and then buttoned his jacket over it.

Paul's attention was drawn unwillingly to all the tiny hairs bristling from the tweed, which gave Majub's air an insectlike alertness. Why someone would wear something like this was beyond him, and he felt increasingly hostile; nor could he shake the queasy feeling that he should know more about this tormenting brown gnat.

"You must understand," Majub said, "that my vital interests are tied to the best valuation we can accomplish. Our fees are a measured portion of the sale. There is no motive for me to understate the worth of this firm. But I cannot be unrealistic, as prospective buyers know they will have to *live* with the facts if they elect to *purchase*."

"Just seemed to me you were a tad aggressive in characterizing my management."

Here an astonishing belly laugh burst from Mr. Majub, who wiped his eyes and said, "Come, come, Paul."

"Mr. Crusoe," said Paul.

"Sure," said Majub, peering up in a pixieish manner. He was having a wonderful time.

"Las Vegas!" Paul shouted. "We met in Las Vegas!"

But Majub just smiled and pointed under Paul's desk. "Is that your dog?"

"Yes, it is."

"What's his name?"

"Whitelaw."

Majub seemed to reflect for a spell before speaking. "America is a marvelous country," he said. "How the world has enjoyed living under your nuclear umbrella!" This confused Paul. He thought Majub *was* an American.

"I grew up in Maine," said C. R. Majub. "My father was a lobsterman, but both my uncles were cowboys. My uncle Olatanji was the champion of the rodeo."

The women turned to each other.

"Look it up," he went on. "Olatanji Majub, world champion of the big rodeo!"

Certainly he sounded very American for someone born, as he'd told the sisters, in the Punjabi state next to the Great Riff. Only occasionally was his English disturbed by a howler, as when he attempted to describe his girlfriend back in Ohio as "red hot," and inadvertently described her as "piping hot."

Natalie found him peppy and well dressed and was pleased to welcome him into her home so recently vacated by her ex-husband, about whom she always reached the same stark conclusion: "Good riddance!"

Word of Majub's arrival had been circulating for days. He'd visited several attorneys and personally done a rapid inventory at the bottling plant among items that must've been quite unfamiliar to him. With each department head he had let an amused glance at Paul's office be glimpsed; when the foreman for procurement suggested tarring and feathering for the CEO, Majub shook his head faintly, implying that something more restrained but definitely along those lines was already in store.

"Girls," said Majub to the women gathered to see him at Natalie's house, "do you know why I am here?" The balls of his fingers rested on a book of celebrity photographs by Annie Liebovitz.

Natalie smiled. "We think so."

"Not sure," Evelyn said.

"I'm here to make the bottle plant go away." He smiled at Evelyn.

"Altogether?" she asked.

"Not altogether, but into something smaller we call money. Unlike the bottling plant, you can carry it in your little purses."

"Where will the plant itself go?"

"Several possibilities, but I'm thinking primarily of an assisted living group out of Texas. They've got the where-withal and I will show them the need."

Natalie mused on how attractive an Indian man could be: refined features, eyes just like a cocker spaniel's! But

Evelyn found his act of being one jump ahead of everybody to be slightly irritating. She also thought that, while justified by the weather, the British clothes somewhat overwhelmed him. Later when he showed them his picture sea bathing at St. Barts in a little bathing suit he called a "banana hammock," he revealed that he was far from inflexible in dress.

"How will you convey the need to own a family business to this Texas firm?" she asked.

"Not just Texas! Fort Worth—where the Basses live!—Evelyn, here's how: I crawl over the portfolio till I find the missing tooth."

Natalie brought out some pastries and coffee while Majub flipped through the celebrity photographs. When he got to Yoko Ono with John Lennon curled up next to her in the fetal position, he cried out in delight, "She'll have him for dinner!" After thumbing furiously through the rest of the book and finding the attention lavished upon subjects he didn't recognize maddening, he pushed the book away and settled down.

"In order to sell this company I have to find its value, which under present management is falling rapidly. I can rough it in by using a multiple of earnings, but there is a trend here and I don't want to risk an opinion and have our sale overturned by a probate court. We'll get a reputable appraiser, maybe even find one in a cowboy hat."

"How did *you* find us?" Evelyn demanded.

"Your father found me. Did you not read the trust instrument? I'm the third codicil."

Evelyn and Natalie turned to each other again. They had thought it morbid to study the estate information too

closely; their mother read it in its entirety and her reports
had seemed sufficient to the girls.

"Your father and I had a long association. He didn't like
to invest in the stock market, and looked to me to find alter-
natives. He felt he had no influence over companies in
which he merely invested. He wanted to own whole companies, and I helped him find them."

"Where are they now?" Natalie wished to know.

"Come and gone, mostly lost money. He really only
knew how to run this one business, I'm sorry to say, but
it has done nicely until now. Your father was not in the best
of health. He never exercised, and he'd been eating those
same big marbled steaks from Kansas City all his life. He
once told me he'd eaten more beef than you see in the
stampede scene in John Wayne's *Red River,* but that he'd
reached the age and state where he couldn't eat another
herd of that size. It was his intimation of mortality. His
hope was that the bottling plant would remain as a monument to, well, to him. But he was a realist. He thought that
your husband—"

"Estranged husband."

"Of course. That *Paul* had the best chance of holding the
asset together." He turned to Natalie. "Whereas I thought
your husband—"

"Soon-to-be used-to-be," said Natalie. "I just gave him
the news."

"Anyway, I considered Stuart the steadier man. However,
your father somehow thought he owed it to Paul, and so
Paul it was. Frankly, he has been a nonstarter because the
fortunes of this company are dropping like a rock. As far as
I'm concerned, Paul is out of runway. I mean, you girls can

look after yourselves, but I don't want to see your mother sleeping in her car."

"Has my mother heard this?" Evelyn asked.

"The doctor is with her now." After giving the remark plenty of time to settle in, he continued. "But look, relax. I will get this fixed, you have my word. And when I'm done you'll see a little security, a little income. You'll need to work, of course, but you'll have some latitude as to the job, not just flipping burritos at Taco Bell."

"How much income?" said Natalie.

"Too soon to tell. And Stuart—"

"What's he got to do with this?"

"He's a stakeholder." He turned to Evelyn. "You're different: you become a landowner. And, more importantly, when the plant goes away, Paul goes away. His claim to fame was to do a good job, and the job he accomplished was sabotage. You're lucky the old man put me in place, or this thing would be an oil slick. And you can thank me for figuring a way to park your marriage until we liquidate."

"Are you being paid?" asked Evelyn.

"I was paid a long time ago. I'll spare you the details."

On the fifteenth of February, the snow stopped and the sun came out. People begin to act crazy. They washed their cars, kissed in public; several suspicions of fire turned out to be barbecues, meat grilling in the shadows of snowdrifts. When the plows finished the town's streets, a pair of hot-rod roadsters drag-raced ten blocks straight east, before being forced to the side of the road by a Montana Highway Patrol car. Both men qualified for senior discounts and had built the cars themselves, starting back in high-school shop class forty years earlier. One driver, wall-eyed with adrenaline, was quoted in the paper as saying, "Officer, you're lucky you ever caught us in that lead sled of yours. These cars are freaky-fast, wind-in-your-hair, point-and-shoot hot rods. They are not for the faint of heart."

The Whitelaw family would have been hard pressed to demonstrate quite such jubilation as they stood and watched a crane lower the WHITELAW BOTTLING sign and replace it with the shorter and graphically more up-to-date ECO FIZZ. It would in time be a memorable gathering— Alice Whitelaw (openly weeping), Natalie Whitelaw (patience rewarded), Bill Champion (out-of-place), Paul Crusoe (ironic leer), Evelyn Whitelaw (uncomfortable), Stuart Cross (nostalgic). Paul's dog stood between the family and the spectacle and alone seemed free of uncertainty. One of the new owners gazed around the neighborhood and asked of nobody in particular, "Whose idea was it to build a town here?"

Looking at the new sign, Natalie feigned cheer as she pointed out to her heartbroken mother, "That's the same lettering they use at Planet Hollywood."

Having felt his gaze, Paul turned to look at Bill, whose cowboy boots were being inspected by Whitelaw, who had sensed Bill's feelings about his master.

"Which planet?" said Alice as Bill looked at her protectively and the dog growled at his feet. Evelyn felt Paul's eyes on her face but declined to turn to him. She shared her family's exhaustion from the negotiations and sale and all the turbulence that went with them. The assisted-living people—born-again Christians, skiers and very tough business people—were openly contemptuous of the Whitelaws, whom they viewed as the dysfunctional family. During one tense moment their accountant said, "We need to wind this up and let this family crawl back under their log."

Natalie and her mother stood shoulder to shoulder, holding the collars of their winter coats to their throats with the same left-handed gesture, and staring at the flashing Eco Fizz sign. Paul walked briskly toward the parked cars without recognizing any of the employees who'd begun to drift out coatless to see the new sign and smoke cigarettes, their expressions revealing their view that this was more management high jinks.

Evelyn's eyes were on Paul when her sister said, "We're going for a victory drink. Care to join us?" Momentarily despising Natalie, she said, "*No.*" Her own mother appeared to her to be a simpleton and an opportunist. Her eyes were on Paul, heading to his car. She wondered why she wasn't happier to see him so utterly defeated.

"I've had two lives, really," C. R. Majub said to Paul, "before my illness and after. In the first I was born, raised in my little town on Lake Erie and educated at Ohio State University. Then the happy days as I built my business. Those *are* the happiest days. I had no family other than my business, which consisted of me and a secretary, a weary old empty-nester I saw between trips and to whom I unloaded my brain like a cargo ship. Then, during a trip to Taiwan to sell a ball-cap monogramming business, I contracted hepatitis. I don't know how, but it resulted in complete renal failure, and very abruptly I began to lose my kidneys and went onto a waiting list for a transplant." Paul felt himself grow queasy and alert.

"Nobody came forward in my little town to give me one of theirs. An old neighbor said he didn't think a white man's kidney would work anyway. At that time, the Whitelaw bottling plant happened to be in trouble. I had done a lot of business with Sunny Jim, but he got himself into this mess without my help. Besides, he had created so many enemies that he was forced to turn to me for the jumbo loan he needed to survive. I was going from dialysis to dialysis and I could barely concentrate when Sunny Jim said, 'Come to Vegas. Bring the check. I think I can help you out.'"

"You sonofabitch, I can't believe you're telling me this." Paul's stomach had turned.

"There's a reason. I never knew where Sunny Jim got it. I mean, I assumed it was on the black market. But I didn't know who the . . . donor was until I sat down with him to help with his will. At first, I was shocked. I thought, People don't do this. Then he explained to me how you'd crossed him and I could at least partly understand. In the end, he was remorseful. He told me, 'Majub, you've got to do right by Paul. You've got to make it up to him. You owe Paul your life; not me, him.'"

Paul followed her out to the ranch. There were black strings of cattle on huge snowfields, and bare trees mobbed with sharptail grouse hoping for a ray of sunshine. Even with snow tires, Evelyn was having a hard time staying on the road. And the silence—*the silence*—inside the car was more than a slight problem. What could she possibly say? Yet she must be prepared to confront the question of whose idea this was, and by the time Paul followed her into the ranch house, waiting diffidently while she undid the latch, she was brilliantly prepared to answer his first question, "What do you want, Evelyn?"

"I want you to give it to me all night long," she said, having elected the shorter version.

"I'm taking this with a grain of salt," he said, a response that conveyed his entire appeal with perfect economy, and they began to laugh like old times, with Paul in his sparkling role as collaborator and demon. Evelyn was reminding herself to keep it light and have a good time. Life was short, et cetera. Amid limbs tangling she made out his voice—"we've got contact"—and despite her alarm at his detached gaze, Evelyn was startled at how quickly she began coming, a long, ashamed experience of relief not unlike wetting the bed. Then she couldn't shut it off and it seemed over and over again that he went well beyond necessity, her own voice sounding unfamiliar and as if from afar. She looked across at the mirror on the dresser and saw a moving image that must've been Paul, though it was too distorted to make out and looked mostly like a black leaf endlessly unfolding, like something terrible.

When Paul and Evelyn were first married, Evelyn had hoped to interest him in the ranch and the land itself. Paul was interested, all right, spotting home sites everywhere and what he called "viewsheds." Paul seemed genuinely puzzled that Bill was unaware of viewsheds, while Bill was baffled by virtually every detail of Paul. Paul's were the first bluejeans Bill had ever seen with a crease. When Paul lurched around on their gentlest horse, Evelyn asked Bill privately if he thought they'd ever make a horseman of Paul. "Never," said Bill undiplomatically. He noted that Paul was "very manicured" and that he "would do well to butter his own toast."

Realizing that Bill was not warming to his idea of home sites, Paul had perversely pressed it. "What's wrong with my idea?" he said. "Not everyone can have a ranch. Should the unlucky ones be cut off from nature altogether?" He tried to push his hands thoughtfully into the pockets of his leather vest, but they were either sewn shut or were not actual pockets.

"They got plenty of houses," said Bill.

"Maybe not the ones they want. Maybe they want different ones."

"Says in Isaiah, 'Woe unto them that join house to house, that lay field to field, till there be no place that they may be placed alone in the midst of the earth.'"

"I guess you can find support for just about anything in the Bible. The big thing here, though, is that Evelyn never wanted to ranch *at all*. She just wants to *be* here."

Evelyn interrupted in order to ease the tension for her beloved. "These aren't choices that concern us, Paul. This is Bill's ranch."

"I got that part," Paul went on, "but this is a beautiful piece of land, and, unless I miss my guess, it isn't doing one percent of its capital value by running cows on it. That's like sitting on an egg that never hatches, know what I mean?"

Now things were even more dire. She looked out the windows made oval by encroaching ice and giving onto an increasingly featureless snowscape. She could see the tracks where Paul had driven away, but light snow drifting in the wind was slowly filling them.

She got up, put on her coveralls and found Bill down in the old sheep shed where he was pouring out grain and medication for the small bunch of locoed calves who'd followed close behind and were trying to upend his bucket. Bill was slow to acknowledge her arrival, and she felt it. Mortified, she turned her attention to the calves who had begun to outgrow the dwarfish faces the poison weed and its alkaloids had given them. They'd become tame with all this hand-feeding, but in the end they'd go on the truck with the others.

Evelyn's father had devised many ways of turning her into Bill's hired hand—for reasons best known to him— and had similarly resolved that Bill would never fail no matter how many small ranchers were devastated by the steadily failing cattle economy. They would call it a partnership. To spare Bill an excessive awareness of his financial plight, he appointed Evelyn as bookkeeper, and she regularly went to her father seeking financial assistance for the ranch. Evelyn began to wonder about her father's generosity. For a time she believed he was trying to acquire the place, which proved not to be the case. Instead, Sunny Jim required Bill to do some estate planning. "You're over seventy," he said. "Let me help you draw up a will." When they finished, they put the document in a safe-deposit box in Harlowtown with Bill's high-school diploma, his grandfather's spurs and a pair of moccasins alleged to have belonged to Gall. Despite that she had been entrusted with the key and had good reason to suspect the ranch would one day be hers, Evelyn never once considered looking.

Today there was an evasive bustle in Bill's movements as he hung the grain bucket on a nail and headed into the corral with the cows closest to calving, giving Evelyn a good view of the back of his coat.

"Scram's got a wire cut," he noted with unusual indifference as he and Evelyn crossed the barnyard to the corral where the horse stood by himself, with a back foot tipped up. Having already been scrutinized once, a thing not every horse likes, Scram watched warily as Evelyn came up for another inspection. She picked up his back foot and rested it heel-up between her knees, the old blood rough between her hands. It was quite a slice, showing white inside, but since it didn't seem there were cords cut, it wasn't crippling. She led him to the hydrant, washed out the wound with water and then poured hydrogen peroxide into it. The bubbling of the wound made him jerk his foot. Then Evelyn wiped it clear, smeared in some Furazin and wrapped it.

"Idiot," she said, and led Scram back to the corral while thinking that Bill could turn into a bitter old man in trying to mind her business for her, but this was an excessive reaction to someone being untalkative.

To Evelyn's great relief, Alice Whitelaw never stayed over when she came to visit and was careful she spent as much time with her daughter as with her husband of long ago. She'd seen Paul around the place, and Evelyn was anxious to avoid conversation that might entail any elucidation of her own marital status. Alice Whitelaw reserved most of her matriarchal concern for Stuart, "—the most *whole-*some, earnest, steady young man" she'd ever met.

"But, Mother, evidently not the right fellow for Nat."

"Oh, but dear, I know you're going to miss him."

"He's not going anywhere. He's doing fine at Eco Fizz."
Evelyn was completely exasperated by her mother's crooning lament, but soon that tone would change.

"So *many* years have passed since my days out here. I was just a girl, but I have never been out of touch with Bill."

Evelyn wasn't about to ask something crazy—such as, were she and Bill in love?—and mostly wanted to snap her fingers and move this thing along. She thought her mother's leaning across the hood of a pickup truck to have a heart-to-heart was an affectation.

"But my God! He lives like a dog! Did *I* live like that? I must have."

"I'm not sure I know wh—"

"Surely I had furniture!"

"Yes, you must've had furniture," said Evelyn dully.

"I suppose that wallpaper in the house was always there. What is it, flocked? And I do hope it wasn't you who supplied that *swag* effect over what passes for a dining room table. I told Bill the only thing that was keeping him from falling into the *cellar* was that greenish linoleum!"

"Could it be that in thirty years your standards of comfort have gone up?"

"I am the same person," her mother said levelly, "I have always been."

"I don't think so," Evelyn said.

Alice Whitelaw straightened up from the hood of the truck and, with a preoccupied air, got into her Buick Riviera and drove away. It was the first of many things to go wrong.

.　　　.　　　.

"What *did* you say to Mother, Evelyn?" Natalie was driving slowly alongside a car dealership, trying to see if there was anything she wanted to buy. She just wanted to be outside. She'd spent days on end chasing the channel changer until general disgust had set in.

"God, Nat, I just *blurted*. I'll have to go straighten this out somehow. Mama was talking about how she was the same girl who married Bill, and I said that I doubted it."

"Oh." She was staring right past her sister, out the window. "See anything you like?"

"They're all covered with snow. What are they?"

"Audis. Maybe she thinks she *hasn't* changed."

"I'm sure she does. And I've just got to get over my irritation and apologize. It's not her fault she's an airhead." A small truck shot past, Hey Culligan Man! on its tailgate.

"I like the idea of all-wheel drive. I want to blast through this shit with German power. I hate winter. I hate it here. I wish to be saved by Germans."

Evelyn just looked at her. "Wait till the snow melts before making your choice."

"It's never going to melt. I want a new car. Tell them to blow the snow off. Get on my cell phone and tell them we're circling the block and will buy anything they blow the snow off of."

"I'm hungry."

"Me too! This weather makes me snack day and *night*. I'm getting a huge ass, and with Stuart gone I can't have some new guy facing a wall of cellulite."

Evelyn sighed. After dropping Natalie off at home with

an armload of car brochures, she drove to their mother's house. The visit proved especially painful because Alice was her usual cheerful self, and Evelyn had to bring the insult up all over again in order to apologize for it. Alice brushed it aside. "I know you're upset with me."

"No—"

"Evelyn, you are, and I accept and understand it. But think of what I've been though. I know I shouldn't tell you this, but I've waited a long time to see my Bill again, to see him like this. And he's just as dear to me as he was when he was eighteen. I never understood whether I was right to have married him or not. I knew there were too many mouths at our table, and my mother and father practically pushed me right out the door before there was a *chance* we'd marry. But after your father's death it all came back, how Bill wouldn't budge, how on a ranch you don't budge or the ranch and the land will beat you, so you don't budge and then all the rest of life beats you."

"You must think Bill's beaten."

"I think he's been beaten for a very long time."

"Maybe if you don't know it, you're *not*."

"You of all people know how the ranch stayed afloat." She adjusted her voice to a complicitous murmur. "Your father was a hard man. Maybe bad. I can live with that. He certainly didn't mind ruining people—but if he was bad, he had a good streak. He made sure you girls went out to the ranch often, from an early age. You spent more time while you were growing up with Bill than you did with your father."

Alice had touched upon something for which Evelyn was thoroughly grateful, her often fabulous girlhood, and she was happy to recall even her most outlandish cowgirl posturing, the barrel-racing mania of her adolescence. As with her mother, it lasted until the appearance of a charismatic male of whom she had yet to rid herself and who had presently, if only in the urgencies of the flesh, rekindled the possibilities.

Evelyn, at least, knew why Bill wouldn't budge, for she had long seen into the congeries of belief that abided him through illness, injury and failure. Bill's piece of ground was a mystery machine that, like soil and weather, occasioned vigilant respect. She unconditionally realized that cattle, buildings, fences—the "improvements"—were stays in the face of general impermanence even as they shared as a principal characteristic the ongoing likelihood of dying or falling down. Alone of her family, Evelyn understood horses and their use, and also that however far back in the legends of horsemanship Bill's talents reached, they were most definitely his gamble against eternity. Perhaps he kept cattle so that the horses would have something to do. If by some now vanished compact he had gotten children by Alice Whitelaw, Evelyn believed that it was only right that at least one of those children should understand his faith.

Had she pursued these intuitions, she might have seen that Bill would have to do something about Paul.

Evelyn moved all her belongings to the ranch and turned her apartment over to Paul. Where else was he going to live, she asked herself in rhetorical indignation as though responding to querulous busybodies. He'd saved nothing of his quondam executive's salary, and his last remaining stake was whatever he shared, as Evelyn's husband, of the ranch when Bill was gone. He sold his Crown Victoria too and bought a pathetic gray Chevette that looked too short for his legs. But it gave him some walking-around money, as he said. Which is what he did: walked around and talked to Majub on the cell phone. Because of the accumulated tensions of recent months, Paul felt he was losing his flexibility and so he signed up for Pilates at the community center. Natalie paid for the lessons on the grounds that any money spent on good health was money well spent. There was also the feeling that getting rid of lower back pain would allow him to put his best foot forward while interviewing for jobs, should he be reduced to that, God forbid.

They were all—Alice, Natalie, Evelyn—living under new restrictions due to Stuart's lawsuit, which had frozen the distribution of proceeds from the sale of the plant. Stuart had managed to stay on at Eco Fizz, and his popularity with both the workers and the new owners positioned him to manage the company. The few times he'd been spotted by family members, he was wearing a dark suit and a top coat. This hardly seemed like Stuart at all.

The calves by now were coming in a steady stream. Bill was staying up for night-calving so Evelyn fed in the morning while he slept, picking up hay with hydraulic arms in the bed of the truck that held big round bales like spools of thread until she lowered them with controls on the dash, cut the twine and rolled out a ribbon of alfalfa. Its miraculous aroma of the previous summer unfolding in the winter air attracted a parade of cows and calves bawling with impatience. Early sun laid an annealed glaze over the snowfields. Tractors could be heard starting at various distances throughout the valley, and a school bus made its solitary way along the base of foothills. Evelyn had so disliked school that even this distant yellow shape still depressed her, all these years later. She went up to Bill's house and cooked breakfast for them both.

The season was changing at last.

Broad community interest followed news of Paul's arrest for parole violation. Only the general fascination he had aroused in himself as a company executive and ersatz man-about-town could explain why the newspaper gave the hearing such attention. He was charged with refusing to meet with his parole officer, Geraldine Cardwell, who not only initiated the charges but also, in high dudgeon, issued sweeping statements as to how she stood as a "firewall" between criminals and society. What turned out to be a coup for the paper, given a repressed atmosphere that played hell with getting sex on the page, was Paul Crusoe's testimony in a crowded, unventilated courtroom. He admitted that he had grown fearful and weary of the sexual obligations imposed upon him by Miss Cardwell, causing the crowd to gasp in delighted disapproval. Trying to restore his relationship with his estranged wife against desperate odds had grown ever more difficult beneath the constant pressure to "service" his parole officer. Arms stretched low at his sides, a renewed vision of jail in his head, the supplicant offered motel receipts and a vague offer of "DNA evidence." Under Geraldine's quiet gaze and in a small, frightened, victim's voice, he said, "I didn't know where to turn, Your Honor. I was afraid that if I requested a new officer, somebody on the parole board would exact revenge. This could happen even now! These people look out for each other in ways that might surprise Your Honor!"

Geraldine Cardwell declined to respond at all. After the hearing, she returned to her office, gathered up the pictures of her parents, sisters, brother, nephews and nieces and, braving smirks in the outer office, returned to her house, where in a state-issued vehicle she closed her garage and asphyxiated herself. The brief note she left on the seat beside her read simply,

"To Whom—"

The next morning's paper was filled with vituperative letters to the editor from citizens who, ignorant of her death, stated that Geraldine Cardwell was a perfect example of why we needed to get government out of our lives; the Constitution was frequently invoked. On learning of the suicide and Geraldine's note, Paul said only that she was "no writer."

Donald Aadfield called Evelyn on the day all this appeared.

"Evelyn, I had no idea you were living such a complicated life!"

"It's news to me too." She felt almost too subdued to speak.

"This man Paul! Is he still your husband?"

"That's unclear to me, Donald."

"But the paper says he's trying to save the *relationship*."

"There's some truth to that. But how are *you*, Donald?"

"Never mind how I am. I can't believe what I'm reading. I've seen Crusoe in the paper *before*. And my neighbors! Two work the night shift at the bottle plant. I mean, I hope I'm not offending you, but according to them, people at the plant actually talk about pushing him into a *vat*."

"That's all behind us now. The company's been sold."

After Donald demanded an immediate visit, Evelyn directed him to the ranch and by afternoon he arrived in his truck, a steel flatbed with a headache rack in the rear and so encumbered with tires, jacks, fence stretchers, spools of barbed wire and fuel drums that it looked like a junkyard on wheels.

Donald jumped out, hugged Evelyn and asked immediately how many acres she had. When she told him, he said, "Ooh Evelyn! And how many cows do you run?" At that, he rubbed his hands in glee and asked to see the calves. She agreeably led him to what had arrived thus far. Bill was in the corral and helped conduct the tour, clearly liking Donald on sight as being a real rancher worthy of Evelyn's company. He particularly admired Donald's crap-laden truck. "I got a tough customer down here to the barn," he said. "Don't want to have this calf, and I think we may be gettin' kind of a crossways presentation."

Donald said, "If they can get in trouble, they will, won't they, Bill? I had an old cow last week started chasing her afterbirth in a circle and ground her calf to mush. I tried to get in the middle of it and got knocked on my butt."

Bill put the cow in the head catch, where she bawled at the calf she couldn't see with just its head out but no legs yet visible.

Donald plunged his hand into his beard in thought, then picked up a piece of binder twine from the barn floor and tied her tail to one side. He took his coat off, rolled up his right sleeve and slid his arm up alongside the calf into the cow. "Once they get junior in the birth canal, they're not too good at kicking. Anyway, here's our problem. . . ." By now he was crouched against the cow, cheek mashed against her dilated genitals, and struggling as though arm wrestling a giant. "I don't like to use the snare here, for fear we'd push something through the uterus, but what we've got is junior's turned one front leg backward, and, wouldn't you know, there's so much musculature to this cow's hymen or else we've got some damn incomplete dilation. But we'll get him sorted out here." He straightened to withdraw his arm, and the small black hooves popped into view behind his hand.

He stood back, and the three of them watched for a long moment until, after mighty straining by the cow, the calf made a little dolphin-dive for his mother's heels and was born. Donald carried him around so that the cow could see him. As the amnion sac emptied its amber contents into the straw, he said, "Turn Mama loose."

Bill was smiling. Later as they discussed calving out the heifers, Donald cried, "No, no, Bill, You mustn't do this to yourself. Next year AI them and calve the whole batch in a matter of days. I'll help you. After doing it for *years* I've got it down. We'll freeze-brand them first, synchronize them and buy straws of semen that *fit* your cattle. Then the nice man comes out from town with his nitrogen tank and you kiss the guesswork of first-calf heifers good-bye!"

Bill even liked the prissy wave at the end wherein Donald said good-bye to all problems associated with heifers.

"These days, Bill, you have to measure everything there is to measure on a cow, test them for efficiency on feed and index them for performance. But I can see you're like my old man: you're not buying any of it."

"Your dad and me are too old."

Over coffee and a sheet of overbaked cinnamon rolls, Evelyn learned that the Aadfields were in an identical rut to the one she'd seen them in last. Donald tried to explain it but even the explanation seemed part of the problem.

"They could sell the place, but they can't picture what they'd do with the money. They never had any, so it doesn't interest them. Realtors come out and it's like talking to a stone. The trouble is, they can't hold that ranch together without me, and there are things about me that they don't need to know. So the small part of me that lives on the ranch and does all the work makes the rest of me too tired to have any other life, and besides, *secret* lives are incredibly tiring and sort of *unreal* in the long run, and I just have this feeling I'm going to end up some lonely old bachelor rancher leaning on a number-two Ames irrigating shovel, and *not one* tourist driving past admiring me as a traditional part of the landscape on the northern route to Yellowstone will ever realize that once upon a time I was an honest-to-God California faggot!"

Afterward Bill said, "Anything ever happens to me, that'd be the feller for you." She liked being drawn out by Donald, by the vigilance and stillness when he listened to her, his hands folded atop his gloves or reaching for his coffee cup but never moving his eyes away. Consequently, she told him a surprising amount about her life. Such as: "The ranch belongs to Bill and me. God knows where *that* might lead, so I guess I'm sort of in transition. It hasn't been that long since my father died, and my mother needs me. I wish I could have my life here, just live it out, y'know? But these little ranches don't work anymore."

"Tell me about it."

"I sell a few horses, but then I don't know where they've gone and it just makes me sad. I don't like pushing calves into a truck the day they're weaned either. I don't like the cows bawling for them for days afterward and looking around where the truck used to be. Sure, we talk about the best way to breed those heifers, but they're too young to have babies in the first place. It scares them and sometimes kills them. You know what it's like to take those old cows to be slaughtered, ones you've known for ten years or more or you raised from the time they were calves themselves. They get broken mouthed, or you can't read the shield, and that year they don't go on the drive to summer pasture. It's starting to get me down." She was silent for a long moment, then added with searing conviction, "I may be the wrong person for my own life."

Donald seemed to have been caught up in her mood. "We had an old longhorn, Luther, we used for a lead steer," he said. "Luther got old but he never got mean. He just went where he wanted, through fences, whatever. Started going in and out of my mom's garden and ruining everything. So we loaded him up—weighed over a ton—and drove around half of Montana to find someone to kill him. Finally located somebody at Martinsdale. Dad wanted the head, but Luther was so big his horns broke when they hung him up." Donald looked desolate. "Just getting in the garden, was all."

"So you headed for California."

"Not for that. I went for basic gender issues, which turned out not to be enough for a whole life. Big surprise, that."

A car drove up in front of the house, and Evelyn, suddenly anxious, went to the window and, separating the blinds with her hand, said, "Paul's here."

She hardly had time to get away from the window before

Paul bounded inside and nearly slid to a stop with a comic back-pedaling of his arms upon spotting Donald, whom he studied sharply as Evelyn introduced them.

"Have we met before?" asked Paul.

"Not that I know of," Donald boomed.

Standing closer to Paul, Evelyn noticed how imposing Donald was. His present western vigor was completely unforeseen.

"You live around here, Don?"

"I ranch at Daisy Dean. Got a hundred-head forest permit. Leased up some spring pasture right there where Mission Creek comes into the river. Where do you run your cattle?" He knew perfectly well that Paul didn't have any.

"I don't have any cattle," said Paul, already crestfallen at this perceived disadvantage. "I don't think I want any. They look like a nonperforming asset to me."

"Don't want any cattle? What do you do to pass the time?"

"I find other ways to amuse myself." Paul was now sufficiently emboldened to let a twinge of acid enter his tone. "Where did you two meet?"

"I got stuck in the snow," said Evelyn, determined not to be interrogated.

"Dad and I dug her out!"

"And now we're all friends," said Paul.

"I hope so!" said Donald, clamping a great paw upon Paul's shoulder, demanding, "How about you, Paul, you got any friends?"

"Enough."

With a hearty laugh, Donald pounded him on the back, "I gotta go, buddy!" He turned to Evelyn and, without a word, gave her a tiny wave at eye level. In the context of the roaring ranch act it was incomprehensible, but Paul seemed not to have noticed.

"Who *was* that overbearing bastard?"

"He's a new friend."

"A 'new friend'? I'd hate to think what *that* means."

"Then don't think about it."

"Oh, I see."

"No, you don't see. He's exactly what I told you he is. He's my friend."

"What's this whole new sacred thing about friends? People used to just *have* friends. Now there's this pixie dust over the entire subject."

"Is that so? I must've missed that."

"I didn't come out here to argue."

"Then you've made a poor start. I don't know what you think the other night means, but it doesn't include the resumption of monitoring my activities."

"Sounds like you've really thought that through."

"As indeed I have."

Paul liked to mimic happy astonishment at various of Evelyn's words. "Monitoring" and "indeed" got such treatment now. It was beyond irritating. It was, Evelyn decided, all part of his routine. "Once they've decided you're the devil," Paul had said long ago, "the gals beat a path to your door."

"Evelyn," he began in an entirely different tone, "I came out to tell you some good news: I have a new job."

"Already?" Evelyn couldn't help feeling pleased. It would all be so much better if Paul would just be happy.

"Mr. Majub must've approved of my work at the plant: he has hired me as a liaison officer for this region."

"I'm afraid I don't know what that is, liaison officer."

Paul had moved to her side. Evelyn sat in an armchair, and his hand was now in her hair.

"It's a fancy word for a scout. I think it involves hoopla. I've always been keenly interested in hoopla. Majub feels that Montana has some undervalued businesses that are ripe for the plucking." She could feel her breathing acquire weight and the heat of Paul's hand was between her shoulders. Though aware of what was happening, she didn't feel inclined to do anything about it. Her mind acted to quickly minimize all reservations as soon as they arose.

"I'll have a company car," he murmured. "I'm just going to follow the old routes, maybe start along the High Line. That feels good, doesn't it?"

"Uh-huh."

"Then work my way down toward Wyoming, and you like Wyoming, don't you?"

"Yeah."

"Just let go, let go, let go."

Her breath kept coming out of her, and some of her clothes had accumulated next to the armchair.

"You get out there around Glendive, Forsyth, Miles City, it's quiet, real, real quiet."

Evelyn could see none of the light in the room. She heard Paul say, "How about now," but waited until her breathing and her thoughts were going at the same speed.

"Now is good," she said.

A retired circuit court judge, T. William Slater, was assigned to mediate the divorce and division of property for Stuart Cross and Natalie. While things were sedate enough at first, Natalie was already offended by Stuart's suit; he'd never dressed like this before, and she wondered about his need to suddenly display such fashion sense. She knew that his fortunes had improved at the bottling plant, that he was climbing fast and making more money than ever before. His modesty, though, was undiminished, and Natalie hoped it indicated that he'd lowered what she considered to be an extreme position with regard to her property. She took solace in the fact that Justice Slater came from a well-known pioneer family. Ranchers and legislators abounded in his background, and since the end of the Civil War there had been much mingling among Slaters and Whitelaws.

Holding a pencil crossways in his mouth and arranging papers at the same time, T. William Slater managed to say, "I take it that we agree that the divorce itself is desirable." He put his briefcase under the table and looked up.

Natalie and Stuart each said yes, Stuart with palpable sadness he was trying to disguise.

"So all that's outstanding is the division of assets."

Both nodded.

"Are there specific items to which either of you are attached?"

They shook their heads.

"What about the house?"

"Not the house," said Natalie emphatically.

"So, what I'm looking at here is house, cars, the proceeds of your equity in the business which I gather here has been sold and probated. Yes, of course it has." Sliding out another sheet of paper. "Because here is all this cash. I seldom see so much uninvested cash."

"In point of fact," Natalie said, "I would be willing to let Stuart have the house."

"Just sell it and we split," said Stuart.

"What's that?" asked a startled Natalie.

Justice Slater said, "I'm assuming unless either of you specifies otherwise that all of this can be made liquid, in which case division is simplified. Would either of you care to give me your feelings on this?"

"Sure," said Stuart cheerfully. "Half and half. Isn't that the law?"

Natalie's eyes were wide with indignation as she turned to Justice Slater.

"Unless it's contested," said Justice Slater.

"Wait a minute here," said Natalie. "The proceeds from the plant only arrived a short time ago. Where's the fairness in that?"

"Does that seem to you to be pertinent?" Justice Slater asked Stuart.

"No."

"Would you care to elaborate, Mr. Cross?"

"Sure. If I don't get half, we won't solve this in mediation. We go to court."

T. William Slater tried to alleviate Natalie's indignation with a colorful observation. "It looks like your husband intends to hang on like a bulldog in a thunderstorm!"

"What's this about, Stuart? You hardly need all this."

"I'm getting married."

"You're getting *married*?" Natalie's lips were tight across her teeth, and she locked eyes with Stuart as though expecting him to flinch. Not often had she seen such a gentle smile on his face. Since he declined to say anything further, she thought she would shake a few facts out of him. "Some *slut* down at the plant?" Natalie's jaw worked slightly as she awaited an answer, and Justice Slater busied himself among his papers.

"No," said Stuart mildly.

"Where else would *you* meet someone?"

"Oh, she's from the plant all right," he smiled at Justice Slater, begging his indulgence, "but she doesn't fit your description."

"Not, I hope, the little brunette by the bottle washer."

"Yes, it is." Stuart smiled.

"I thought Paul had already been through that one."

"I don't think so," said Stuart, staring red-faced at his unblemished legal pad. "He was busy with you."

With a sudden flurry, T. William Slater resumed his role. "My job is to help us avoid a jury trial, and I heartily suggest you join me in that effort. I have noted that a spectacle is imminent, and I urge you, as long-time residents of this community, to avoid the damage to your standing that *public* resolution of your dispute will likely produce."

Natalie had locked on to part of Judge Slater's remark, and with a chivvying, rueful laugh made several observations. "Yes, Your Honor, we *are* long-time residents. But there is a difference. There is a difference. I am a Montana native, born here, raised here and *still* here. Stuart is an out-of-stater. There, I've said it. Stuart is from out east. The Whitelaw family established our fortunes by supplying the miners and cattlemen who built this town in territorial days. We're the same Scots-Irish stock that fought the Indians, pioneered trails, brought cattle up from Texas and built these good towns. Stuart's name isn't even Cross. It was Crozoborski until his grandparents arrived here from

Poland. I've got nothing against immigrants, Judge Slater, but you and I grew up here. We can still make out the old sign for Slater's Blacksmith Shop on the side of the beauty parlor. Some of what we feel is just not part of Stuart's world."

"I get half or we go to trial," Stuart practically sang.

Judge Slater, who'd barely peeked up from his papers during Natalie's speech, said in the gingerly tones of one avoiding an explosion, "There seems to be plenty here to go around." He extended his palms upward toward the ledgers and documents in a scooping motion. Clearly, he was hunting the exit.

Natalie shouted: "You have any idea what this guy spent on the adult channel? Forty-eight bucks to see *Lewd Trooper* three times in a row."

Slater was gone. Natalie made a face of hideous detestation at Stuart. "Bad cop busts barely legals?"

By the end of the week, a chinook had started to blow and the temperature rose sixty degrees in four hours, turning the corrals into a sea of mud. Dirty water backed up into the barn where the cows had tramped snow into icy ridges. Bill and Evelyn dragged straw bales to make a dam around the head catch in case they had to pull a calf, then they saddled their horses and pushed the cows out of the mud into the closest pasture. The new calves, thrilled by the sudden warmth, played crazily as the sun flattened the snow.

Evelyn was glad to be back on a horse and sat for a long time in the hard south wind watching calves overcome by the wish to meet each other, while the cows, after a spell of absorbed eating, grew fearful of losing track of their babies and abruptly lumbered around the herd, each lowing among the crowd for the only acceptable calf. Part of Evelyn's thrill of watching cattle from horseback lay in observing the distinct personalities in what at a glance seemed anonymous: the contented young mothers, the belligerent matrons, the bad mothers who wished they'd never had this calf, the poor milkers whose abraded udders pained them, the cows who seemed to know their calves were sickly and would not live. Some viewed the horsemen as the enemy and hurried their calves away, while others seemed to recognize the drivers of the hay truck in another guise. And on certain occasions Evelyn felt less herdsman than predator, protein viewing protein. In this game, the poor milker, the indifferent mother, and the mother who was also a grandmother were slaughtered alike. At the end, there were no exceptions. Man must dine. But Evelyn was tired of man.

When the chinook stopped blowing, it stayed still for two days. Skies were clear and the cattle scattered out to look for patches of bare ground, old grass and a change of diet. Bill and Evelyn took their horses into the summer pasture, Evelyn riding her colt Cree, crossing drifts until the Crazy Mountains arose like a silver wedding cake to the north. From there, the water courses, tree lines on a white expanse, made spindly courses to the Yellowstone. The Bridgers could be discerned, as well as the bench of Sheep Mountain, the low-humped Deer Creeks and, to the south, the blue crags and high, dark canyons of the Absaroka. This was altogether too much for the colts, who kept trying to turn toward home and were afraid of the crowds of deer at the bottom of every snow-filled bowl. Evelyn was aware of a great weight lifting off her as they rode along. The notion of not ever going back made her smile and think of the trail: Texas to Montana and never once turn your horse around. Her happiness began to be felt by Cree, who looked eagerly in the direction of their travel while Evelyn made plans with Bill for next year, the following year, the next five and ten years. A three-mile cross fence was in the wrong place and should be moved a half mile to the east. Springs needed to be improved, salt grounds moved, pastures rested, loafing sheds built. Somehow the money must be found for the tractor they coveted, a four-wheel-drive New Holland that would let them bale wild timothy for the horses. From the ridges, they could look down into their small valley and see flocks of pigeons trading between the barn and hay sheds, wings sparkling in the brilliant light.

That night, Paul beat her.

He arrived at suppertime, already upset, and sat in Evelyn's front room with his coat on. "Rural peace," he said spitefully. "I wish I had a taste for it." Evelyn had already decided that she would try not to see him anymore, but she knew not to expect too much of herself and, because he was somewhat crumpled, decided to at least allow him to speak before explaining that their separation must resume.

He was clutching his cell phone.

"I went around to see Stuart," he began, eyes ablaze with indignation. "He's looking quite spiffy in my old office. He's got people coming and going with armloads of paper. He's got a phone ringing off the hook. He's got my old secretary doting on his every need. He's got his little girlfriend working down on the shop floor and a movie poster from *Down to the Sea in Ships* on the fucking wall. He's got this whole hearty manner like a sea captain. It is to puke over."

Instead of the intended picture, Evelyn imagined a Stuart unbound.

"I told him about my arrangement with Majub as a liaison man. I realized that you don't find companies you can sell every five minutes. I told Majub that. I told him I need something to carry me between sales, to keep gas in the Chevette, for Christ sake."

Evelyn could smell the liquor on his breath.

"But Majub is like, 'Finders fee, period, and don't ask again.' When I tell him I can't live on that, he tells me not to get my panties in a wad. So my proposal to Stuart is why don't I go on calling on some of my old customers, kind of earn my way, use my own car and so on, can't be anything but good for one and all. And Stuart says no. When I ask for clarification, he *spells* it for me: N-O. You believe this? I go straight over the top of his desk, and next thing I know he's got goons dragging me out into the alley, where I receive unnecessary roughness at their hands. You have to understand, these are *my* former employees."

Evelyn's heart did pull somewhat toward Paul, but she thought she should be candid with him, despite the tight look of his face, the wildness of his eyes, and tell him how in her own view he was merely bringing trouble upon himself. The first blow astonished her with its ferocity. He had not beaten her before, and she was not expecting it. Soon he was knocking her through the furniture with such fury that she wondered if he meant to kill her. Curled on the floor, her head muffled in her arms, there was a sudden lull during which nothing could be heard at all. Then she heard Paul say, "Okay, Pops, I'm going," and looked up to see Bill training his Winchester on Paul's head, his finger through the trigger guard, his face the same expression of unemotional focus he bore when he cut the worms out of an old bull. After glancing toward Evelyn to see if she intended to intervene on his behalf, Paul laughed without humor and went straight out through the door.

Before Evelyn could explain the situation, which she badly wanted to do, Bill was gone too. Evelyn almost expected to hear a shot, but it never came.

She hardly slept. Her bruises were such that if she drifted off, moving or rolling over, pain awakened her again. Anxiety that she could have been so vulnerable ran through her like voltage, her life turning into one jagged question after another. She was ready to run, not from Paul or the place itself or her family, but from her own abasement. Around four, she gave up and went into the kitchen. From there she could see light from the barn, which meant Bill was pulling a calf. Evelyn began to feel some relief from her self-hatred as she imagined the calf's craving for oxygen. Then after filling a thermos with coffee, she put on her coveralls and went out to face Bill. The snow danced in the halo of the barn door.

He sat on an old car seat that he had arranged for just such vigils. An unhappy young cow was secured in the head catch, and Bill was half asleep. He said nothing as Evelyn handed him a cup of coffee and poured herself one. She sat down next to him and they watched the cow, a pair of tiny black feet projecting from her rear.

"Hadn't moved," he said of the feet. "How are you?"

"I'm all right, I'm fine."

"I don't think that calf's comin' on his own. I kinda dozed. Nothin' don't happen, I'll pull him. Drink this coffee first, though."

"Okay."

"I hate to use that puller, but I can't get at this one."

"I'm so sorry about what happened." Here was the disease again, and Bill said nothing at all. "For what little it's worth, that never happened before." She knew this was just one more side of the same thing, embarrassment where rage should be. There was nothing censorious about Bill's quiet. He never took on other people's questions, and he always knew what to do next.

He put his cup down and got up, attached the calf puller to the protruding legs, looping its chains above both fetlocks, fitted the breech spanner to her hips, made sure the ratchet on the cable drum was pointed in the right direction, then slowly turned the crank. Once the cable had tightened, Bill tried to time his downward press to the cow's contractions.

Finally, the calf was drawn out in its glistening caul, sliding forth in a tumble of afterbirth. The mother clanged against the restraints around her head, and Bill pulled the calf around to the side so she could see it, wet and luminous, then wiped the membrane away from its head and seal-bright eyes. "A little bull," he said.

Alice Whitelaw brought so many covered dishes to the ranch that Evelyn and Bill worried about gaining weight, and since she periodically checked their housekeeping or did it herself, they became conscious of their sloppy habits and began doing things they had never done before, such as hanging up their coats.

Bill looked on all this with quiet amusement. Sometimes, as Alice marched around laying down the law, he remembered her as the slender girl of their courtship, that night in the Martinsdale Hotel, when she said, "Cowboy, I can beat you to the floor anytime you want to try." Time, he thought, all it is is time. All it will ever be.

Stuart and Natalie settled their differences without a trial. After Stuart announced his engagement to Annie Elvstrom, things went quickly. They would be married in Two Dot in June. Since Natalie did not want Miss Elvstrom living in her house, now grown sacred in memory, she kept it and compensated Stuart right down to the penny. She was currently angry at Paul for saying, when she'd announced her plans for a face-lift, "Quick thinking, Natalie," and she seemed to be acquiring a lot of hard-to-pin-down ailments including chronic fatigue syndrome, Epstein-Barr, seasonal affective disorder. She bought a light box and put travel stickers on it. Bought a cute little Audi. Sideswiped a parked car while chasing the first robin of spring.

Nobody had seen Paul for a while, and reports were scanty: he was a stamp collector, a ham radio operator, a car salesman; he'd been spotted at the Guns Galore emporium out on the interstate. Violet and Claire at Just the Two of Us assured Natalie that they had seen a section of State Road 287 with Adopt-a-Highway signs with Paul's name on them. Donald called Evelyn to say he'd bumped into him in Helena but was in drag, testifying against a restrictive farm bill, and thought better of striking up a conversation.

Then, after a month or so, Paul began paying visits to Evelyn, but with Bill there, these remained formal. Evelyn didn't want him on the ranch at all, and she distrusted herself in the face of his narcotic appeal. She was never unaware of the bruise on her soul, and wished he'd fall in love with anybody else.

Paul felt he was making better headway by turning his considerable skills on Bill, who never wasn't watching him. Despite that, Paul found numerous ways of being useful, running parts and supplies out from town, revealing some surprising mechanical abilities and, more important, filing for cost-sharing and farm subsidies, which entailed hours of tedious paperwork. He began to persuade Bill that the burden of the ranch on Evelyn's modest estate could be alleviated through imaginative forays, even beyond tapping into the federal subsidies which of late were the only real crop. Appealing to Bill's fear—some by nature, some age-related—of being a burden, particularly on Evelyn, was a rich vein in terms of gaining Bill's acceptance.

In observing his reliable alertness, Paul failed to understand its purpose. He explained that he was facing a difficult, very important decision that might also produce opportunities for Bill but that he had decided to leave it, if not to chance, then to Punxsutawney Phil's forecast on Groundhog Day. When it was reported that the rodent had indeed seen his shadow, Paul packed his bags and left without further explanation.

Bill's vigilance was rewarded when Paul called from Medicine Hat, Alberta, quite late at night. Paul was at his best and made what he clearly thought was a great case for Bill to lend a hand in bringing a boat into the States duty-free. "I knew you'd come through," Paul said, prematurely celebrating his loss of respect for the old coot. Then after supplying the operator with further coins, he gave Bill his instructions. "It may be coming a little late in life, Pops, but I'm going to show you how the big boys make money."

Evelyn drove Bill to the bus station, an errand she would recall for the rest of her life, as though Bill had borne the shame of her beating upon his own shoulders, believing him to be headed off to his neglectful daughter in Miles City.

But Bill rode to the High Line. He had nothing but his coat, his gloves and his worn Open Road Stetson. In his pocket a wallet contained photographs of Alice, and of Natalie and Evelyn as children, and a pair of reading glasses with only one earpiece. He didn't speak to the other passengers and stared out at the weary landscape emerging from snow as from time to time mountain ranges rose and fell in the distance and the bus followed the wet black road north. They went through some open country that reminded him of a twenty-thousand-acre pasture without a division fence in which he'd once tended cattle. Most of the time, he had been alone with a saddle horse and had slept on the ground. The crew boss left him food the first and fifteenth of every month at the shipping corrals, but Bill never saw him do it. He was eleven years old.

He looked out of the window at low cliffs, sage-covered pastures, fences poking out of snow and enclosing nothing. Ranches looked like remote fortresses in the distance, white crowns of snow, blue shadows of road cuts. He smiled to see Angus cattle strung out and feeding toward the horizon, willows growing out of flat panels of ice. The land was wired together with telephone and electrical lines, railroad lines and highways, as if it might otherwise drift apart. Every now and then, a treeless new subdivision showed up, looking much the same as a car lot. They passed yellow stacks of lumber and a sawdust burner at a prosperous little mill. A distant, vertical plume of smoke suggested a rare, windless day.

He changed buses at Great Falls and two hours later stepped off at Havre, where three men awaited him. One a sandy-haired fat man whose face reminded Bill of a cat's. The beetle-browed man in an old sateen jacket advertising auto-racing products never once looked at Bill and spoke only French to the third, who was small, startlingly better dressed than the others and wore a long mackintosh over a sports coat. He looked like an Asian sort of fellow. The three of them drove Bill across the Milk River, where the man with the cat's face pointed and said, "There's your river, *monsieur*. That's how you get back to the U.S." Bill didn't know what he'd been told, but now he was patient as a wolf, watching the three with cold absorption. The only snow left here was in the still-filled ditch forming an enormous white worm that raced alongside the car. The second man said something in French and gestured at a ridge where antennae bristled in every direction. The natty one replied in French, and Bill joined them in gazing up at the structures, some sort of border surveillance, he assumed. All he could make out from the signs was "Alberta 880." At Aden, they crossed the border itself without pause, and it seemed to Bill that the men exaggerated their Frenchness to produce some sort of effect on the Canadian border officer. The small, well-dressed man held all the passports and handed the guard Bill's driver's license.

After a short drive, they turned into a road that was little more than tracks in the sod. Their headlights picked up the ridges and the gates through fences, but the well-dressed man was hunched over the wheel, cursing incomprehensibly as they pushed through miles of badlands. Bill could no longer determine what part of the middle of the night it was, mostly aware of the cursing that had been omnipresent since he got off the bus.

At length they struck a line of cottonwood trunks blazing up into the headlights. Then Paul appeared in front of them, a jack-in-the-box shielding his eyes against the glare. Bill, the last to get out of the car, hardly took his gaze off him as he chatted with the others, apparently making the acquaintance of two of them for the first time but greeting the small and dapper man with familiarity.

"Where'd you learn your French?" Paul asked.

"At my mother's breast."

"Bill," said Paul, "meet Mr. Majub."

Majub shook Bill's hand warmly and said, "How thoughtful of you to join us."

While the men conferred, Bill examined the boat that was drawn up on the riverbank, an oversized wooden rowboat with iron fastenings bleeding through its gray paint. From beneath tarpaulins and cargo netting drifted a sweet odor Bill had never smelled before. A pair of oars rested in their locks, and a single thwart spanned the middle of the boat.

"I'll row first," said Paul, clapping his hands together as he climbed aboard. Bill got in and sat facing him while the men on the beach exercised terrific caution in keeping their feet dry as they pushed the boat into the flow. Majub caught Paul's glance and held a finger under his eye and nodded.

Bill listened to the steady creak of the oarlocks as the bright bands of headlight receded on the bank. The current underneath made the subtlest throb, and Bill's eyes grew accustomed to the dark so that he could discern the gloomy country around them, sandstone bluffs and hoodoos divided by the dusky gleam of the river.

"Don't let me hit anything," said Paul with a friendly trill in his voice.

"How far we goin'?"

"A long damn way."

Sometime before sunup, waking from a restless nap, Bill said, "What's the cargo?"

"It's medicine, Pops. And it's had a long trip: Afghanistan, Siberia, Alaska, the Yukon, Alberta, and next stop Montana. Once it hits the High Line, it goes all over, and a lot of sick folks are going to get well. It'll be a new morning for a bunch of folks who right now are trying to remember their own names."

At first light, Bill took over the rowing. A cold, black storm was forming to the west. Daybreak had given him infinite keenness, whereas Paul complained of backache from rowing. This, Bill wanted to tell him, was not going to be a problem.

When it was Paul's turn to row again, he gave a great yawn and stood up clenching his fists behind his head, elbows out in a luxurious stretch. Rising silently behind him, Bill followed the outline of Paul's face against the black current. Paul bent back from the waist, rotating this way and that, bent his head back for a long gasping yawn. With deceptive ease, Bill shoved him over the bow into the river.

Paul made a tremendous splash close alongside and surfaced with a shout at the shock of the cold. Bill stood with one of the oars and fended off his attempts to return to the boat.

"Let me in, Pops. Honest, I'm not mad at you!" Only Paul's head showed among the shapes of floating ice. "I can help you get ahead!" The absurdity of this remark was not lost on its author, and he began to laugh.

Bill could hear the scream inside the laugh even before it dissolved into curses, and stood there, imperturbably trailing the oar by one hand, and sat down only when Paul's head went under. Bill suddenly thought he was going to be sick. The boat began to drift unguided as he leaned on his knees with his head in his arms.

He didn't know how long he'd been sitting when Paul's voice brought him upright, not a word but a groan that came from deep within his chest.

Paul was crouched in the bow gasping, arms hanging at his sides, a length of pipe in one hand, his eyes fastened on Bill. As soon as his breath quieted, he said, "I need the clothes, Pops."

He began to undress, throwing his clothes in a sodden heap onto the floor of the boat. Slowly, Bill took off his old stockman's coat, folded it carefully and handed it to Paul, who gestured impatiently for the rest and put them on as fast as Bill could get them off, including the boots with the undershot heels that he could barely pull on. Sitting at the stern, the wind blowing snow against his bare body, Bill declined to shiver.

Paul took the oars and angled toward shore, crossing several streams of current before the boat ground softly onto the sand. "Here's your stop," he said, slumping at the oars. "I know you're a religious person, Bill. Think of this as a rain check and curl up some place warm."

Bill climbed out and waded barefoot through the thin sheet ice rimming the shore, then watched the boat move away from him, just a smudge on the silver of river and then not even that, only the river and its steady sound. He turned away from it and began to walk.

Watching him, Paul thought, I'm not a violent person like that old cowboy, I let God decide.

But he was not happy with these clothes. It was like being in a costume. He hated that everything had gotten so serious and his head hurt. He was comfortable with the idea of the old man walking into nowhere, though he felt this without great emotion because Bill had been, when you got right down to it, a worthy adversary. He knew how Bill saw him, had seen him from the beginning, and he had to hand it to him. At seventy-five, you've got to know something.

Whitelaw had thought of himself as tough, but he was crippled by his fanatical ideas about loyalty. Paul's mother taught him long ago that we are acted upon by forces, period, and that imagining we go through life with those principles was just further evidence of the arrogance of man. Still, it was hard to avoid. Paul would deliver this load and take his reward down there to Evelyn and save the ranch, just as Whitelaw delivered all the bottles for half a million square miles and saved the ranch. Old Bill was heading into his last snowstorm to save the ranch. It's as if, Paul thought, we're all in some Gary Cooper movie and can't get out! He hung on the oars and let his most genuine smile warm his face. Thank God I still have my sense of humor, he thought, then threw his old clothes into the river.

He was a new man.

The river wound on into a distance that was darkening under a winter storm, and Paul kept looking to the south for Devil's Tower. But he was happy and continued to have thoughts like, I gotta find a better way to get to Great Falls!, which helped to pass the time. At last his monument appeared, just a stack of rocks, faintly lit by what light got through scudding clouds, and the river seemed to slow, making a deep bend to the east; the lantern appeared on the bank.

The three men dragged the boat ashore and the first thing Majub said was "Where's the old guy?" The cat-face man lifted the lantern high over the boat, then peered under a corner of the tarpaulin. The others watched Paul as he stood up and stretched.

"He fell overboard," Paul said blandly.

"Fell overboard! Didn't you try to save him?"

"Not too much."

This delighted Majub. *"Not too much?"* Then he turned to the other two and repeated it in French—*"Pas beaucoup!"*—which produced laughter all around until cat-face commented grimly, *"Putain de merde, eh!"*

Turning back to Paul, Majub said, "Well, that is how it is, isn't it? If you dance with the devil, you don't want to step on his toes. Unless you're tired of living."

Removing the tarpaulin that covered the cargo revealed numerous small bricks wrapped in dark cloth and tied in bundles, and emitting the same sweet smell that had filled the rowboat. Paul helped move these to the truck, where they were covered by heavy bales of alfalfa and piled to the height of the cab's rear window. The tarp from the boat went over the bales and was lashed down by its grommets to the stake pockets of the truck's bed.

Majub looked closely at Paul and said, "Hey, your outfit is shrunk. You need to buy stuff in your own size." Then he turned to his crew. "One more thing to do and we're on our way."

Paul and the other two followed a game trail into the brush and before long Paul got the feeling he was being escorted. He remembered what he'd learned in prison: Never let them see you sweat: That's ignorant. Something was gnawing its way up his spine, and he knew he had to let it go right through and out. Peace was the goal: Easy Street. But Paul knew that he wasn't going to make it.

There was a small clearing you couldn't discern from twenty feet away; in the middle was a deep, rectangular hole, and the shovel used to dig it sticking up beside it in the ground. "Seems like a funny place to put an outhouse," Paul said. It was his last joke but much appreciated both in its original form and in translation.

The three men found his sobs almost deafening. Afterward, Majub said to his companions, "The music has stopped. Let us return to our seats."

Bill didn't know where to go so he walked straight away from the North Star. The air was so cold it felt like heat. He ought to be running, he told himself, but he was too old to run so instead he imagined that he was walking toward his babies, Evelyn and Natalie, all the while doubting he would make it very far. In fact, no straight line worked long before it came up against a sandstone ledge or the base of a hoodoo that made him turn toward the North Star, and with every turn that way there seemed to be less of him able to go in any direction. At the same time, he was growing comfortable and the earth around him more accepting. Night birds flew off between his legs, and when he walked past a snowy owl perched at eye level, it merely rotated its head with his passing; but when he'd gone another while into the darkness, he noticed the owl was not far behind him, easily seen because of its terrible whiteness. Several coyotes returning from a hunt came downhill, and he stepped aside to let them pass, thinking that if they had anything to say to him, surely they would've stopped. They must have known he had his own appointment to keep. He did think about having a word with the owl, to make it clear that he didn't mind company but being followed was an abomination. Otherwise, he was enjoying the new lightness in his step. He felt, even as he fell more and more frequently, that his lightness made every sort of contact a delicacy. Keeping a watchful eye on that owl would be a good thing. This far away, he may be the only fellow that can tell us anything, even if he don't want to just now. The North Star had got in behind a cloud—a really good cloud all white and tongue-shaped and lit up at its edges by stars—that Bill thought to follow until he couldn't make out which way he was pointing and turned back to the owl for advice.

There is a man there. I don't think I can stand up no more. So I don't and I get there where the ground can help me since I'm right on it and it wants to help. The man wears a straw cowboy hat and long sky-colored coat. It so happens I know this man quite well, John Red Wolf or, as he was known in the navy, John R. Wolf, my good friend. Even though we went from Montana to Alameda and then on to the Solomon Islands on the same cruiser, we only met after I rode half of a forty-millimeter gun mount over the side during a suicide attack. It was a low overcast day, and the Japs were coming out of the cloud cover. We never heard this one. At least I didn't after what living between two five-inch guns had done to my eardrums. This plane dropped like a rock and blew up fifty yards in front of me and just tore my gun mount to pieces and I went over the side with a bunch of dead and dying guys who'd been passing shells from the ammunition bay. The minute I knew I was alive and floating in the big ground swell from the Philippines, I'm thinking about the sharks that shadowed us from mid-Pacific all the way to Saipan, looked like submarines. They got right into the dead guys and were cleaning them up when John Red Wolf pulled me into the lifeboat.

The next day we were playing catch on the stern. I'd loaned my glove to an officer who never gave it back. John just went up and retrieved it from his quarters so we could play catch, two guys from Montana anchored off a little island covered with abandoned bunkers and a blowed-up ammo dump that looked like a hole right in the middle of the world. He wasn't particularly afraid of officers, old John.

We almost got used to the kamikazes, they was such a regular feature there toward the end when the emperor knew the score. Every now and then something would happen you couldn't forget, like the Zero that came from between two little islands near Jolo and Tawi-Tawi about five feet off the water, weaving every which way until he elevated just enough to catch the stern catapult and blow up. Even before the firemen could move, this hand come whistling down the deck and stopped right next to the sick-bay ventilator. Me and John went over to look. That air show was right out of the Olympics, and here was this little brown Jap hand. Remember that, John?

When we started up the boxing matches on the fantail again for the first time since the New Hebrides, I went along with my new friend. This big farm kid from Indiana put on the gloves with a smaller but savvier Mexican from California. The Mexican danced around till some of the guys was booing, but he kept it up till the farm boy run out of gas and then started whaling on his head. It was no good. You'd see his face flatten, with hair all pointed one way and the sweat drops just flying out over the ocean. I remember, John, you saying, "Yes, sir, this makes a lot of sense."

How that ship stank! The captain didn't want submarines following our garbage so we kept it all and the ship smelled like a city dump. Red Wolf says, "I'll take the subs." It was hot. We slept on deck with sea bags for pillows and swapped theories about the stars that swarmed right into the ocean. Sometimes it got too hot to sleep, like on our way down to Borneo, so we just talked about home. I told you I ranched a little and you told me you was a diesel mechanic and medicine man. I have to admit I didn't much care for it when you said that your people were the real owners of my ranch. That kind of talk was so much like the talk we had with the southern boys on the ship, about the War Between the States, and I'm glad we dropped it. At first, guys would show off, reciting every state of the union and its capital, but that give out long before the equator. By Subic Bay, the only country we had was that light cruiser.

One of the last things our task force took on was shelling a bunch of islands near New Georgia, if I remember right, where we set off a Jap ammunition dump, better than any fireworks display. That's when Red Wolf showed once and for all what kind of stuff he was made out of. A five-inch shell hung fire in the gun, and the whole crew waited for it to discharge and blow a hole in the side of our ship, but John worked that shell free and dumped it over the side. Said it wasn't nothing, that he had extra powers.

Sometimes, when Roosevelt broadcast to all hands over the loudspeakers, John and me would find a quiet spot to visit about things that was so amazing to young fellows from the sagebrush. Like when a torpedo bomber hit us in '43 and we had to seal off a flooded compartment with seventeen of our buddies still inside. Funny thing was, we shot that plane down after he cut his torpedo loose. The pilot bailed out and we turned him to hamburger with the twenty-millimeter. Later we find out that's against the rules of war. Tell it to those seventeen boys. Or close calls, like seeing a periscope on a moonlit night and zigzagging all over the ocean to keep from getting sunk. We talked about the guys that couldn't take the heat and concussion and boredom and finally went Asiatic and had to be shipped home. We looked out there at all the flying death and told each other it was like a movie. Or the big powder magazine that went up on Tarawa, a rolling ball of smoke and flame, jam-packed with dead Japs. You start to get the picture about the human race, that most of it's dead. Other stuff going up all the time: pill boxes, assembly areas, truck depots. Never a dull moment. How about Magicienne Bay when Jap shore batteries opened up on the *California*? We watched those dark hills with little tongues of light from the flamethrowers. That's how some of them boys went out, at the wrong end of a flamethrower. Bodies always floating past us, Jap and American both, just bobbing meatballs that used to have mothers and hometowns. I'll bet you'll never forget the day the ship got caught in the gigantic oceanic whirlpool with Bing Crosby on the air from Radio Tokyo, the ship swinging in smaller circles like it was headed down a giant drain and we're listening to this crooner. Wasn't that war something? Like we always said, never a dull moment. But the world has changed, John, and guys like you and me don't really exist.

The last time was when that suicide plane lost its bombs and the canopy peels away, then a wing, and it comes over the stern bouncing sideways. The motor tore loose and slid across the ship, killing the mount captain on the other forty-millimeter. They found his earphones wrapped around a roll of his scalp about a hundred feet away. Remember him? He's the one tried to show us how to play chess. By then, we were gettin' pretty squirrelly every time they called general quarters, having to be good in the clutch whenever the Japs felt like playin' ball. Lord, it was stormy out there. Like you said, enough wind to blow the monkeys right out of the trees.

It didn't matter though, did it? The war was over. Truman said so on the radio. You and me heard his voice on the loudspeaker while we stood on the fantail, two nobodies from the boonies, waving good-bye to the dead. Now John, here is how I remember the rest of it: We get discharged at the navy receiving station in San Diego and ride a bus all the way home, but when we crossed the Montana line the only thing you said was, "Looks better with a few hills," and when I asked if I'd see you again, you said, "Yes." I got to my ranch and there was nothing there, cows gone, machinery rusted into the ground, saddle horses stolen or eaten. But fifty years comes and goes and you wait for a time like this. The *Gazette* ran a picture of a battleship graveyard around Mobile, Alabama, and I seen our little cruiser in the pack of wrecked ships but I ain't seen *you.*

Well here I am, said Red Wolf, and I followed him into the canyon where the sky was upside down and we could walk straight into the stars.

ALSO BY THOMAS MCGUANE

NINETY-TWO IN THE SHADE

Tiring of the company of junkies and burn-outs, Thomas Skelton goes home to Key West to take up a more wholesome life. But things fester in America's utter South. And Skelton's plans to become a skiff guide in the shining blue subtropical waters place him on a collision course with Nichol Dance, who has risen to the crest of the profession by dint of infallible instincts and a reputation for homicide. Out of their deadly rivalry, Thomas McGuane has constructed a novel with the impetus of a thriller and the heartbroken humor that is his distinct contribution to American prose.

Fiction/Literature/0-679-75289-7

NOBODY'S ANGEL

Patrick Fitzpatrick is a former soldier, a fourth-generation cowboy, and a whiskey addict. His grandfather wants to run away to act in movies, his sister wants to burn the house down, and his new stallion is bent on killing him: all of them urgently require attention. But increasingly Patrick himself is spiraling out of control, into that region of romantic misadventure and vanishing possibilities that is Thomas McGuane's Montana. Nowhere has McGuane mapped that territory more precisely—or with such tenderhearted lunacy—than in *Nobody's Angel*, a novel that places him in a genre of his own.

Fiction/Literature/0-394-74738-0

PANAMA

Chester Pomeroy is a washed-up rock star turned casualty of illicit substances and kamikaze passion. As he haunts Key West, pestering family, threatening a potential in-law with a .38, and attempting to crucify himself on his ex's door out of sheer lovesickness, Chester emerges as the pure archetype of the McGuane hero. Out of his struggle to rejoin the human race—and the imminent possibility that he may die trying—McGuane has fashioned a harrowing and hilarious novel of "alligators, macadam, the sea, sticky sex, laughter, and sudden death."

Fiction/Literature/0-679-75291-9

THE BUSHWHACKED PIANO

As a citizen, Nicholas Payne is not in the least solid. As a boyfriend, he is nothing short of disastrous, and his latest flame, the patrician Ann Fitzgerald, has done a wise thing by dropping him. But Ann isn't counting on Nicholas's wild persistence, or on the slapstick lyricism of Thomas McGuane, who in *The Bushwhacked Piano* sends his hero from Michigan to Montana on a demented mission of courtship whose highlights include a ride on a homicidal bronco and apprenticeship to the inventor of the world's first highrise for bats. The result is a tour de force of American Dubious.

Fiction/Literature/0-394-72642-1

THE SPORTING CLUB

When James Quinn and Vernor Stanton reunite at the Centennial Club, the scene of many a carefree childhood summer, Stanton marks the occasion by shooting his friend in the heart. The good news is that the bullet is made of wax. The bad news is that the Mephistophelian Stanton wants Quinn to help him wreak havoc upon this genteel enclave of weekend sportsmen. In this hilarious novel, Thomas McGuane launches a renegade aristocrat and a mild-mannered fly-fisherman onto a collision course with each other and with the overbred scions of Michigan's robber barony. Escalating from practical jokes to guerrilla warfare, *The Sporting Club* is a foray into the sclerotic heart of American machismo.

Fiction/Literature/0-679-75290-0

ALSO AVAILABLE

Keep the Change, 0-679-73033-8
The Longest Silence, 0-679-77757-1
Nothing But Blue Skies, 0-679-74778-8
Some Horses, 0-375-72452-4
To Skin a Cat, 0-394-75521-9

VINTAGE CONTEMPORARIES
Available at your local bookstore, or call toll-free to order:
1-800-793-2665 (credit cards only).